MYSTIC GIFTS TRILOGY
Mystic Perceptions
Dream Visions
Inner Reflections

ANCESTOR'S ENCHANTMENT TRILOGY
Witch Within

<u>**Writing As: J. Risk**</u>

REALMS BOOKS:

THE ALTEREALM SERIES
1 *The Huntress*
2 *The Seer*
3 *The Empath*
4 *The Witch*
5 *The Chronos*
6 *The Warrior*
7 *The Telepath*
8 *The Healer*
9 *The Kinetic*

THE SOLRELM SERIES
Coming soon:

Concealed

GEMINI LEAGUE
Coming soon

Dark Moon

PRIDE

Animal Senses Series Book 9

Jacqueline Paige

I need to thank my daughter, Jaii, she is my external memory when it comes to my writing. Without her, my characters would change, age, and appearance and sometimes be renamed in error. She remembers every little detail that prevents me from changing the rules I established in book 2 of a series, so in book 9 I'm not creating a time paradox or committing plot sins of indescribable horror.
I can't thank you enough for reading each story almost as many times as I do.

Xox

As I (Jaii) beta/proofread the final copy of this, and I didn't know this was here! You create worlds that I can temporarily retreat to. I like finer details and I love a good book but cannot write, so helping process and organize your thoughts and seeing them come together is one of my favourite things. I'll read anything you write a thousand times and never be bored.
Jaii

Chapter One

Tripp reached in and grabbed his pack. Shepard Addison asking him to do this personally wasn't unheard of, but he had to wonder if this missing female was more important than he was told. Not that all females weren't important—they were, but why have the King ask and not his team leader? Could be he was the closest, but his gut said otherwise, and it was never wrong. Pulling out the map, he opened it on the seat and then checked his phone to see the last location she'd been at.

He stabbed his finger into the map at the location and then dragged it along the map for a few inches. Mountains were close to where she was last tracked. If she'd gone in that direction to head to the meet-up with the teams, it wasn't going to be a good time. If she wasn't just lost and someone did get to her, there were a hundred different ways they could move undetected and vanish, especially with the help of the snow heading that way.

"Shit." Folding the map, he stuffed it back in the pack. It was a long drive from where he currently was. So much for his being the closest theory. He'd wanted to be in on the ops to get more of Konner Flores people out. He smirked, remembering how much spunk Terah had when he'd found

"

them. Curiosity had him wondering if they were all that fast and strong. Now he would never know.

He was going to need enough supplies for a long trek. He looked down at his bare feet, and his boots, those would be a good start. He'd only stopped to go for a quick run and grab a bite to eat before driving to the rendezvous location for the ops.

Walking to the back of his SUV, he opened it up and grabbed his boots. Before he could get the first one done up his phone rang. No number came up. "Carson."

"It's Zain Sanders, I'm the office director for Jesse's team."

Director? aka office guy. Pulling the sock out of his boot, he sat on the bumper and pulled it on.

"I checked your location and have arranged a flight for you to get to Amari's last known location."

He paused for a second and then jammed his foot into his boot. "A flight?" Only one thing in this world turned his stomach, or rather his animal's, and that was flying. Tripp had been in planes, and helicopters, and even tried cliff gliding and all of them were a big nope. His feet needed to be able to always reach the ground—like a nervous ass noob learning to swim. He clicked his teeth together, it *would* get him there faster, then he might be able to get in on the second wave of the ops. "All right."

"I'll send you the location." This guy's voice told him he was one step from freaking out.

"Can you give me more details on this Amari?" If he could get a sense of what she was like, he might better understand what he was walking into. If she had been taken, would she fight her abductors or just shut down and accept her fate? He'd dealt with both before. He honestly wasn't sure which was the hardest to deal with.

"Like what?" He heard a door close and then boots on tiles. "Sorry, just mad at myself, I'm the one that told her to start heading to the meet and not wait for one of the incursion team," he snorted, "not that she would have waited."

That explained his next question as to why she was alone. "How long since her trackers went offline?"

"She hasn't checked in for four hours and the trail stops three hours ago."

Shit. Three hours in that area could have her anywhere. He opened his mouth to ask if it was possible she was offline on purpose, but Zain hissed out a deep breath.

"I don't want to have to call her family. It's not going to go well if I do."

Tripp was glad that task was never part of his job. He liked doing his job and someone else dealing with emotional people. "Hopefully you won't have to."

"It will be a shit show if I do." A door slammed and he could hear the echo of traffic now. "The last thing I need right now, that Jesse needs is an angry Alpha all up in his face, not to mention Amari..."

It was like fireworks went off in his head, "Alpha?"

"You weren't told? She's an Alpha's daughter."

Tripp straightened and squeezed the bridge of his nose. "No." She was an Alpha's daughter, which shed some light on the urgency in everyone's tone—light brighter than a thousand-watt lightbulb. He opened his eyes and then stood up, "Okay," he nodded and then shut the hatch. "Any chance she's just lost?" He went back to the front and climbed in, "there's a lot of mountains in that area, the signal could be..."

"No. She's not lost."

Closing the door, he realized he didn't have a direction to go yet. "Can you send me a pic, so I know who I'm looking for?" The chances of seeing a crowd of people in that area were slim, but he still needed a confirmed target. He cringed at his own thought, she wasn't the target...

"Uh, yeah, but she's easy to notice, blond, attitude."

Tripp shrugged; attitude could describe ten different personality types. "Okay, send me the location. I'll head there now."

"Right. Okay." He could hear him running now. "Update me as soon as you get there, so I can let the team know." He swore, "the last thing we need is them distracted."

Tripp nodded. "Will do." It was an automated response and the only one he had right now. When the line went quiet, he looked at the phone and then opened his team leaders' number and typed *123,* and hit send. That was their way of saying, call me if you're able.

An Alpha's daughter. Fucking A, just what he needed.

His phone lit up and he looked down at the information on it. He didn't need to look at the map to figure out where he was meeting his lift in, he'd driven by it a half-hour ago. Jamming his phone into the holder, he started the SUV and turned around.

He didn't get fifty feet before his phone lit up again. That Zain was fast. He liked that. Tapping the screen, he opened the picture and then slammed on the brakes. In the photo was a man and his daughter, all dressed up. He barely looked at her, but the man, he knew all too well.

It was Alpha Vesper Hughes, the leader of one of the two cougar clans in Ontario. Tripp stomped on the gas and would have given himself whiplash if his muscles hadn't already been rock-hard with tension.

Alpha Hughes was an asshole. How did he know this was one hundred percent correct? He'd met the man eight years earlier. It had been a dark and trying time in his life. His father had been killed, for the Alliance and for the protection of another clan. Staying with the clan just brought it all up for his mother over and over again. So, she and his younger sister wanted to leave. Tripp had traveled with them for three weeks, staying off the radar to get them to Ontario only to hit a brick wall at the end of it. That brick wall was Vesper Hughes. He didn't want any outsiders added to his clan unless they were mated in. If it had been up to Tripp, he would have taken his family to Mae's clan instead, but his mother wanted to be with a cousin—he still wasn't sure of the connection, just knew that sometime since the dawn of time their bloodlines had crossed.

When Hughes had called for assistance against the rouge shifter, he met Kenzo Dean. *Rouge shifter*, he sneered. Kenzo was the first man in Tripp's life he'd feared. He smirked, now he worked with him on the same team. He wondered if Kenzo remembered that first meeting too.

Shortly after that, he'd met Shepard Addison and the second man he feared, Calum Dante. He didn't know Calum that well, but since then had worked with him a few times and he respected the hell out of that man, he truly did. He scowled at the picture again, then tapped the screen so it wouldn't go to sleep. The result of that turbulent time was his mother and sister were allowed to be part of that clan and Tripp—was never allowed to step a foot on the clan's land again.

Now—he had to go rescue that man's daughter. He blew out a breath and grabbed the phone. Balancing his wrist over the steering wheel, he enlarged the picture so Alpha Asshole wasn't on the screen. The daughter was wearing some off-the-shoulder dress and smiling like the princess she undoubtedly was. He squinted at it, okay, she was cute as hell with her big, beautiful eyes and pouty lips, but still, she was Alpha Asshole's daughter. "Fuck." He jammed the phone back in the holder and glared at the road. If it weren't for all the ops happening right now, he'd beg one of the others to take over and do this instead of him. Rescuing those held by one-forms was much more rewarding than going in to get some pampered, precious Alpha's daughter. Seriously, what the hell was she doing on one of the Alliance teams? He rolled his eyes, probably whining to daddy, who arranged it and got her the position—and he was going to have to go in a plane to go get her. His knuckles were white as he gripped the wheel and growled at the road in front of him.

Chapter Two

The first thing that dawned on Amari, was that her head was pounding like she'd whacked it against something hard. The second was her eyes were open and she couldn't see jack all. The last thing that registered was she was being carried over someone's shoulder, if the ache in her guts were any indication, she'd been in this position for a while now.

She could taste blood. It was her own.

With a dry tongue, she tried to lick over her lips and felt the swelling. Her mouth was busted up. Why was her mouth that way? She tried to move her hands to see if she'd decked someone—her wrists were bound together behind her back. She sucked in a breath and prepared to find out what the hell was going on, when her stomach heaved, rebelling against that idea. She blinked again and tried to reach her cat, to see if she had any idea what was going on. She was there, just barely. Trying to stay lax for a minute more, so whoever was carrying her wouldn't realize she was awake, she fought through the fog to remember what happened. She'd been driving. Made no stops. Hadn't gotten out of the van—

"She's waking up." She felt the words rumble through the body carrying her.

"Shit. Already?"

There were two of them. She didn't recognize either voice. With the blood rushing to her head, she was barely able to think at all. They stopped moving.

"Right here." A large hand slapped her on the ass.

Before she could struggle, she felt a sting and the only thing that came to mind was she'd just been tranq'd in the ass. Clenching her teeth, she tried to fight the effects. If she could just get her cat in on it, some adrenalin might help counteract it.

A rocking motion brought her out of the thick haze in her head. What was going on? She was sitting in a vehicle. Sideways on a seat, she thought. Her head felt like it was pulsing with each beat of her heart. They'd knocked her out again.

"She's awake." A male voice said.

"Don't dart her again, too many will stop her heart." That was a different voice than before, she thought, the fog in her brain was heavy, so she could be wrong.

The words 'stop her heart' registered *very* clearly though. Her next thought was to kick and scream, but her cat moved closer to the surface to settle her down. She was poised, as if she were in hunting mode. Amari took a deep breath and breathed it out again. Calm and watchful would get her further than freaking out. Okay, she could do this. Closing her eyes, she started to take stock of the situation.

There was something over her head, and from the smell of it, she wasn't the first recipient to wear it. Her feet weren't bound, that was a good start. Wiggling her toes, she realized her boots were gone. So much for the knife in her boot. Her wrists were still bound, but her hands were in front of her body this time. She could work with that. Rolling her head to the side, she tensed. There was something around her neck. Cold, thick, she dropped her head forward, it felt like hard leather. The bastards had collared her. Amari *really* had issues with restrictions, physical or otherwise. Now she understood her cat's stance, shifting was out of the question. *Calm, just stay fucking calm, figure this out.* She took short breaths and blew them out.

"How's her shoulder?"

She stiffened. Her shoulder? Relaxing her arms, she tried to ignore the way the binds were cutting into her wrists. Her one shoulder was stinging. There was something on it.

"No fresh blood through the bandage," one of them said.

"You're lucky she didn't get more than a few bumps and cuts," a voice growled from her left. It had to be the driver. "What the hell possessed you to shoot her through the window while she was driving?"

Amari opened her eyes wide. Through the window? She tried to focus to think. Shit, she had been driving with the window open so she wouldn't get tired. Wait—if they'd tran'q her while she was driving, she crashed the van.

"Why the hell did you make us walk all the way back to the jeep?" Someone said from the same seat as her.

She was in a jeep, but couldn't feel the air brushing over her, so it was closed in, which meant she couldn't just flip herself out and take off.

"They'll come looking for her." The driver said, "tracks leading from the crash site are a huge beacon."

She had cashed the van. All her stuff was left there—*focus, figure out their weaknesses.* She closed her eyes again and tried to relax her whole body, hoping they would keep talking.

"What are you bitching about, I carried her." From the direction of his voice, he was sitting in the passenger seat. He'd slapped her ass. She'd be communicating with that one later.

"So, what's the plan?" That one was sitting across from her asked.

"We'll go to the lookout and wait it out for a few days, let them chase their tails around in the bush." The driver said. "Then we'll head down and make us some nice money."

Amari dug deep to stay relaxed, but her mind was processing possible ways they could make 'some nice money'—with her. *None* of the reasons were good.

"Female, if our intel is right, Alpha family, we should get double the fee for this one."

Her restraint broke, she kicked out with her foot in the direction the voice came from. When she connected with a body, she did it again with twice the anger.

"Son of a..."

"Grab her legs."

Amari tried to kick again, but strong hands pinned her legs down. "Are you going to be okay?" He sounded amused.

"I think she broke my fucking nose." His voice was a lot more nasal than it had been a few seconds ago.

Amari clenched her jaw and relaxed in the hold on her legs. There was no sense in expending more energy until she was out of this vehicle. She felt a small measure better knowing she'd landed the kicks on his face. When she got loose—and she would somehow, he was getting a lot more than a kick in the face.

"She probably came to and panicked." The hands loosen on her calves, "she'll be too dopey to do it again."

Wanna bet? She clamped down on her anger so she could listen and learn more. *Intel.* Someone had sold her out. A thought hit her, if they had the information on her this long since they discovered the leak in their system, how many other women were at risk from the Alliance databases? *Shit.* She needed to get out of here.

The girls on the team could be next. She went to bite her lip and then winced when her teeth brushed over her swollen split lip. Gia would be fine, she had Deacon to watch over her. Calla and Deva didn't have a mate to ride shotgun all the time. Taking a deep breath, she tried to keep calm. They'd be more inclined to wait for their partners from the incursion team though. Clenching her jaw, she cursed herself. It was her own fault; she was hell-bent on proving her balls were just as big as any male out there and now—*now* she was going to have to listen to all the I told you so's.

Turning her head, she rested it against the seat. This wasn't over. There would be no sales taking place. She just had to wait and listen and find that opening. She could play the docile frightened female. Until her hands were free, then these men better run fast and far. Shifting in the seat, she winced when her shoulder objected. How bad was it? She needed them to take this hood off her head, so she could see. Moving her hands to the side, until she found a position that didn't make her shoulder throb, she rested them against her belt. A slow smile moved her swollen mouth. They'd left her belt on. Now, she just needed the opportunity to turn it so she could reach the back of it, then she owed them a large order of payback, with a side order of revenge.

Chapter Three

Tripp rolled the chute up and dropped it on the ground. Never again. He was *never* getting on a plane of any sort *ever* again. He'd thought for a few minutes he was going to lose the internal battle with his cat and shift inside that tin can with wings. That would have ended badly for everyone. He'd fast roped from choppers before but jumping out of a fucking *moving* plane—not happening ever again. He dropped down and sat on the chute and took the backpack off his front. He'd honestly thought the pilot was joking when he asked him if he'd ever parachuted before until he held one out to him and told him there was nothing to it.

Nothing to it, my ass. The ground was coming upon him so fast he'd almost froze and not pulled the damn cord. He was sure he looked nothing like the pros that landed gracefully and hit the ground running. Not him, no, he'd dropped like a wet fish and then got rolled up in the lines from the chute and ended up looking like a big burrito with strings of cheese hanging out.

His cat rolled through him. He blew out a breath, "yeah, I know, if I'd had more warning, we wouldn't have had a full stomach."

Pulling off the black beanie, he ran his hands through his hair. The cool air on his head felt good. Getting up, he stuffed the hat into his pocket and then pulled the elastic off his wrist. Pulling his hair back into his 'man bun', as the guys liked to tease him, he looked around. The trees were sparse here, and he was glad of it because dropping was one thing, there's no way he could have steered that thing. "If I was meant to fly, I'd shift into something with wings." He mumbled to himself as he adjusted his run pack that was bunched under his arm beneath his jacket.

Taking out the map and compass, he squatted down to figure out where exactly he was. Turns out his parachuting wasn't all bad, he was only a mile off target. He looked around again and then back to the map, if he shifted, he could make up that time fast. A shiver moved over his skin; his cat was all for a run. Folding up the map, he looked at the backpack, betting his animal wouldn't be so eager when he found out they'd be carrying the full pack. Which his cat hated.

Tripp chuckled, hopefully, there were no hikers around, seeing a two-hundred-pound mountain lion wearing a large gear bag would not be good for their mental health. He started stripping down and jamming the bulkier items into the bag. His cat caught on fast and let his displeasure be known. "There's a female out there, probably scared out of her mind, and bad guys to educate." That did it for the creature, now he was all paws in. He would pick up a better scent in his animal form.

Adjusting his run pack so it would sit on his side, he went bent down to extend the straps to the spots marked on his bag. It had to fit tight and not shift around or he could get hung up on a branch and throw off his cat. It had taken many hours of running with this thing on his back to find balance while wearing it. He got down on his hands and knees, like a noob shifter, to get into the straps. Whoever had designed the bags to do this, was a genius, it helped his team, and probably others, get places fast with all their gear. Unfortunately, it added a solid fifty pounds to his back, but his animal loved a good workout. "Hold on, princess, we're in the game now." He whispered into the wind and then shifted.

He didn't need to have a map out, his cat let him know the van was through the trees up ahead. He could smell it. Pausing, he checked the ground around them, there were no tracks or scents that didn't belong out here, so no one came this way. He moved with slow steps, so he could get eyes on the van and assess the situation before he burst through the trees. He wasn't picking up any sound that would indicate that there was anyone with the vehicle.

Hunkering down, belly to the ground, Tripp made sure to stay in the shadow of the growth while he took a quick look. When he got a clear line of sight, he huffed out a breath, the van was slid sideways down the steep ditch, the front end of it embedded on a large boulder. The doors he could see were sitting wide open. That confirmed for him that she hadn't just hitched a ride with someone. However she'd left, it wasn't on her own accord.

He circled around, so he wasn't trampling any tracks and then shifted. Climbing out of the straps, he pulled his cargo pants and weapon pack out of the bag. He didn't plan on being here long enough to get completely dressed. If he left barefoot prints, there would be no way to confuse them with any booted ones.

Wrapping his hand around the grip of his 9 mil, he walked slowly toward the van, scenting the air as he went. His cat was alert and would let him know if there was anyone nearby, wild, or otherwise.

Tripp approached the driver's side first, the door was open, and the window was down. Laying on the ground beside the door was a red-tipped dart. He looked at the door again, she'd been tranq'd through the open window while driving? He nodded his head slowly, that was a precision shot. Leaning in the door, he inhaled slowly. Blood. It was dried but still stood out like a beacon to him. Examining the inside of the door, the steering wheel, and the seat, he found traces of it on all of them, but thankfully not enough to be life-threatening injuries.

He climbed in through that door, not wanting to disturb any tracks on the other side. The snow hadn't arrived yet, so any tracks would still be there. The gear was still in the van, nothing had been gone through. It wasn't tucked under seats now, having slid around from the force of the sudden stop, but it was all closed. *Shit.* He was going to have to get the cleanup team here to remove all of it.

Squatting down, he grabbed her run pack and then saw a worn backpack and picked it up too. When he found the princess, and he would, she'd be more settled if she had some of her own stuff. He opened it and glanced inside. Pulling out the material on the top, he confirmed it was a shirt and there was denim right beneath it. Setting the backpack and run pack beside the door, he leaned out and looked at the ground outside it. There was an impression in the snow that pissed him off, it was from where they put her on the ground unconscious after they pulled her out. A few spots of blood were in the melting snow. Nothing that alarmed him, so this was good. He tilted his head and studied the boot prints, two sets of them if he wasn't mistaken, but he'd confirm that once he was following them.

Hopping out, he made sure he stood only on the spot where they had laid her down. First, he needed a direction and then he'd look for a scent to give his cat. There were so many prints, it looked like they did a dance in this area. The tracks thinned out and went into the trees on the left. Okay, the direction is confirmed. Tucking his gun into the waist of his pants, he turned around and looked at the van.

Phone. Where was her phone? He walked to the front of the van and opened the already unlatched hood. The wiring was ripped out in a hasty way. This vehicle wouldn't be running for a while. Reaching in, he lifted the bundle and saw that the clip that should be carefully hidden among them was gone. Tracker one down. He bent down and looked under the front;

it lay there crushed into pieces. How the hell did they know where to find it?

Standing back up, he looked around for her phone. They wouldn't leave it on her, no one was that stupid. Going to the passenger door, he was about to open it and then paused. Someone had to go in through this one to get her out the side or moved to the side for the other one. Leaning down, he held his nose close to the door handle and took a slow sniff of it. His cat perked up, bingo, they hadn't been wearing gloves. "What do you think? Bear of some flavor?" He sneered, he hated going head-to-head with the bear clan, they were like God damned tanks with teeth and feet. Opening the door, he looked down. Found the phone, the many pieces of it. "Fucking bears and they're braggart strength."

Closing the door, he went back to the side one and looked at the handle, hoping this one hadn't worn gloves either. Moving closer to it, he took a slow breath and paused to filter the smell of metal from it. Opening his eyes, he cocked his head to the side, "and you're a mystery flavor."

He grabbed her packs and closed the door. He needed his bag, so he could leave a chip behind for the clean-up team to come to erase the evidence of this sloppy abduction. Setting hers down, he jogged to where he'd left his own.

Placing the chip under the driver's seat, he got out his phone and brought up the number for Kaid Rivera, the leader of the clean-up team. He punched in the code for the tracker he'd just used, typed van, and then hit send. Kaid would have the tech team trace it and send someone.

He paused and looked at the signal strength on his phone. It wasn't great. Glancing in the direction the tracks led, he blew out a breath, it was probably going to get much worse. Tapping Kenzo's number he typed in, *Vehicle found. Evidence of minor injuries. Two idiots. Following trail. Cleanup notified.* Then hit send.

Stuffing her run pack into her backpack, he strapped it onto his and then looked down at it. If he had to hike any of this on paws, it was going to be a balancing act. His phone buzzed in his pocket. Pulling it out, he read the reply. *Will notify Jesse. Bring her back.*

Shrugging, he sent back a thumbs-up emoji. Kenzo hated when they used emojis, but it summed up what he needed to say.

He pulled out his boots, shirt, and jacket and quickly put them on. Tripp learned a few years back that keeping his run pack under his shirt and jacket made for faster shifts. Next, he checked the map of the area. If they were still on foot, this was going to be short and sweet. If they'd stashed a vehicle somewhere in all this wilderness, he'd still be able to track them, but it gave them a big lead on him. Tucking the map in his run pack, he checked the time on his phone before he sealed it in a waterproof bag. If they had driven at some point, he wasn't going to catch up until dusk, maybe later. Dusk worked for him—he could see without being seen then. Zipping the pack up, he hefted his bag onto his back. "Hang tight, princess, we're on the way."

Chapter Four

Amari jolted and tried to sit forward and couldn't. Something was restraining her. The cloth against her face reminded her of the recent events. Had she drifted off or had they darted her? How long did this crap stay in her system? Her mouth was throbbing, her tongue felt thick and so dry, there was going to be no swallowing or licking her swollen lip.

She rested her head back against what felt like a tree and closed her eyes. She felt like she'd drank about ten more drinks than her body could handle. Had a hangover ever felt this bad? She didn't think so. Taking a deep breath, she snarled at the smell of this material, it was rank. Her cat was there, more alert than she was, so that was good, if she'd had to wait for her animal, she would have been a little bit miffed with that. *Okay, girl. What do we know?*

The information was a shortlist. She'd been shot with a dart through the window, while she drove. She quirked an eyebrow, that was almost an impressive shot. Too bad the one that had done it was going to regret it when she got out of this. Her arm, face, and shoulder throbbed, so clearly, she'd crashed the van. *Assholes.* They'd put some stinky thing over her head and carried her. She scowled and then shot her in the ass on the walk. Oh yeah, the one that had a fondness for the tranq darts was due some hurt, courtesy of her. Blowing out a breath, she clamped down on the rage, she couldn't afford to expend the energy she might need later. *Focus*, her cat reminded her. Next, it was a ride in the jeep. She smirked and then winced; her mouth hurt. At least one of them, the one that shot her in the ass if she wasn't mistaken had a messed-up face from her foot. Score one point for her. And then—a big blank until she just woke up. She was tied—she tried to rock to assess how and didn't like the result, her hands were bound behind her, and she was tied by the freaking collar around her neck. How had she forgotten the collar part? Last, she didn't have her jacket or boots on, and her ass was cold from the ground. Overall, none of it was encouraging at all.

What she needed was this thing off her face, so she could see what time it was and where she was. Slowing her breathing, she listened for her new friends. Someone was moving to her right. She held her breath for a second so her breathing inside the hood didn't funnel to her ears. There were two voices further away, sounded like they were getting closer, so they were walking. *Okay*, she huffed out her breath—*you've got this. Assess the situation.*

"I still don't see why we're all the way up here." That was a new voice, one she hadn't heard before.

"Dead zone." The one that had been driving said. "We don't know if they're using an internal tracker or not."

Amari had to work on not chuckling, letting someone stick a tracker in her body—not happening.

"Wouldn't we have been told if they were?" That was the one that had carried her.

"Last I heard access was cut off," he sounded very nasal, must be the one that met her foot, "chances are they found the breach and have fixed it."

All of this fit with what Jesse had already told them. The tech team was already all over that. There were four of them now. Four was more of a challenge than two, but she loved a good challenge. The longer she sat here playing like she was still unconscious, the more she might learn.

"How long are you going to be gone?" Nasal asked.

"By the time I get down from here to where I can get a signal, it will be late."

Where the hell had they brought her? Down? *Shit—the mountains.*

"I'll be back up tomorrow, or whenever they reply."

"She's worth double." The new one said.

"I know what she's worth. Just make sure she's undamaged—in every way." He was obviously in charge, the authority in his voice was clear. She might go a little easier on him for that order, maybe. Doubtful.

"We know the drill." The one that had carried her said, he sounded bored.

At least they had no plans to hurt her, that was a plus for them—even with her hands bound, she wouldn't go down easy if they didn't drug her anymore. Her cat rolled through her, telling her to stay calm and figure this out.

"When she wakes up, make sure you get some water into her, those darts dehydrate you."

"We'll feed and water her, no worries." The new one answered. "Just bring back some extra blankets, that storm moving in is going to suck up here."

She frowned; a storm would slow her down when she got out of this mess. Her cat had a nice warm coat, so she'd simply just stay in that form until she cleared it.

"See you tomorrow."

Amari listened to him walking away and noticed none of the others moved as he did. Was he Alpha, or just the one in charge? Not that it mattered, one less for her to deal with was fine by her. Now, she just needed to get them to take this damn thing off her head.

They didn't talk to one another, she could hear one of them walking away, one of them moving around on something that sounded like canvas or plastic of some kind and the other one hadn't done anything.

"Give me a hand." The new one said, "I want to get the tarps over these to insulate them from the snow."

At least he had brains, she decided. Okay, time to see the faces that went with the voices. Play it calm her cat reminded her. Moving her head, she moaned like she was just coming to—hopefully it inspired them to check on her.

She heard the pause in movement and moaned softly again.

"I'll check on her, you go get some wood for the fire." The new one said.

Amari didn't move while he walked toward her. Her cat was still, waiting with her, reminding her once more to stay calm and quiet, they needed them to believe she was harmless and write her off as a cooperative hostage. If that was even a thing.

"I'm going to take the hood off," his tone was quiet, "just behave and it can stay off."

She stiffened and waited.

The first breath of fresh air felt so good she almost smiled. Blinking, she let her eyes adjust to the light again. It was barely daylight, so that was a plus, they hadn't traveled too long.

"That's it," he spoke from beside her, "I'll get you a drink and see what we can do about finding you a more comfortable position in a bit."

If it weren't for her situation, she might give this one a pass, she thought for a second, but he was still part of it, so that wasn't going to happen. Lifting her chin, she watched him walk away. He was a big son of bitch, but she'd taken down bigger in her life. She didn't know how long he would have his back to her, so she took the opportunity to look around. They were on some plateau surrounded by trees. She was *on* the mountain she'd been admiring as she drove.

They'd erected some tents, that weren't new if the faded material was any indication. A smaller man was securing tarps over them. She looked behind her to see she was tied to a young tree. There were only traces of snow on the ground, so that was a plus because she was sitting on the wet ground and at least it wasn't numbing cold snow.

When he started walking back toward her with a bottle of water, she kept her chin down and looked him over from under her lashes. He had a big scar across half his face and despite his gentle voice, his expression was not. He was a killer and there was no mistaking that void expression in the back of his eyes. That eliminated the possibility that she could play on his soft side.

When he squatted down beside her and uncapped the water bottle, he glanced over his shoulder, "told you stopping her was a better plan than taking the shot while she was driving," he turned back to her, "this is going to be a challenge with your mouth all messed up."

Amari flicked her gaze to his briefly, how bad was her face? She was still numb all over from the drugs and the cold. Tipping her head back until it rested against the tree, she opened her mouth as far as she could. Her neck muscles were tight, no doubt from the impact when she crashed the van.

"That's a girl." He leaned closer and poured some of the water into her mouth.

She tried to rinse it around her dry mouth and ended up drooling half of it out because of the swelling. Swallowing it, she winced and then tipped her head back again. This time she swallowed it and repeated her action without making eye contact with him once more. They needed to believe she was scared into compliance and too afraid to do anything about her situation.

When half the bottle was gone, she nodded her head slightly to tell him she'd had enough. The last thing that she needed was to drink too much and have to go to the bathroom. That, with three males watching, wasn't happening. She'd go in her pants where she sat before she went in front of them.

He capped the water and set it beside her. "You were a hard one to track." He smirked at her and then stood up.

Was that supposed to make her feel better? How had they tracked her? She never took the same route twice, and never made a predictable move. The phones, she was told were now secure and the vehicle tracking was only known by a few—so, *how* had they tracked her? She needed to get out of there and get a hold of Zain and Jesse and let them know they knew about the new tracking methods. So many were at risk.

When he reached the tents, he shook his head and looked at the smaller man. "Why don't you go shift and fix your face." He sounded amused. Turning to the other big guy, he motioned to one of the tents. "You don't need to stand guard. We'll hear anyone approaching. Grab a blanket and get it on her. We don't need her half-frozen."

The one that had carried her, nodded and moved to the other tent. The big one with the scar was in charge when the driver was gone. Good to know. Now, to figure out which one of the three jerks was the easiest to con. She tried to reach the back of her belt and couldn't. Reaching to the side, she bent her arms in an uncomfortable way, if she could turn the belt to the side, she would be able to get the knife out of the hidden slit she'd put in her belt. The case was sewn to the backside of her belt and that little knife had saved her ass more times than she could count.

She was able to touch the leather, but the belt loops on her jeans prevented her from turning it. Of course, she wore real denim and not that elastic stretchy shit the new ones were made with. Scowling at the ground, she decided she might have to rethink that for the future—not that she had plans to be abducted again.

Amari watched them set up more of the camp. The little one went into the trees, probably going to shift to fix his face. If she could get him to come close to her again, she'd have to give him something more permanent to worry about. The big one with the scar carried a small gas can over to the dug-up firepit area and poured a bit on the wood. Not how'd she'd light a fire—but okay. The smell would be a great indicator of where they were located though.

Zain would have sounded the alarm by now. How many check-ins had she missed? Three, four? She couldn't be sure. Someone would be tracking her whereabouts by now. With any luck, Calum was close enough to lend a hand or Blair. She hadn't seen him in action yet, but she'd heard the stories and could only hope to see him in action sometime.

The one that had carried her came out of a tent, dragging a blanket along the wet ground behind him. When he reached her, he grabbed her shoulder and jerked her forward, almost choking her when the rope on the collar hit the end. He draped the blanket over her in a half-ass way, then walked away.

She tried to sit back and stop it from sliding off again. It fell off her injured shoulder but still covered her other side. Amari sent him a look that marked him with a silent promise. First, he'd carried her like a sack, then smacked her ass, and now this. Oh yeah, she was going to have to balance the scales before they parted ways. Big snowflakes started to fall, just what she didn't need right now.

The small jerk came out of the trees and stopped, motioning to his face, "all pretty again?"

Scarface snorted, then went back to what he was doing. "Go see if she needs another drink."

Amari dropped her head, trying to come up with something to bring him closer to her. *Calm,* her cat reminded her. No worry there—she was so bloody calm right now; he might mistake her as dead. She would have smirked if it weren't for her mouth. *Perfect idea.*

Chapter Five

Tripp took the heavy bag off his back and leaned it against a tree. It had taken him a lot longer than he would have liked to follow this trail. With the snow coming down now, the tracks were covered. If it hadn't been for the narrow path in the trees, he would have lost it—but a vehicle could only fit there.

The sun was going down, but that was to his advantage, the hazy period between day and night made it harder for him to be seen and easier for him to move through the shadows and glares the departing sun left in its wake. His cat was just as annoyed as he was that the woman had been out there this long. He didn't have time to pause and reassure his animal.

The trail from the vehicle headed down through the bush and he debated for a moment on following it, but the smell of a fire burning piqued his interest and he'd learned a long time ago that following his gut paid off more than misleading signs laid out before him. It wasn't a coincidence that the trail led past someone with a campfire going. With the storm, it was doubtful it was just some hikers out enjoying the fresh air.

Pulling a bottle of water out of the bag, he drank it down and then stopped all movement and listened. With the snow coming down, he couldn't be sure of the distance as it tended to muffle sounds, but if his estimated location was right, someone was at the top of the hill. He looked in the direction the vehicle had gone. If he were a criminal douchebag, he'd send only one to make contact and stay back with the prize in this dead zone in the middle of nowhere.

Picking up the bag, he hefted it on his back. If he was wrong, he'd shift and make up for the lost time following the vehicle. The map showed the nearest town wasn't that far from this location—if you went straight down the mountain. His cat could go places something on wheels couldn't.

He moved up the hill, keeping in the trees, so he could see, but not be seen. If it was them, they were idiots for having a fire going. He liked idiots; they made his job much easier. As he got closer to the top, he could smell more than just a campfire. His cat analyzed the other scent without hesitation, it was blood. Not a lot, but still blood. There was also a strong smell of gasoline. Did they have rec vehicles up there? It would save him the energy of walking back out of here after he dealt with them—the princess would probably be happier with a ride out of here.

As soon as he could hear the crackling of wood, he slowed his step and tapped into his cats' better vision to help in the low light. The burning fire was like an invisible trail showing him the exact direction they were. He moved toward the left, not wanting to walk right into their camp when he got to the top.

Pausing just before he could see their location, he took the bag off and set it where he'd be able to find it again. Moving his gun to the back of his pants, he pulled out his knife and then proceeded to move in that direction. Staying low to the ground, he crept along much like his cat would have if it was stalking something.

With the snowfall, he had to stay in the shadows, or else he'd stand out like a flashing sign against the white. When he reached the point where the hill leveled off into an open area, he felt the satisfaction of being right. There was a camp set up.

Three tents grouped together. Motion in front of one of them had him zero in on it. Two large men were crowded around a third one. *Shit.* The possibility of two from the bear clan was something he didn't relish. If three were here, that meant he had to deal with four if he waited too long.

"I told you not to get too close." The one said, sounding more annoyed than anything else.

"It's not going to grow back even if you shift, you idiot." The other one told him.

Tripp held this position, breathing into his hand so it filtered his breath toward the ground, and couldn't be seen in the cold air. What wouldn't grow back? His interest was piqued now.

The smaller man stood up and jerked his head away from the other one. He was holding a cloth against the side of his head. Tripp's eyebrows went up in surprise. He looked at the tents, trying to see if there was anyone in them. Whoever had done that to that man wasn't friendly. He didn't detect any movement. First guess, the princess wasn't as docile as he'd pictured her to be.

"Pouring gas on her was stupid," the one closest to him growled and waved his arm, "now we can't move her closer to the fire to keep her warm."

He didn't like the sound of that. They'd poured gas on her. Who did something like that? He shuddered, something that strongly scented on *any* shifter was just cruel.

"The bitch bit half my ear off." The other one growled, "let her freeze."

Tripp's lips twitched with amusement, but it was short-lived. He needed them to move out of their little huddle so he could see if they had any weapons on them—and he needed to find the princess with the sharp teeth. Chances were she was probably halfway to unconscious now from the gas fumes.

Moving back down out of their line of sight, he crept along the ground to find another vantage point to see if he could spot her. He didn't have to go far; the smell of the fuel gave his cat the direction now that he was out of the smoke from the fire.

She was tied to a tree, facing the tents. Her hands were bound behind her, and they had a collar around her neck as well—he wasn't sure from this angle, but it might be the leather. They'd secured her to the tree by the neck. They were treating her like some kind of pet. He'd bite someone's ear off too if they'd done that to him. Her face was banged up and he hoped the blood on it was from her biting that guy. He studied the way she sat; she didn't appear to have any other injuries. In fact, she was holding herself board straight, not leaning against the tree at all for support. That simplified getting her down from here if she could move on her own.

Tripp took his time assessing the situation, trying to plan the best way to take out three of them without her being in the line of fire. He couldn't just outright shoot them, might prefer to, but he needed to know where the vehicle went, who was in it, and what the plan was. Anything less would yield him a major berating from Kenzo and other higher-ups in the Alliance. The fact that they got their hands on a member from one of the teams pushed all the wrong buttons and they'd need answers

If he cut her binds, would she freak out and make them aware of his presence? She showed great initiative, biting the ear, so maybe she would stay still and silent and let him do his thing. The gas had to be burning through her clothes, so she could try to struggle out of them and alert them that she was free. Before he could come up with a solid plan, she turned her head and looked right at him. Not in his direction, but *right* at him. He was impressed, and from the look on her face, she was beyond pissed. Anger was something he could work with, just as long as it was cool, calculating anger and not the inferno kind. He moved his hand from his mouth and held up his finger to tell her to hold tight. She turned her head back to look at the men like he wasn't even there.

Now that she knew he was here, he couldn't just leave her sitting there getting buried in snow, he decided. Staying low, he backed up, so he was in the darkness of the trees again, all while keeping his eyes on the three that were still debating on how stupid the little man was. In any other situation, he'd happily offer his opinion on the matter.

He moved up behind the tree she was tied to, it was not big enough to hide his presence if anyone turned and looked at her. The only advantage he had was they were occupied, and the fire was far enough away to not cast light on her. Touching her hand, he winced when he felt how cold it was. Carefully, he worked the blade between her wrists and hoped she kept still. "I'm going to free your hands." He whispered no louder than a breath and hoped her hearing was as good as her eyesight. She kept her head still and looked in the direction of the men. The smell of gas almost gagged him and he had no idea how she was keeping her breathing so steady. His animal was not impressed that his sense of smell was voided out right now. "Are they armed?" He glanced up to see she gave a quick shake of her head.

"Dart gun." She whispered.

That was a plus, no dodging bullets, although if he got tranq'd he'd be very unhappy. "I can't get to the collar without giving away my position." He felt remorse for offering her so little hope. "Hold tight, darlin, I'll be right back." He rolled away so he wasn't in their line of sight.

Once he was no longer visible, he made fast work to get back to his bag, he was going to need a few more toys to pull this off. His cat was prodding him internally as he did, trying to convince him to shift so he could deal with it. It was a great idea, but in cat form, having a conversation was a little limited and he needed information out of those idiots, not to mention alive worked better for having discussions. He needed to know when the fourth was coming back, and if he was bringing others with him—any details after that were all bonuses.

Tucking the wire into his pocket, he reached into his weapon pack and pulled out another blade and gun. Most of the teams used zip ties, but a big shifter could pop those apart without breaking a sweat. Wire cut into flesh and prevented any further thought of misbehaving. He'd learned that the hard way when he'd gotten a little out of hand that first time he met

Kenzo. It was terrifying to feel the wire cut into your flesh—afterward, of course, he thought it was brilliant.

Picking up the bag, he carried it further up the hill, so he wouldn't have to leave them long to retrieve it. He had one shot to pull this off without incident. The *incident* being he didn't sustain injury. Three against one, he shrugged, seemed about even to him. Moving fast, he went back up the hill with soundless moves.

He found a tree big enough that he could hide behind it and checked their positions before he walked into it. They were all still close to each other. The tents being near were a worry if they had weapons in there that she hadn't seen. He glanced to see she was watching them, not looking around. *Good girl.* He'd been worried she'd be looking around trying to figure out where he went. She even had her hands behind her back still. That surprised him, which didn't happen often.

Just as he stepped out of the tree, the two big men turned to move away from the little guy. He held the gun out in front of him, so they would be sure to see it. The first one froze and stood there. Tripp had his other hand hovering near his side, so he could access a knife or gun, whichever might be required the most.

When the second one noticed, he glanced at one of the tents. "I wouldn't," Tripp said loud enough that even the man with one and a half ear would hear him. The little one jolted and spun around. "Let's do this the easy way, okay?" Tripp moved toward them, watching their feet more than the rest of them. The funny thing about a body is it didn't matter where you looked or what you planned to do; your feet were the first part of a body to move to do it and always pointed the way if you watched close enough.

His cat was scenting the air, monitoring it for him, trying to get a sense of what they might do. Adrenalin and fear were easy emotions to pick up on.

In a blur of movement, the woman that was bound to the tree went screeching past him, both in movement and sound.

Tripp moved closer, then pulled out his knife. How the hell did she get free and *what* was she doing?

She lunged at the little one, growling a low eerie sound. Her cat was closer to the surface, making his cat come forward even more.

One of the big ones started to move, so Tripp flicked the knife and landed it in his foot. Right through the boot. "Don't." He advised. The other big one dropped to his knees and held his hands up. That was more like it. Later, he'd internally bitch with his cat about how easy this had been and how they hadn't gotten a single swing in.

Tripp stepped to the side so he could see what she was doing while keeping an eye on his new friends. Buddy was on his knees now in a chokehold. He wanted to blink to make sure he wasn't hallucinating but didn't take the chance he'd miss something else. She leaned down, close to his whole ear and he wondered if she planned to bite that one off too.

"This is for shooting darts in me," she moved her hand to his throat and that's when Tripp saw the glint of metal, "and the gas." She started to straighten up and he figured she'd gotten it out of her system. In a move he could never have imagined, she stabbed the knife into his carotid artery and held his chin up, so it spurted out all over. It got her right in the face, she licked her lips and then looked at the dying man, "just like candy," she whispered.

He knew his jaw was close to hitting the ground, but he honestly couldn't decide what to do at that moment. The princess he'd pictured evaporated right before his eyes. He glanced at the other two. The one was hunched over his foot, reminding Tripp he'd left a weapon too close to him. The other one was reflecting his thoughts, of 'what the hell just happened?' Stepping closer, he, motioned with his gun for the injured one to move back. He shuffled back. "Hands nice and high." When he complied, Tripp ducked in and picked up his knife.

Backing up, he kept those two in his sight as he turned to see the princess standing there, blood all over her hand and cheek. She wiped her hand back over her hair, streaking it red too, and didn't seem to care. When she moved toward the other two, he quickly cut her off. "We need information." He gave her a wary look, "they talk better when they're alive."

She looked him up and down and then held her hands out from her body. "Fine." Backing away, she went over toward the first tent and opened the flap.

Turning his head, he looked at the two men and lifted one eyebrow. The horror on their faces told him that they were regretting the most recent decisions in their lives, the ones where they had abducted that petite little bundle of anger that was now standing beside the tent pouring water over her face. He looked down to see she had boots on now too. "All right, gents, who wants to be tied up first?" He wiped the blood off his blade and secured it in the case on his hip. Neither of them moved. Pulling the wire out of his pocket, he held it up for them to see.

"Allow me." Amari went by him and yanked it out of his hand.

Tripp shrugged and stood back, keeping the gun up, but not pointed in her direction. The first man winced as she bound his hands behind him. Tripp almost felt bad for them—almost.

When she was done with the second one, she kicked his bleeding foot as she walked back over and held out the wire to him. He took it, trying not to look as stunned as the idiots in front of him. "My bag is about twenty feet down there." He pointed, "I grabbed your pack," he glanced briefly at her, "might want to put on something that doesn't smell like a fuel station."

"You found my van?" She scowled in the direction he'd pointed, "is it totaled?"

"No one will be driving it any time soon." He shrugged.

She huffed out a breath, followed by a growl. "I'm going to get my stuff." She walked away.

Tripp glanced at her, then turned back to the other two. "She's a surprise." He smirked. Crossing his arms over his chest, he let the gun hang over his elbow so they wouldn't get any stupid ideas. "So, I need only one of you alive to share the juicy bits of information I need," he looked from one to the other, "which one gives the orders?" He glanced over at the one lying in a pool of his own life juices, "I *really* hope it wasn't you." He gave his head a quick shake. The one who had a hole through his foot gave him a dirty look, "I don't like you much either, but the difference is I have a bullet with your name on it and you got nothing but hate, buddy."

He heard her come back into the camp. The smell of gas was still strong.

"I'm glad you picked up my bag. Thanks."

He shrugged one shoulder but refused to look away from the males. "No problem, I'd have done some take-out too, but we're in the middle of absolutely nothing."

She made a sound that could have been amusement or annoyance, he couldn't tell without looking and the injured idiot was staring at him like he was getting ideas. "There's some jerky and bars in the top part of my bag, help yourself."

"Thanks."

He could hear her digging around in what had to be her bag, he didn't have things that made crinkling noises in his. When she moved over and squatted down where he could see her and the men, he felt better. She had her head down and was digging through her bag. Her hair was wet, and she had to be cold, the snow on her shirt was caked on it a few places. "You might find a jacket or blanket in one of the tents." He offered.

She jerked her chin up and looked him over much like someone would to another that offended them. "I'm good." She pulled her hand out of her bag and stood up, turning to look at the two watching them.

Tripp couldn't see what she had in her hand but hoped it wasn't another knife. He frowned, it dawned on him he still didn't know where she'd had the first one hidden. Also, if she had a knife on her they hadn't found, why was she still bound to the tree when he got here? "Which one gives the orders?" He glanced back to the men, "tell me it's not the one you bled out."

"It wasn't him."

She moved fast to stand in front of the one with the sore foot and he figured it was him and felt better about the blade through his boot now. In a lightning-fast move, she lurched so she was leaning down in front of him and the man screeched a sound that cut right through Tripp's body. Then he spotted the flash of electricity she was holding something between his legs. His stomach seized and he rushed over and grabbed her by the waist and pulled her off the man. When they were clear of his feet, he pointed the gun toward them and held his arm clamped around her waist. The smell of gas burned his nostrils. "Are you trying to set yourself on fire?" Wrestling the taser out of her hand, he looked at the man and a shiver of pity went through him. He may not like the man, but a jolt of electricity to the balls was never a punishment he'd use on any man—*ever*.

"Shit." She jerked out of his arm and paced away. "I didn't even think of that." Issuing a low growl, she turned back to the guy that looked like he had either swallowed his tongue or was trying not to throw up, possibly both. "That's for slapping my ass," she pointed at him, "when I was slung over your shoulder."

Tripp winced and looked at the guy, "you are having a *really* bad day, aren't you?" He wiggled the gun in his direction, "I'll give you a break if you start talking." He checked that the taser was definitely off and slipped it into the side pocket of his pants.

"I'm going to see if they have coffee in their gear." She stomped to one of the tents.

Tripp watched her walk away and then slowly turned his head back toward them. He needed some answers before she did something to them—again. "When is your friend due to drive back up here?"

Amari came back out of the tent, carrying a worn kettle and can. "He said tomorrow or whenever he heard back."

Tripp shifted so he could glance to see her going to the fire, "how about you come here and watch them, I'll make coffee."

When she stopped and looked at him, he could see it register why he was trying to steer her from the sparks and flames.

"Shit." She shook her head and came toward him.

When she stopped in front of him, he leaned down and looked at her face, "you could go shift and heal that up." He glanced at the wet bandage on her shoulder, "Is your arm okay?"

She nodded and jammed the coffee pot into his chest. "I'm fine." She looked at the two men, "if I shift now, I'm liable to come back and maul them until they're shredded pieces of flesh." The way she said it made him realize she'd thought it through.

"Fair enough." He cleared his throat and held the gun out to her. "We do need them breathing for now."

She took the gun and just the way she shifted it in her hand told him she knew how to handle one. "I got it."

He glanced at the men and silently told them not to move a muscle and then turned to the fire. "Did you hear anything else?" He set the kettle down and then went over to the tent she had gotten it from.

"Yeah, they know about the new tracking and that I'm—" she paused, making him stick his head back out of the tent, "worth more than an average female."

Her expression had changed from anger to something he couldn't read in the low light but feared for whomever the emotion was directed at. "Because you're Alpha family." He reached back in and grabbed a few bottles of water, "they ripped the tracking out of the wiring in the van." The fact that they'd known about her status pissed him off. He gave them a side glance as he went back to the fire. The one was still swallowing bile from the looks of it, the other was watching Amari and Tripp was sure the expression on his face was admiration. He bit back a smirk at the man's misplaced loyalties—she was never going to reciprocate that.

"Do you have anything that gets signal here?"

He squatted down by the fire and poked it with the stick resting beside it. She probably wanted to check in with her father. "It's a complete dead zone." He looked over to see her scowling at the men.

"I wanted to get in touch with Jesse." She gave him a quick look, "I'm concerned about the girls on my team." She waved the gun at the one she'd tasered. "I need to give them a heads up."

Tripp focused on getting the kettle on the fire in a spot he'd be able to get it back out without frying his hand or arm. Standing up, he waited until she glanced at him and then motioned for her to come closer. Then he remembered the fire and her new body wash and stepped over the log and met her halfway. "The teams will be fine right now." Hoping he didn't have to spell it out to her in front of their audience. They were all together with enough weapons to take down a city.

Her eyes flicked up to his then back down, "right." She nodded, "it's about that time, yeah?"

Tripp nodded. Unzipping his jacket, he shrugged it off and held it out to her, "put this on, temperatures are going to drop more at this elevation and until we can get you a bubble bath, you can't exactly warm up by the fire."

Without lifting her chin, she looked up at him and he was momentarily taken back by her eyes. They weren't blue or grey but a mix of the two. When they weren't shooting daggers out of them, they were likely the prettiest eyes he'd ever seen. That thought faded when they hardened again, and he remembered her very aggressive streak.

She held out the gun and took the jacket. "Thanks."

He watched her put it on. She was favoring one arm. It was going to piss him off if she was lying about being okay. Tripp opened his mouth to tell her to go shift, but her words about mauling them came back to him. Maybe she struggled to control her animal? That's the last thing he needed right now. Wrangling a she-cat that was out for vengeance. Tranq'ing her was out of the question, he looked at the one she'd stabbed. Yeah, it was best to just keep an eye on her and not suggest shifting again—or anything that might set her off. The next time he rescued a female, he was going through the backpacks and seeing what torturous devices they hid in them.

Chapter Six

Amari stood a good distance from the fire and sipped the strong brew. It could have been mud at this point, and she wouldn't have cared, anything to get the taste of fuel out of her mouth. Her cat was going crazy inside her, not being able to process any scents. If it hadn't been for—she didn't even know his name.

He came out of the tent dragging sleeping bags behind him, then surprised her when he draped one over each of the men. She could have cared less if they were cold, wet, or breathing for that matter. He glanced at her as he picked up his cup, "I'd sooner put a bullet in each of them and head home," he gave her a lopsided grin, "but until then, I can't be inhumane. "

Amari lifted one eyebrow at him, "I can."

He stepped back from them, so he was closer to her again, "Yeah, I caught that."

Moving just her eyes she looked over at the two douchebags that were responsible for her being here. The one with the bad foot was slumped forward, he hadn't moved in a while now. The other, Scarface, she was going to call him, just watched them. He hadn't made a sound or moved since she'd gotten a little retribution on his friend. She tried not to smirk. She looked back at her rescuer, "they go around abducting people," she shrugged her good shoulder, "my job mostly comprises of relocating the lives they've damaged, so yeah, they get no sympathy or soft touch from me." She pointed a finger at them, "and they made me crash my van."

He watched her, his gaze moving over her face slowly, "that's a valid point." He nodded his head slowly, then took out his gun, pointed it, without looking, and pulled the trigger with zero hesitation.

Amari looked to see the injured one flop back onto the ground. His friend's eyes were so rounded now, she thought they might pop out of their sockets. Keeping a straight face, she turned back to see him sipping his coffee like this was some sort of cafe. "Special ops, right?"

His grin was slow, "good guess, darlin, what gave it away?"

"Well, you're a little bit crazy," she would have smirked, but it hurt to do it, "I'm not judging, it's not a *bad* quality," she looked at the other man who was staring at the dead body beside him, "and S.O. team are the only ones I know of that work solo."

"The others are a bit busy right now." He straddled the log, brush the snow from it, and sat down so he could keep an eye on her and the last surviving jerk.

"Hope that goes right." She was not impressed that she wasn't going to be there to help. There was nothing that made her feel like all the shit she'd gone through was worth it like seeing the faces of those freed when they realized it was true. She moved to the log the furthest from the flames and sat down. Her ass couldn't get any wetter than it was, so she didn't bother with brushing it off. She needed to get this smell off her, but even if she shifted, she doubted it would work. Her legs were cold now, which was a plus, the irritation from the fuel against her skin long had been driving her crazy.

"There's no reason it shouldn't. It's all planned like a beautiful ballet." He waved his hand around.

Amari grinned, then winced when her mouth hurt, "let's hope none of the ballerinas fall off the stage." She wiped at her lip, "I actually thought they'd send Calum and Blair to find me."

"No such luck," he was quiet for a second, "Blair—he's the one that took out Lindon Elden in cat form?" He blew out a breath, "his own brother, I hear."

Amari still wished she'd been there to see it. She liked working for the co-ord team, but it was a pretty chill job and she liked to be in on the action once in a while. "Yeah, the guys gave me the rundown on that. From what I hear Lindon went down in about two minutes."

The man beside them sucked in a breath, she turned to see him giving them an intent look.

"Was he a friend of yours?" He asked him.

The hatred was plain to see on his face as he shook his head. She filed the fact that all the dirtbags knew each other. It was too organized for it to be any other way.

Her hero laughed a quiet deep chuckle at the man's expression and then looked back to her, "I'm Tripp, by the way, Tripp Carson."

The name seemed familiar, but she couldn't put her finger on why. "I guess I don't have to introduce myself."

He shook his head.

"Okay, Tripp Carson, what's the plan here?" She motioned to the other man. "I don't think he's going to share much."

Tripp turned to look at him and then nodded his head slowly like he was figuring out what was next. "I plan to chip this location and get room service to come and clean it up," he motioned to the body of the man she'd stabbed and then the one he'd shot, "but I don't want them walking in on their friend when he returns."

"We're waiting for him to come back?" She didn't mind that idea at all, she couldn't leave the other one breathing to do this again. She's already decided that when Tripp had shown up. "He's going to have the information of who they contact."

"That's the information we need." He mused quietly. He set his cup down and reached up and pulled his hair loose. She was surprised it reached his shoulders. With the sides of his head shaved, she honestly didn't expect the thick wavy hair to be in that sexy little man bun. "I'm going to go for a run and check the trail to see if he's headed back or waiting out this storm."

She looked at the trees, wanting to go for a run as well, but still didn't trust she could control her cat enough to not come back and add some more scars to the man that was watching them. "Is your car nearby?"

Shaking his head, he picked up his coffee and held the cup in front of his mouth. "They made me jump from a flying tin can to come to find you."

Amari noted the unamused tone in his voice. "Okay, I guess we have to run to get out of here?"

Setting the cup down, he stood up, "at least until we can get a signal." He motioned to the fire, "I'll bring back something we can cook up." Pulling the gun from his waist, he glanced at the man still breathing, "try to leave him alive, security is going to want to have a chat with him."

She took the gun he held out to her, "I wouldn't want to ruin their fun."

He grinned and then sobered quickly, "are you sure you're okay?" He tilted his head and the way the fire reflected off his face she could see the genuine concern.

"I'm fine. Go grab dinner," she put her hand over her stomach, "I'm starving."

He pulled his knife out and flicked it at the ground. "I'll be back shortly."

She watched him walk over to the tent and then lean down and take off his boots, he took the time to take his socks off and then tuck them in the boots before setting them inside so they wouldn't get wet. When he peeled off his wet shirt, she paused to admire the muscles of his back. They weren't overdone and huge like a lot of the men she worked with but sculpted nicely. She turned her head away and took a sip of the coffee. She had a weakness for fit male forms. Looking at the fire, she ran her tongue along her fat lip and then rolled her eyes at her own thoughts, this wasn't a weekend getaway with another stranger she'd picked up from a nearby clan. Amari didn't have many rules, but at the top of that shortlist was never screw someone you worked with. So that labeled Tripp Carson's fine body off-limits.

When she turned back, he was gone. The man moved without any sound at all. She looked at the gun in her hand and then at the man watching her with a wary look on his face. "Relax. I'm not going to shoot you unless you piss me off." She shrugged.

A large mountain lion came out from behind one of the tents, she was momentarily shocked, then annoyed that her sense of smell was impeded, or she'd have known what type of clan Tripp was from. He walked over to the man and emitted a low warning growl, basically telling him to behave while he was gone. With a quick glance at her, he took off into the trees.

He was from the same clan as her. She frowned and looked at the trees where he'd vanished, he must be from Mae's clan, because if he was from her fathers, she'd know him. It didn't matter that she hadn't been back there for several years, those dark green eyes she would have remembered. Still, his name was familiar.

Setting the cup down, she got up and went over to the asshole she'd stabbed. If he had a wallet or phone on him, it might be worth a look. Doing something was better than sitting here trying not to think about being with the teams, or worse her past. She was proud of who she was and her abilities, even if *some* weren't.

Tucking the gun into the back of her jeans, she eyed the other man, to make sure he hadn't moved. She knew how tight she'd put the wires on, any movement from him would yield him sliced-up wrists, but some people liked to learn things the hard way.

She had just sat back down with the two dead men's wallets and phones as Tripp came trotting out of the trees, a rabbit hanging out of his mouth. He came over and dropped it by her feet. She looked at it and then into his dark eyes. Most didn't retain the same eye color when they shifted. "Good kitty." She smirked as much as her mouth would allow her. He huffed to show he wasn't fond of being called that and then turned and took off back into the trees.

Amari looked at the wallets and then at the rabbit, even if she did skin it, she wasn't going anywhere near the fire to put it on. Shrugging, she opened the first wallet and looked through it. Fake ID, wasn't nearly as good as the Alliance's work. Pulling the cards and bills from the wallet, she tucked them into the jacket pocket and then tossed the wallet into the fire. She repeated her actions with the second wallet.

Opening the screen on the first phone, she glanced at the man watching her, "so, what you woke up one day and decided kidnapping people was a good career move?" This phone only had three contacts stored in it and a few text messages. Little man wasn't very popular, she thought, then again, he was a jerk, so it made sense. The messages revealed nothing of interest. Sticking it in her pocket, she glanced to see he was still watching her.

"The Alliance shouldn't turn outside clans away." He said in a low steady voice.

She was surprised he'd spoken at all. "You came here from somewhere else and were rejected, then got all butt hurt and decided to destroy lives was the best course of action?" She scoffed, "clans take in outsiders all the time, maybe you should have improved your people skills before asking to join one."

He looked at her with hard, cold eyes, then turned his gaze to look at the ground in front of him.

Amari shrugged and opened the screen on the second phone. Again, very few contacts, but the text messages on this one had locations. Turning, she looked at Tripp and her bags under the tarp they'd put over the tents. Going over, she got her map out of her pack to see if she could find these locations. She knew the first one, it was the little town she'd slowed down going through to gawk around. Getting the map out, she squatted and shone the light from the phone on it. She was pretty good with directions, so it didn't take her long to figure out that the other location was a town at the base of the mountain on the other side. It had to be where the driver went. Folding the map back up, she put it back in her run pack and set it inside the tent.

She was happy Tripp had found her, but her conscience wasn't going to let her just leave. Not with the driver still out there. The teams were up to their asses shutting down more locations and she couldn't take a chance that this one would slip through the cracks and disappear. He could always round up another crew and continue doing what they did. She thought of her little sister and the other women on her team, one of them could be next on his shopping list. Moving back over to the log she'd sat on, she looked down at the rabbit. Her stomach gurgled with hunger. She was going to find the driver and turn him over to security to unravel his network of abduction, with or without Tripp Carson's help—or anyone's permission.

Chapter Seven

Tripp watched her eat in silence. She hadn't said three words since he'd gotten back. Not that he was the chatty type either, but her silence made him wonder what she was thinking about. He still couldn't believe she hadn't shifted to heal her injuries—and get rid of some of that stink. It wasn't going to leave easily, even after he'd taken off down the mountain, he could still taste it. His animal was less than impressed with the strong odor.

"Visibility down from here isn't great." He picked up his water and opened it, "I doubt he's coming back up tonight."

She paused in picking off another piece of the rabbit and looked over at him, "he said he wasn't returning until he heard back."

He watched her put another piece in her mouth and chew it slowly. "Any idea what they were driving?" Pulling off a piece of meat, he got up and went over to the silent prisoner, "open up." He placed the piece of meat in his mouth and then turned to see her giving him a void look, he shrugged. He wasn't for starving anyone, that would be an awful way to go out. His preference was a quick death, none of this seeing-it-coming shit. *That* sort of death was reserved for those that deserved nothing else or the ones that pissed him off. So far, this one hadn't and the fact that she hadn't already killed him yet meant he hadn't done anything to warrant her revenge.

"Jeep." She said and then took an awkward drink, pouring the water past her sore mouth.

Sitting back down, he stared into the fire. "He might be able to navigate back up here, but visibility is still crap."

"Are we waiting up here for him?"

She'd shared the phones with him when he'd returned and they knew where he'd gone, but he wasn't comfortable with the idea that she would still be here when he did come back. He'd found her relatively unharmed and didn't want to take a chance that anything would happen to the Alpha's daughter. "I'd like to cut him off before he gets back up here." What he really wanted to do was to chip this place and go down far enough to get a signal to call in the cleanup. He glanced to where she'd dragged the two bodies, those would be bringing animals to investigate once the snow let up. Popping the rest of the meat in his mouth, he got up again and went over to the smallest tent, and pulled the stake that was holding the tarp over it.

"We can do that," she said quietly, "go cut him off."

Tripp paused on the last stake, "we?" He shook his head, "you need to stay clear of the action, so I can get you home to your family intact." Pulling the stake free, he yanked the tarp off the tent and dragged it toward the bodies. "These two are going to be advertising a free buffet for every wild animal in the area soon."

She got up and came over to him, "I'm not going back to my *family*," she tugged the tarp from his hand, "I'm finishing this and then heading back to the teams."

He went over and helped her cover the bodies and then stabbed the stake into the ground and stomped it in with the heel of his boot. "I don't think so." He did the next two stakes and then stopped when she stood where he'd have to put the last one in. He'd already figured out she wasn't the princess he thought, but she should still go home to her family.

She jerked the stake out of his hand and then stomped it into the ground. "I'm staying."

Tripp's cat was alert and intrigued. He made fast work of telling him to settle down, Alpha daughters were not on the menu, *ever*. Even more so, Vesper Hughes's daughter was a *never-ever*. He watched her spin on her heel and go over and look at the tents. She glanced over at the man sitting under the snow-covered blanket and a look of annoyance came over her face.

"We should move him to one of the tents, then take turns watching him," she motioned toward the tree she'd been tied to, "we'll tie him over there before we head out," she paused and looked at the sky, "if we leave before first light, we can find a good vantage point to catch him on the way back up." She didn't wait for his input, just went over, opened one of the flaps on the tent, and looked inside it, "this one." She announced and then turned around and gave him a look that said he should already be moving to do what she said.

Tripp rubbed the animal grease off his hand down the side of the jacket. He'd grabbed it out of the tent, so he didn't care about the state of it. He was all for equal rights and women's equality, but that all sounded too much like taking an order and he didn't do that very well. Hell, he had to bite his tongue often when it came to Kenzo's orders, so bowing his head or saluting her and then jumping to do her bidding wasn't going to happen—even if her plan was a good one.

He started to go over to her to clarify it and then decided doing it from a distance was a better idea. He'd confiscated her taser, but he still had no idea where her little blade was or if she had more on her and wrestling the rescued princess to the ground, would be frowned upon. Getting stabbed by the person he'd been sent to find wasn't a good outcome either.

Instead of getting in her face, he went over to the man watching them with great interest, like they were here for his entertainment. "Get up." His good mood was plummeting more with each second. He flipped the blanket off him and grabbed him under his arm to help him up. Even with the little movement he'd made since being bound, his wrists were a bloody mess. *Shit.* He was going to have to look like a soft heart in front of her, but if he didn't bind the wrists and then put the wire over it, the bad guy was going to slowly bleed out before he made it back to the Alliance holding area. The man struggled to get up without moving his wrists and slicing deeper into his arms. "In the outside pocket of my bag is a med kit, grab it."

She gave him a look that clearly said, why the hell would I do that?

"If we don't bind his wrists, he's going to bleed out before he's picked up."

She gave the man a 'how dare you' look, then turned and went to his bag. With jerky movements, she got the kit out for him. Standing beside the tent, she chucked it at him with great accuracy, it hit him in the chest. He caught it and then looked at her.

"I'm going for a run, the burning on my legs has stopped, but I don't want permanent marks on them to remind me of this adventure."

Tripp looked at her legs like he could see them through the denim. Was her mood like this because of that? Instead of taking a chance of saying anything else that might piss her off further, he nodded and then turned the guy toward the tent. "Did you destroy that collar they had on you?" He glanced to see her stomp over toward the tree and start kicking in the snow to find it. When she did, she picked it up and hucked it at him much like one would throw a knife. "Enjoy your run." He said with a very big fake smile. Neither he nor the prisoner moved as she grabbed her backpack and walked out of sight.

He picked up the collar and looked at him, "maybe a run will improve her mood," he shrugged, "or she'll come back and maul us both."

"Taking an alpha female wasn't my idea."

He paused and looked at him, that was the first sound he'd heard from him. "Pretty sure your friends," he jerked his head toward the bodies, "regret their choices too right now." He put the collar on his neck and then twisted it, so the buckle wasn't near the front. They'd brought a big dog collar with them. Tripp didn't care who or what, no one deserved to be shackled by the neck, not even dogs. He glowered at his wrist again. He needed to fix them up before his temper got the best of him. He motioned to the tent. "I'll get the wire off and stop the red trail you're leaving." *They'd had her chained up like a pet.* His cat wasn't happy with that any more than he was.

He checked in the direction she'd gone at least ten times while he did that. His cat was just as distracted by the ornery female and that was bad news, both needed to focus on what they were supposed to be doing. He scowled as he wrapped the second wrist. What was that again? Find Alpha's daughter, check. Subdue bad guys, check. He smirked, okay one survivor so far, but close enough. Get intel, call in backup or clean up. Tripp glanced in her direction again, backup was a possibility, and it wasn't going to be for the reason it usually was.

When the man grunted, he realized he'd put it a little too tight. An apology almost came out of his mouth. What *the* hell was wrong with him? Normally, he was hyper-focused on what he was doing. His cat was all over the place, which happened, but usually, he would ignore it and carry on. Maybe a short rest would be a good thing, he couldn't remember when he'd slept last. That had to be it, he was tired. Even an energetic, crazy asshole needed downtime occasionally.

Pulling the wire out of his pocket, he wrapped his wrists and then stepped back and motioned to the tent. "I'm leaving the flap open, so you don't hatch any stupid ideas." He watched as the big guy lowered himself down to sit. Glancing at the wet sleeping bag, he went over and picked it up, then tossed it into the corner of the tent. Hopefully, the big guy had enough body heat to stay warm.

Moving away from the tent, Tripp pulled his phone out and checked for a signal, he knew wasn't going to be there. He'd been so worried about her doing something stupid while he was gone, he didn't go far enough down to get a signal and send an update. Even if they were in the mix of shit getting

Konner's clan folk out, Kenzo would still have the message waiting for him when they were done. He needed her to get back to where she belonged, so he could focus.

Pushing the wet hair back from his face, he studied the fire. With the snowfall increasing, it wasn't exactly a roaring fire now. The coals hissed as snow fell on them. Dropping his hands, he went over and grabbed a few more branches and dry-ish foliage to toss in. With the amount gathered, the big guy must have been up here for at least a day to get all of this set up. He glanced to see him looking out the open flap, then again what else was he supposed to do? "What was your job in all of this?" He motioned around them, "find the locations and set things up?" He cocked his head to the side and studied him, he'd seen some action for sure, "are you the real brains behind this or the backup muscle?" He held the man's look; he was definitely thinking about answering him.

"He's butthurt the Alliance didn't welcome him with open arms."

Tripp spun around to see Miss-bad-timing coming out of the trees, nowhere in the direction she'd gone in. How long had she been there? He probably wouldn't talk now. Recovering, he turned back to him, "Is that right?" He clenched his jaw for a moment, he understood all about being rejected. Keeping his eyes on the man, he couldn't look at her right this second, the emotions were a little too close, and he might end up telling her that her own father had no problems turning others away.

"Snow's coming down heavier in the direction we need to go." She said and went over to put her bag in the tent.

The gasoline smell was less, but still there. Until he could get her somewhere to bathe, it wasn't going to leave. "I'm hoping it lightens up closer to daylight," he glanced up at the sky, "so the team can get in here."

Amari turned and grinned at him, "they'll come in choppers for this location." She zipped up his jacket. "I've seen them drop from the sky before and twenty minutes later, they're lifting shit up to them and gone." She turned and looked at him, "one of us should head down and let our team leaders know what's going on."

Tripp kicked the end of the branch into the fire and put his hands on his hips. "We both need to grab some rest before we go running anywhere." He motioned around them, "wildlife is sparse in weather like this, so hunting is going to be hard, and I didn't bring a lot of rations with me because I was en route somewhere else when I got the call and had no time to stop and shop."

The hard look left her face so briefly, he thought he may have only imagined it. "You made good time getting here." She nodded her head twice, "thanks for that."

Tripp was shocked but kept his mouth clamped shut. Maybe the run had helped her disposition a bit, or she was exhausted. He motioned to the tent, "why don't you try to catch a nap."

She studied the man watching them from inside the other tent, "Yeah, two hours. No more."

Tripp had just been about to say a two-hour rest for each of them would refresh them. "Then I'll grab a couple and we can head out after that."

Amari looked him up and down for a long awkward moment and then turned and went into the tent without another word. Tripp stood motionless until she zipped the tent, then looked at the man and raised one eyebrow as if to convey how intense she was. "You should get some rest too; you have a long wait ahead of you." Turning back to the fire, he leaned down and wiped the snow off the log he'd been sitting on earlier. It was going to be a good two-hour hike down to find a signal, then the team would have to get here.

Rubbing his jaw, he decided he'd have to do a little hunting before they left so he could fill up the man's gut before they set out, big guys like that probably burned through the calories like wildfire. Tripp was used to be around large, bulked-up men—most of the teams were filled with them. He wasn't exactly scrawny, but he kept his muscles toned without adding fifty extra pounds to his body. On two or four legs, he could outpace most others without needing to take a break. With the weather on this mountain, he was glad for it. He looked at the tent she'd gone in, it would probably be a slower trip down than he'd like with her trailing behind him.

Chapter Eight

Tripp sat up and then froze, listening. He blinked to focus, then remembered he was in a tent on top of a mountain with the unpredictable daughter of a man he hated. Not the wake-up recollection he would have preferred. Stretching the stiffness out of his neck, he flipped the sleeping bag off. Taking his turn after she'd been in the bed, meant he'd got to smell the pungent scent of gasoline the whole time. His cat was tripping on something he decided, with the inclination to roll around on it like it was a sweet-smelling chunk of grass or something. If his animal had a penchant for the smell of fuel, this was the first he'd known about it.

Getting to his knees, he grabbed his boots and shirt. At least his animal had cranked up the heat and kept him warm enough that he hadn't needed to sleep fully clothed. Pulling on his boots, he unzipped the door and looked outside. The snow had stopped, so that was a huge plus. Inhaling, the scent of cooking meat filled him. Grabbing his shirt and the borrowed jacket, he scrambled out of the too-small door and stood there like he was expecting a disaster to be in front of him.

Amari turned from where she was squatted down in the door of the tent their guest was in. Tripp went over so he could see if the man inside was still breathing. He was chewing. Tucking the jacket under his arm, he turned his shirt so he could pull it on. "You left him and went hunting?" Was she that naïve?

The look she gave him resembled someone asking if he'd fallen and hit his head. She glanced over to where they'd covered the bodies. Tripp's stomach clenched. She wouldn't…

"I dragged one of the main entrees into the trees and set some snares." She stood up and then pointed to the fire.

Tripp yanked the shirt over his head and turned around. Beside the fire looked like the remaining parts of a small wolf. She'd used a dead body to lure a wolf into a snare—and then killed, cleaned and it cooked. *Damn.* He was starting to see why his animal was so intrigued with this she-cat. Coffee, he needed coffee, ASAP—

"The coffee's fresh."

Tripp blinked, was she reading his mind or some shit? Shaking his head, he jammed his arms into the jacket and then went over to the fire pit. He kept his head down and his mouth shut as he tapped the snow out of one of the metal cups and then picked up the coffee pot. At this point, he didn't care if the cold cup chilled the liquid or not. Caffeine was caffeine regardless of temperature.

"I thought we should fill him up before we head out." She came over and sat on the log across from where he was standing. "We don't know how busy the teams are right now."

Tripp glared into the cup; he was annoyed she was coming up with all the right plans—plans he'd already thought. Taking a sip, he turned and looked to see the guy in the tent wasn't any worse for wear. "Yeah." Was the best he could come up with right now. When he'd finally admitted he needed a short rest and gone in the tent, he'd laid there for what felt like forever, just listening. None of what he'd been afraid of happening had. He cleared his throat, "I'll take our guest for a bathroom break, just before we leave," she quirked an eyebrow at him, causing him to stop speaking.

"I fed him, so he didn't die, I don't care if he's comfortable." She gave a little chuckle, "at all." Getting up, she went over to the tent their gear was in. "I think I have some bags in my pack, we could take some of this meat with us," she glanced back to him, "so the animals don't come looking."

Tripp glanced to the tarped body, "where's the other one?"

She stuck her head back out and looked at him, then pointed to the third tent, "we'll have to move the big one there too. The tent material won't stop the animals, but I have an idea for that."

Tripp looked at the flimsy tent, "you have some kind of magic that will deter wild animals from a rotting corpse?"

When she stepped out, she smiled at him, and he had a flash of the sexy woman in the picture with her father. *Father.* He frowned; how could he forget who she was?

"This," she held up a tube of something.

Now he was curious and took the tube from her when she offered it to him. He read the label. Liniment was going to deter animals? Opening it, he started to raise it to smell it and then straightened his arm as far from his body as he could possibly get it. The stench of it made his eyes water. "Where the hell did you learn something like this?" Capping it, he handed it to her like it was going to burn through his hand. It was a brilliant idea, that would deter anything with a nose. She smiled again and he looked away so his cat wouldn't get stupid ideas about that sexy grin of hers.

"Blair's mate has these cheats for tracking and covering scent."

Tripp stood up and took another drink. "I heard she bested Calum tracking a pelt."

Amari nodded, looking proud. "Yes." She shrugged, "I think it's sweet justice that the first to beat him was a woman."

Tripp cringed. "What do you have against Calum?"

"Nothing," she went over to the tent the body was in and opened the tube, then putting her other hand over her face, she rubbed the tube along the material. When she straightened up again, she moved her hand, "I just think we need some good female leaders," she glanced over at him, "I mean it is about time, right?"

Tripp took a big drink of the coffee, needing to feel the burn on his tongue so his mouth didn't get him in trouble. Lowering the cup, he leveled her with a look, he hoped conveyed anything but him wanting to roll his eyes at her. "Have you met Wynter?" He shrugged, "she's the team leader of the incursion team."

She nodded and went to the tent the man sat in. He was intently watching the two of them, "I have. She's great, but one female leader out of how many?" She opened the tube again and held it away from her face, "we could use more."

Tripp looked at the man in the tent as she went around it, the smell of the ointment was getting to him, no question about it by the grimace on his face. He needed to pack up his gear and put the fire out, but instead, his mouth started flapping, "what do you have against males?" Even the guy in the tent looked at him with a look that said, 'are you dumb?'

Amari stepped from behind the tent and put the cap on the tube and then pulled a plastic bag out of her pocket and sealed it in it. "Nothing." Stuffing it in her pocket, she went over to the tarped body and flipped the tarp back, "I'm just tired of competing with penis'."

"Hey, let's not bring body parts into it." Tripp lifted his hands to show he was trying not to offend, "it's based on skill and…"

"Skill?" She dropped the tarp and came toward him.

He refused to step back. He wasn't afraid of her, cautious maybe, but he wasn't intimidated by the little female. He nodded, "a lot of females don't—" when she stepped right up in his face, he stopped talking, not out of fear, but because his cat was losing his mind and Tripp had no idea why.

"More often than not a female is overlooked just because she doesn't have," she reached and cupped him between the legs, "these," she dropped her hand.

Tripp's eyes widened, but he didn't move an inch.

"I can do anything a man can," she smirked, "except pee standing up, and I haven't even tried that yet to see if I can." She turned and went back over to the body, then stopped and looked at him, "give me a hand moving him."

Tripp started to open his mouth and then snapped it shut. He picked up the man under the arms and waited for her to get his feet. Thankfully, the cold had slowed the odor from getting too bad. "I'm not doing the he-verses-she thing, but a lot of women prefer having a family to what we do." He hoped she noted he'd said *we*.

She ducked down and went into the tent backward, "that's true, and all the power to them."

Tripp waited for her to get out of the way and then heaved the upper body in and dropped it. He didn't agree with her or disagree for that matter. He knew he should just nod and let it go, but his mouth was never good at doing the right or easy thing. "I think gender has nothing to do with it, if a body wants to do something, then they need to prep for it and get good at it. Then do it."

She stepped out of the tent, and he almost put his hand out to make sure she didn't trip over a body part, then grabbed the canvas and held it back instead. Now was probably not the time for any move that could be construed as chivalrous.

"Right. That's it there, but the higher-ups don't see it that way, do they?" She frowned, "why is the king always in charge? Why not a Queen?"

Tripp bent down and did up the tent, almost relishing the strong scent of the ointment burning his nostrils so he'd have to pause before he thought. "Well," he moved from the tent quickly, "in my experience it is the woman leading, the man is just the face of that leadership." He shrugged, "most of the population is more comfortable being led by a male than a female." He flashed her a grin, "whereas I don't like to follow either."

Amari stood there, hands on her hips, and looked him up and down. "I guess we agree on a few things then." She bobbed her head once. "Good, saves me stabbing you for being a jerk." She spun on her heel and went over and started kicking snow at the fire. "You going to do the chip thing so they can find this location?"

The snow started again, making him pause to debate if tying their friend to a tree was a good idea. What if the cleanup was busy? Tripp turned to look at the captive and went over to zip up his tent as well. The man looked amused, and Tripp thought it was too bad, in different circumstances he might like the idiot. "It was a pleasure meeting you, the team won't keep you waiting long." He zipped it up and turned to go get his bag. "I plan to walk out on two legs," he glanced over to see her bending down to lace up her boots, "easier to find a good spot that way."

She looked over at him as she switched feet, "yeah, the cats move too fast to find the best location."

Tripp nodded like it was important they'd settled that, of course, he planned on shifting and booking it to where he got a signal as soon as possible so the team could come to clean up this campsite. He needed to talk to Kenzo because damn, he was at a crossroads with this she-cat and didn't know which way to turn. Technically she should wait here and go out with the team, but after the comments yesterday, he wasn't stupid enough to voice that out loud. He needed to clear it with his leader though, because of who her father was, he didn't need a landslide of shit landing on him for her not returning home right away.

An hour and a half later, he stopped and dropped the pack off his back. He was impressed as hell right now and that annoyed him further. She'd kept up with him, actually came close to moving by him. The gun was secure in her hand the whole time, and she hadn't said more than three words. In fact, a few times, he'd had to look back to see if she was still behind him. Pulling the hat off his head, he jammed it into the jacket pocket and bent down to get a bottle of water. He looked at the sky as he drank it, not needing to check his phone to see what time it was. They still had roughly an hour until dawn.

Amari stopped a few feet away from him and took the pack off her back, she squatted down and opened it.

Getting out another bottle, he did a quick count to see there were five left. He held it out to her. "I'm going to book it ahead and see if I can get a signal." He glanced back up in the direction they'd come from, "if the animals are hungry enough that stench won't hold them off long."

Amari took a drink and then nodded. "Makes sense." She motioned into the trees off the trail, "I'll keep heading that way and try to get higher and see if I can find a spot to ambush that jackoff when he comes back to collect the prize."

Tripp looked at her, then to where she'd pointed. For some reason, he thought she'd just chill and wait for him to come back. Looking down at his pack, he was just about to say she should wait, when she chuckled.

"Don't worry I can haul your gear for a little while."

He looked back to her and nodded, literally clamping his tongue between his teeth so he couldn't speak. Taking the jacket off, he opened his bag and stuffed it in. Pulling his run pack over his head, he set it on top and stripped his shirt off, then put the pack back on. When he looked up, she was eyeing him like he was her favorite flavor of candy. Normally he wasn't shy around a woman, but the way she looked at him, made him uncomfortable, to say the least. That was a very foreign and strange feeling for him.

"Sorry," she motioned up and down his body, "I appreciate the work that goes into making a body that fit."

It wasn't said in a derogatory or sexually suggestive way, so he shrugged, "the job helps a lot," he motioned around them, "lots of running, climbing, and carrying." He pointed to the bag.

Nodding her head, she capped her bottle and came over. Taking the shirt out of his hand, she jammed it into his bag, then smirked at him, "don't worry I'll turn my back while you get naked." She stood up and rubbed her hand across his chest, "if we weren't on the clock, it might be a different story."

Tripp honestly didn't know whether to be turned on or offended. His cat was right there and all for any play that might take place. He had never realized his cat was such a pervert before. "Thanks." He smirked, "I'm shy."

Amari laughed and turned around, so her back was toward him, "I'm sure you are."

Tripp made fast work taking off his boots, socks, and jeans. He shifted so fast he was almost dizzy from it.

She glanced behind her and then turned around and bent down to pick up his stuff. "Make sure you reach out to Jesse or your guy, let them know that they're onto our new tracking." She paused after she did up his pack and stood there holding his boots by the laces. "You are one fit cat. Maybe once this is done, we can go for a good run." She smiled and then tied the boots to his bag.

Tripp's cat had the insane idea of going over and rubbing against her, but he wasn't having any of that. Swinging his head around, so his cat had no choice but to follow, he took off down the snowy trail.

Tripp sent the chip number and message to the clean-up team. He'd told them two bags and a chair, to let them know there were two bodies and one prisoner for pick up. He knew from experience the chips got signal damn near anywhere. Why they couldn't make their phones the same was way beyond his knowledge of electronic stuff.

Blowing out a breath, he looked down at himself. Nothing strange about a naked man standing in the middle of the snow-covered bush using his phone. He still couldn't believe he'd been so distracted by her that he hadn't put his pants in his run pack. She was probably laughing her ass off about it right now.

Shaking his head, he brought up Kenzo's number and sent *123!!!* He needed him to call as soon as possible, Tripp didn't care if he was in the middle of wrestling some guy to the floor, he needed him to call him. Looking down at the ground, he realized he could only stand here and wait, sitting was out of the question. This was completely ridiculous. Nothing usually got to him, he was rock steady. A little hot-headed from time to time, but things didn't rattle him the way Amari Hughes seemed to be. He didn't know what was going on, but it needed to stop. Now.

His phone rang, and he answered it before a full ring could finish. "Carson."

"You good?"

It was Kenzo. He nodded, "I found her, last night."

"I knew you would."

He sounded out of breath, "is this a bad time?"

"No. No, we're just taking out some trash."

Tripp grinned, "everything went well?" He was having issues, but the operation always came first. He glanced up the mountain, or it normally came first.

"Like a well-oiled machine." Kenzo sounded happy, that was good. "Konner's Flores' clan has just increased in size, and we found a few extras we'll have to rehome."

"That's great."

"How is Amari?"

Tripp scowled at the ground, he knew he was asking about health-wise, "she's uh, good, no complications. I just sent clean up the number to come and pick up a few bodies and one live one."

"Bodies? Things get messy?"

Tripp pushed his hair back from his face and then rested his hand on top of his head, "she was tied to a tree one second and then stabbing one of them in the neck the next, Kenzo, I-I didn't even have a chance to react." He hadn't meant to say any of that, but well, the cat was out of the bag now.

Kenzo laughed. *Laughed.* "Sounds like Amari."

"That's not all, she took a taser," shit, he'd left that up there with her, "to one of the guy's balls…"

"Fuck, tell me you shot him and put him out of his misery."

"I did, well, not right that second, I was too busy worrying about it sparking off the gas they'd poured on her and her going up in flames…"

"They did what? Were they planning to burn her?"

He dropped his hand, "she bit half an ear off, and the guy was a bit pissed before I got there," he felt like he needed to clarify that he hadn't let *that* happen. There was a long silence, "Kenzo?"

"Yeah," he sounded like he was laughing, "hang on, Jesse is here, I'm going to put it on speaker." He heard voices in the background, "seems your girl bit one of their ears half off before Tripp got there. Then he poured gas on her as payback."

"Shit, is he alive?"

"No." Tripp said louder than necessary, "she's uh," he frowned, not knowing how to even word it, "unpredictable, Jesse."

Now he could hear more than one of them chuckling.

"That's one way to say it." Jesse answered, "she can look after herself. I'm glad she's all right."

He blinked, almost forgetting, "they know about our new tracking. The unit was ripped out of the wiring unit on her van, and she said they'd been following her for a while..." he stopped when he heard cursing.

"I'll go tell Devin and Illias," Jesse said.

He heard Kenzo shifting the phone around.

"Sounds like you're having all the fun." That was what he said to him.

Tripp raised his eyebrows and looked down the mountain, "she is not what I expected in an Alpha's daughter, Ken, like," he waved his hand around, "she's refusing to get a lift back to her family and says she's staying here to get the last one."

"Tell me about that."

That was it, just okay, next? "The fourth one went down the mountain to make contact with the buyer I guess, he should be heading back up today sometime," he turned around and looked up in the direction he knew she'd be, "I was planning to ambush him on the way back up and see who he was contacting..."

"That sounds good, Amari will likely help with that."

"I don't think I have a choice. She won't leave."

"I've never heard you this rattled, if it helps Amari does that to everyone," he chuckled again. When the hell did Kenzo become such a jovial man? "First time our paths crossed, I feared for my own life, never mind the ones we were tracking."

"Tracking? She's on the co-ord team…"

"I'd welcome her on this team if that's what she wanted, Tripp, she's good, she just prefers to be alone and not work close to others," another goddamned chuckle, "sound familiar?"

Tripp glared at the phone for a second and then put it back to his ear. "Fine, she stays, but know I have no problem tranq'ing her if she puts herself in danger…"

"Good luck with that." He said something with his hand over the mouthpiece, "if you can find out who was planning to purchase the *feral* female, I think you should follow up on it…"

"You want me to stay and meet up with them? I imagine they'd be coming to get her because no one would want to transport an Alpha family member, it's too risky."

"You're probably right, if they're coming to meet up with your mark, then stay and get them too."

Tripp nodded, that was more like it, an objective that he could sink his teeth into. "If there's anyone remotely close to this damn mountain, you should send them this way and they can pick up the driver once we're done with him." The scary princess too, he thought.

"I would prefer it if he was alive when he was picked up."

Tripp rolled his eyes, "I'll see what I can do." He was starting to get cold standing still, "what's next for the team?" He would never admit he'd forgotten his clothes to anyone.

"We've got a hit list about the length of my leg now, so it's been decided we're doing multiple breaches at the same time for about the next week—bouncing directions so it's not predictable."

Tripp rolled his shoulders, "I'll finish up here asap so I can come to play too."

"The more the merrier, and Tripp?"

"Yeah?"

"Be careful around Amari, she's a bit *quirky* sometimes. Oh, and she has a knife in the back of her belt, both boots, and probably her pack too—thought you should know so she doesn't kill anyone she shouldn't." The line went quiet.

As he was jamming his phone back into his run pack, he paused, how the hell did Kenzo know where she kept all her concealed weapons? Belt? That's where she'd gotten it that she'd used on the one guy with half an ear. Quirky? What the hell did that mean? Quirky, how?

His cat took control as soon as he shifted, starting back in the direction she was. Tripp let him go for a few minutes, trying to sense if he'd picked up on something he'd missed, when he couldn't smell anything but trees and the odd wild creature, he slowed him down and took the lead again.

Still, how did Kenzo know about her knives? It could have come up in conversation if they'd worked together. He picked up the pace, it was still strange that he knew. Quirky, he still had no idea what the hell that meant. What was he some kind of dictionary? How was he supposed to know what a stupid word like quirky actually meant?

Chapter Nine

It was a good plan, but he still didn't like it. It might be the only plan that would work, but if anything went bad, his ass was going to be on the line—with Kenzo, Jesse, her father—

"Come on, how else are we going to get him to stop?"

Tripp looked over at her, trying hard not to look at her boots again. Damn Kenzo for saying that. "Using you as bait is a bad plan. What if he's not alone?"

She shrugged, and looked back down at the trail, "shoot whoever isn't driving."

"We need the contact too." He set his pack down and squatted down behind a tree, "from here they wouldn't see you..."

"He'll stop if he sees me down there," she pointed to the only place the vehicle could drive back up to the campsite.

Standing up again, he moved over to stand in her way, blocking the view of the trail, "it's generally frowned upon to use the one you were sent to rescue as bait."

Her eyes brightened as a slow smile formed, "and you always follow the rules?"

Tripp frowned, "no, but—" if he'd been smart, he would have left her tied to a tree at the camp for the crew to take her back with them. "Fine." He pointed his finger at her, "we need him alive though, so we can find out who he's dealing with."

She looked at his finger, the smile gone from her face, "okay, I won't kill him."

Dropping his hand, he studied the look on her face, trying to figure out if she meant it or was just trying to placate him. "You know, revenge isn't the answer, right? It will eat you up inside," he should know, it had fed him for years, "until you can't think straight." He turned away from her when his cat started warning him not to upset her.

"That's your advice? Revenge isn't the answer?"

He opened the pocket that held his binoculars and took them out, "yeah."

"You've never wanted to get back at someone and settle the score?"

Tripp lifted them to his eyes and searched down the mountain, following the trail any vehicle would have to take, "I have."

"And how did it feel when you settled it?"

Tripp ground his teeth together for a minute, "I wouldn't know." He hated to admit it, but he couldn't exactly tell her that his unsettled score involved her father. Because of that man, he couldn't go home to his family, and he had to meet them off clan land anytime he had free time. He couldn't tell her that his whole reason for being on the team had been fueled by his hatred of that man. At the start at least, now he did it because it was what he was good at and—he enjoyed it.

"I see, well no one crosses me and gets away with it."

The sound of a chopper had them both searching the sky to see where it was coming from. They couldn't see it from where they were, but the direction it was going could only mean it was the clean-up headed to the camp.

"Hope they're fast." She said quietly.

"If we can't see them, no one on this side will either." Tripp turned back to look down toward the town at the bottom. He followed the road that led from the town. With the low light of dawn, it was easy to see any lights that way. There was one set that looked like they were starting up the long trail, but he couldn't be sure until they went past the last turn-off outside of the town. "This might be our target."

"Good. You watch, I'm going to make some footprints in the snow."

Tripp turned to see her running down the incline toward the trail. She was doing what? Less than a minute later, he understood. She was making it look like she had come down the vehicle trail and was wandering around. His guts were tight, his cat anxious. This was a bad plan. He looked back down to see the lights going by the last turnoff. It was too hard to see what kind of vehicle it was, but the chances of someone going for a leisurely drive up the mountain at dawn in the snow were pretty slim. "Shit." Squatting down, he turned to see where the best vantage point was for him to see the trail. If she went too far up or down it, he wouldn't have a good shot. He silently cursed every swear word he could think of as he looked. He'd have to use the darts, and the accuracy with those wasn't as good as live ammo. Amari stopped and looked up at him and pointed to the ground in front of her. At least she knew to find out where he could see. He lifted his arm in the air giving her a thumbs up. Nodding, she backtracked on her own footprints and then headed back up toward him.

Tripp was watching the lights come up the mountain when she came up behind him. "This has to be our guy."

"What's the plan after we get him?"

He figured they had at least fifteen minutes before he was close enough to execute the plan he was hating right now. "First, we're confiscating his jeep," he flashed a quick smile, "so we can get down off here with dry feet." She smirked. "Then we'll find somewhere to hole up and ask him a few questions."

Amari nodded, "there's bound to be a motel down there." She took off his jacket and set it on her backpack then glanced at him, "wearing an Alliance-issued jacket is a huge tell that things have changed since he left." She tapped her finger on the emblem on the shoulder of the coat. It was grey and hard to see right away, but she was right. "Hopefully he doesn't realize I'm wearing different clothes. Do you have any zip ties?" She held out her hands.

Tripp raised an eyebrow at her, "I'm binding your wrists?" That was a stupid plan, taking away her options for defending herself.

"Not for real, just make it look good, leave one loose so I can get my hands out."

His cat was in the process of gouging his insides to shreds and Tripp couldn't blame him at all for it, he wasn't happy with this plan either. Leaning down, he opened a pocket on his bag and pulled out the carefully looped zip ties, that were always ready to slip over hands and tighten. He showed them to her and then turned and lifted the binoculars, "let's see how fast he's navigating the road."

Tripp's cat was going crazy inside him, "cool it, I have to focus," he whispered. He couldn't see the Jeep yet, but he could hear it. He wasn't taking his eyes off her until this was over. She stood there right now, her hands on her hips, the zip ties hanging from one wrist. He still wasn't sure what she planned to do, just standing there like 'here I am', and it was driving him to distraction.

Taking a deep breath, he exhaled slowly and relaxed into his position. He had the dart gun in his hand, but his weapon with the real ammo was sitting beside his hand in case he needed it instead. As long as it was just one person in that vehicle, things *should* go according to plan. Unfortunately, experience told him things rarely came off without a hitch.

When Amari put her hands behind her back and slumped her body like she was completely without strength, he knew the driver was close enough. She walked along, dragging her foot behind her like she was injured. Tripp grinned, she was a smart one, and he was impressed. Right now, she looked like she was completely helpless, but the poor unsuspecting sap driving into their trap didn't know that. Even tied, she'd proven she was never helpless. He heard the vehicle come to a stop and flicked his eyes quickly toward it to check if it was more than one. He didn't see another person in it.

"Help me," Amari whined; the tone even made Tripp look back at her.

"How the hell did you get down here?"

Tripp followed him with the sight on the weapon, keeping it lined up with his neck with each step he took. He was a big son of a bitch, and he hoped one dart was going take him down in time.

When he reached Amari, she leaned into his body, Tripp had to bit back a snarl with the man being near her, "I don't know how you got down here, but someone's getting their ass kicked." Amari slumped into him like her legs had just given out. "Shit." The idiot leaned down to pick her up, but before he could, she launched herself, landing on his back, and wrapped her arms and legs around him. He broke her fall when they hit the ground.

Tripp was now on his knees, prepared to run down there when she rolled to her back and got the big man in a sleeper hold. Jesus, did she watch wrestling matches much? He wasn't even sure if he could do what she had that efficiently.

The man was struggling, trying to break her hold on his body, he couldn't get his arms out of the grip with her legs to reach the arm wrapped around his neck. Tripp stood there for a few seconds, trying to decide if he should wait it out or do something. His cat made his opinion known, the big one was probably crushing her. Without further hesitation, he shot a dart into his leg and then a second one. He kept the gun aimed at him and waited until he slumped in her arms.

Amari dropped her head back at an awkward angle and looked up at him, she didn't look happy. Releasing him, she shoved him off her.

Tripp grabbed their bags and went down the hill, sliding most of the way.

"I had it under control." She gave him a hard look as she came over and jerked the coat out from under his arm.

"I did it for his safety, not yours." He went over and bent down and checked his pulse, "if he struggled too much you could have snapped his neck."

Amari went over to the Jeep and leaned in the opened the door. "I know how to do it; I wouldn't have killed him."

The growl in her tone made his cat sit up and pay attention. Standing up, he picked up the bags and went over and opened the back of the Jeep, and tossed them in. "He'll be out a long while now." Slamming the tailgate, he looked at the man lying on the ground. He was going to be a heavy one. "Anything in there?"

She climbed into the vehicle and leaned down. "Phone and," she held her hand out the door and rattled a key in her hand, "motel key." When she smiled at him, he forgot what he was going to say. That sexy smile could stop traffic he was sure of it. Amari hopped back out, "you can have a chat with him while I grab a shower."

Tripp's cat nudged him to speak, "uh, let's hope we can get him in the room without being seen."

Amari looked down at him, then grimaced, "he's going to be heavy."

Smirking, Tripp went over to stand by his head, "maybe next time we should ask them to climb in the backseat before we knock them out."

She laughed and went over to his feet, "does that method work for you usually?"

Hefting him up, Tripp grunted from the weight of him, "no. Those ones up there were the easiest I've ever had," they shuffled toward the Jeep. "Although this crazy blonde chick screeching at them and stabbing one of them is probably why they gave up without a fight."

She smirked but made no comment.

Getting him in the backseat was not fun, he almost hit the ground a few times. By the time he was in, and the door closed, both of them were panting like they'd just done a five-mile sprint.

"Okay," Tripp pulled his beanie off and jammed it into his pocket. "What's the ownership on this say?" He looked in the driver's door, "pretty worn if it's a rental."

"You think we can get information from his ownership?" She went around to the passenger side.

"Unless you want to take him out and frisk him for a wallet, we can hope."

Amari climbed in and sat in the seat, then closed the door. "Let's go find this motel." She smiled at him as he climbed in. "Shower, food, then phone calls?"

Tripp closed the door and then looked over at her. Of course, she probably needed to call her family. She looked so happy right now, he wasn't going to chance saying something to piss her off. Turning the key, he looked around them, "I should be able to get this turned around if we go up a bit further.

When they got to the motel, he was calling Kenzo and telling him to send transport for her and the heavy bastard in the backseat. The sooner he got things back to normal, the better off he was going to be. Yeah, she was cute and smart as fuck, but she was so off-limits, it wasn't funny. Crazy blonde chick. He smirked, it was true and because he wasn't masochistic enough, he really liked her. The last thing he needed in his life right now were attachments, especially a cute, blonde, lethal Alpha female.

Chapter Ten

Amari stood beside the door and watched to see if anyone came around the corner. It was impressive that Tripp was able to pick up that man and carry him in like he weighed no more than a child. Her cat noticed too, and Amari quickly tramped down on that kind of interest. He was the last thing she needed right now, a strong-headed man that ran around killing people and shit. Okay, he was her kind of male, but they didn't exactly have a few free days. She liked the violent ones, not the beat her up kind, but the ones that knew the score in this crazy shifter world of theirs. A strong man, but one strong enough to know how to back off and let her be who she is. Tripp was checking all the boxes and her cat was completely purring over him, which was rare, she usually hated Amari's choice of short flings. Did she want a fling with him? He was S.O. and a total loaner.

He navigated through the door without issue. He didn't even look like he was straining under the weight. He might even have the potential for a repeat performance. It had been months, at least eight since she'd had some fun. Although, being in her cycle had made it more necessary than fun. Too bad they were on the clock right now.

Tripp dropped him on the closest bed and then turned around and looked at her. "The sparse diet at the holding center will do his heavy ass some good." He smirked, "I'll go get our gear. See if you can find a receipt or something that says how long this room is rented for."

Amari nodded and went over to the table that was cluttered with dinner and breakfast takeout containers. She didn't care how long it was rented for, she was having a shower and anyone that tried to stop her—she was going to bite, literally.

She found the receipt and looked at the date, she had no idea what today even was.

Tripp came in the door with the bags.

"What day is it?" She held out the receipt when he set the bags down.

Taking it, he looked at it, "it's paid for another day." He turned the receipt sideways, "hang onto this, there's a number on it." Handing it back to her, he turned and looked around the room. "Step one, go through his stuff and see if there's anything useful." He went over and rolled the man to his side, so he could check his pockets.

Amari looked over at the bag sitting on the chair. "Step one is I'm going to wash off this smell." She smirked when he looked up from the man's phone at her.

"Right." He motioned with the phone in his hand, "I'll message Kenzo that we got the driver." He glanced back down at the phone, "several calls were made, but no messages."

She looked at the unconscious man, "I guess we wait for him to wake up and share." With a shrug, she picked up her backpack and headed toward the bathroom. "Better put the do not disturb sign on the door." She went in and closed the door. Setting her bag on the vanity, she looked around the bathroom, either the big man was exceptionally clean, or he hadn't bothered to bathe while he was here last night.

Taking off Tripp's jacket, she hung in on the back of the door and went over and looked at her reflection in the mirror. There were no scars, but she looked like she hadn't bathed in a week. Being kidnapped wasn't a good look for her.

Shrugging, she pulled the shirt over her head and dropped it on the floor, briefly wondering if there was a washer she could use to get the gasoline stink out. Her backpack only had one change in it and that's what she was wearing. She'd tossed the other clothes into the fire when it was her watch, not wanting to ever wear that outfit again. Stripping out of the jeans, she lifted them and checked to see if they smelled of that stench. They seemed fine. Then again, her sense of smell wasn't one hundred percent yet. How long was this going to last? Maybe she could use one of the unconscious man's shirts, he wasn't going to need a change of clothes where he was going. Grabbing a towel, she wrapped it around herself and went back out.

Stepping back out, she stopped. Tripp had taken off his jacket and shirt, she looked at his bare feet, and boots as well. It wasn't uncommon with her kind, clothes felt restricting if your animal was close. He'd also taken his hair out of the elastic, and she paused for a few seconds to admire his profile. Damn, it was too bad this was a business stopover.

He turned and gave her a concerned look.

"I don't want to put the smelly shirt back on after my shower." She looked at the size of the man on the bed, "thought I'd borrow one of his."

Setting down his phone, Tripp went over to the man's bag and opened it. "It's going to look like a parka on you." He pulled a blue shirt out of the bag and held it up.

Amari smirked; it was huge. Holding the towel together, she went over to him, "I'll make it work." She noted his gaze was on her bare legs and working his way up her slowly. The expression on his face was definite interest. Her cat rolled through her, and it was hard not to smile, rarely did they agree on her choice of bed partners. Tugging the shirt from his hand, she gave him an obvious once-over and then turned and walked slowly back to the bathroom. "Did you message your boss?" She watched in the mirror outside the bathroom door to see he was still watching her.

"Yeah. No reply yet."

"Do you have any water?" She licked her lips, "I can't get this taste out of my mouth, and I hate tap water."

He jolted and turned for his bag, "right, that chemical taste is so strong, I can't stand tap water."

Tossing the shirt into the bathroom, she stood at the door as he brought the bottle over to her. He moved like a predator, and she had to admire that—lithe movements, not a sound. "Thanks." She took it and opened it, "how long will he be out?" She motioned to the bed.

Glancing back at the man while he pushed the hair back out of his face, he shrugged one shoulder, "probably a few hours at least." Tripp turned back, amusement in his eyes, "I wasn't sure one tranq would be strong enough."

"He's a big one." She took a small sip, "I felt bones crunching when I rolled to my back holding him."

Concern flashed through his eyes, "are you okay? You should have said something."

Capping the bottle, she set it on the edge of the sink, "I'm fine." She watched his eyes; they were such a dark green a quick glance made them look almost black. They were bad boy eyes if that was a thing, she wasn't sure, but she liked them. Moving down, she watched his chest rise with a silent deep breath he was taking. If sexual tension could be a visible thing, then she'd be seeing it right now. Her cat confirmed that both he and his animal were interested. She looked in the bathroom and then slowly back to him, "I could use a hand in here," she watched his eyes flick to the shower then back to her, "scrub off this stench," she stepped out of the doorway and put her hand on his chest, the muscles tensed under her touch. Her sense of smell might be inhibited, but this close she could still pick up on the male pheromones coming off him.

When his eyes locked on hers, the look he gave her sent a shiver through her. Oh yeah, he was her type of fun. Shoving him back against the wall, she stretched up and kissed him softly on the mouth. She loved the conflicting feelings of a rough movement than something tender. She hoped he wasn't one of those men that had to make the first move because she'd never been one of those women that could stand back and flutter her eyelashes and wait for the man to decide.

Looking up, she saw the look he was giving her wasn't anywhere in the spectrum of being offended, in fact, he was very interested, indeed. Grasping his hair, she tugged his head down closer and kissed him softly again, then nibbled his lip lightly. "How about it, special operations, want to lend me a hand?"

A low growl rumbled through his chest, and she found herself lifted up into his body. Letting go of the towel, she put her hands behind his head and accepted the assault on her mouth. His muscles were rock hard against her, but his touch was gentle. He wasn't gentle in his kiss, a heat went through her, and he knew how to play the game too.

Her back hit the door as he walked her backward without breaking the kiss. Amari dropped her hands to the waist of his jeans, fast and frenzied was fine with her. She preferred that to slow, emotional, feely romps. The abundance of feelings trapped inside her from being abducted needed a good purge and this man was going to do the job just fine.

Jerking the towel out from between them, he shoved his pants down off his body and then lifted her as he stepped out of them. Her body was already shaking with need, and she chastised herself for denying it so long that she was acting like a virgin as he kissed her again. When another rumble went through his chest, she moaned in response to it.

He gripped her hips and hiked her up higher, bracing her shoulders against the wall, and then thrust into her without that awkward fumbling that usually happened with two strangers. Amari tore her mouth from his and moaned as he slowly lifted her up, as he slid out of her body. *This* was what she needed, a man to do the driving for a few minutes and just let her ride along. The gentle touch combined with the hard entry had her almost off the charts as far as being turned. When he thrust into her again, she threw her head back, knocking it against the wall, and didn't care at all.

Slowly, he pulled out again and she was too busy trying to remember to suck air in that she didn't realize he moved away completely until her feet touched the floor. Her eyes popped open to see him watching her, a focused look of promise on his face. Normally she wouldn't trust a man for anything, but she sensed with him he meant to follow through.

Wrapping his arm around her, he moved to the shower, pulling her along with him. Yanking the curtain back, he leaned down and turned on the water, his eyes stayed locked on hers the entire time and she was almost squirming with anticipation and need.

She heard the spray of the water hit the tub but was too caught up in him to care whether she got that shower now or not. He turned and pulled her into his body again, kissing the side of her neck gently, it sent shivers through her. Grasping her hips, he lifted her back up against his body and stepped in under the spray.

Ten minutes earlier her only thought was to have a shower, now that she was under the spray, bathing wasn't a priority. Tripp nipped her neck with his teeth and then moved back to her mouth. Amari wasn't usually big on the kissing part of this, but his mouth she couldn't get enough of. She took a hold of his hair this time and held onto it, so she could stop him from pulling away from her again. The little prelude before the water was barely a taste and she loved it—needed more of it.

Tripp shifted so she was completely under the spray as he kissed her, his tongue stabbing into her mouth and stroking hers. The taste of him felt more intimate than she'd ever felt before and it accelerated her need even more.

Later when she was clear-headed, she would blame it on being so long since she'd been close to someone or that it was the adrenaline from being taken—but right this minute, right now she knew it was the man and not any other circumstance. Her whole body was going into overdrive, his hands moving over her, the cool tile against her back, the heat from the water pelting off her and his mouth, it was almost more than she could stand right now.

Tearing her mouth from his, she gasped for a breath and then lowered her mouth to his shoulder, she bit into it lightly before continuing down his chest. Her mouth followed her hands as they traveled over the taut muscle. His hand moved to her hair and gripped it, but he didn't pull her away, just held it and let her explore his body. When she gently bit one of his nipples, his hand tightened, and he pulled her head back. The kiss she was rewarded with was rough and consuming.

Her cat was going crazy inside her and Amari couldn't think through the lust haze to figure out why. She wasn't objecting to him; it was almost the opposite. When Tripp lifted his mouth from hers and boosted her up higher on his body, her cat went completely still. Anticipation filled her and she wasn't sure if it was her own or combined with her animal.

A deep growl came from him, and it was more animal than man, the sound turned her on even more than she already was. She needed him to touch her, everywhere, *now*. She needed to feel him fill her but didn't want this part to end either. She rarely lost herself in someone's touch, often she yearned for just that and now, this right now was more than she'd ever felt before.

He turned them so the spray was at their backs and then she found herself looking at the tiles. With slow, but not too gentle movements, he placed her hands against the wall and ran his down her arms, then over the front of her. His mouth moved roughly over the side of her neck and shoulder. She shuddered with anticipation.

The slow movements ended when he lifted her one foot to rest on the edge of the tub. He entered her from behind with a hard thrust, lifting her leg as he did. Amari moaned with each movement from him. She was spiraling fast from the sensations. He was pressed against her back, one hand holding hers in place on the wall, the other hand exploring the front of her. She could barely focus to stay standing.

Each stroke grew faster, and harder and she was so close to the edge of the promise of sweet release that she frantically tried to move with him to obtain it. He pinned her with his arm, lifting her just enough that she couldn't. His lips traveled roughly along her neck and even her cat went crazy. "Use your teeth," she gasped needing that painful-pleasure sensation.

Tripp complied with her prompt and everything inside her blurred as she crashed over the edge. She may have cried out, but she couldn't be sure, the feelings rippled through her in never-ending ecstasy that rendered her helpless and unable to think. He growled with her flesh still clamped in his teeth and then went ridged.

Amari almost slid down the tile when he released her and stepped under the water. She wasn't a cuddler, but normally her partner at least let her catch her breath. She sucked in a breath and then realized her neck was stinging. Touching it she felt the warmth from blood and the outline of teeth marks on her neck. Eyes wide she looked at him, "what did you do?" She smirked, not even caring. He looked like someone had stabbed him in the gut—not the look she expected after that shattering moment.

Tripp put his hand over his mouth and then held it out toward her, "I'm sorry." He flipped the wet hair back from his face, "you told me to use my teeth, and," he motioned to her neck, "I got carried away in the moment."

Struggling through the fog to suck air into her lungs, she closed her eyes for a moment as an aftershock rippled through her. That was the most satisfying release she'd ever had. She smiled and opened her eyes. The guy still had a shocked look on his face, "it's not the first bite I've gotten." She smirked, "no biggie. It will heal up next time I shift." After what he'd done for her, she could forgive him for just about anything.

Tripp opened his mouth and then snapped it shut. "I better go check on our friend."

Amari blinked; she'd completely forgotten about the tranq'd man in the other room. "Yeah, I'm just going to scrub the gas smell away." She wanted to kiss him again, knowing that as soon as he got out of the shower it would be back to business. It was too damn bad this was the only opportunity they were going to get; she wouldn't mind a repeat with him at all. "Thanks for the assist, special operations." She stepped under the spray with him and stretched up to kiss his mouth softly. He returned the kiss and even lingered for a moment, making her think he wouldn't object to another few rounds at some point, but then he lifted his head and stepped out of the tub, closing the curtain behind him.

Her body was buzzing and content, and she refused to overthink his reaction. She didn't need attachments and she knew the job he had didn't leave room for any of that relationship stuff either. Picking up the sample bottle of shampoo, she squeezed some into her palm and decided her hair needed the scrubbing of a lifetime after the last few days.

Her cat was quiet and content right now, making Amari smile, he was good enough to settle her uptight cat down. "Bonus points for you, special operations." She whispered and then lathered her hair up.

Chapter Eleven

Tripp yanked his jeans on outside the door as the water dripped from his hair down the front of him. He turned and looked at the door, then shook his head, he wasn't going back in for a towel. Walking across the room, he glanced to make sure the man was unconscious, he was, which was a good thing, he couldn't deal with that right now.

Lifting both hands, he rested them on top of his head and stared at the wall in front of him. She wasn't going to be so forgiving when that bite didn't go away with her next shift. He'd fucking marked her. Worse, he'd done it without her consent. Without his own knowledge as well, a second's notice didn't count and that was all the warning he had, from when her scent registered in his brain to his cat biting her.

Closing his eyes, he reached for his animal. As soon as they weren't within earshot of anyone else, they would be having a talk. Like why the hell hadn't he let him know she was their mate? Tripp couldn't smell shit, but the gas smell, but his cat's weird behavior made sense now. Opening his eyes, he turned his head, with his hands still on top of his head, and looked at the bathroom door. He couldn't blame his cat, hell, he'd been drawn to her too, which should have set off all the alarms for him. He was never this distracted on a mission, *never*, not even with some of the crazy shit he'd seen had his attention ever strayed from the object he was tasked with.

Blowing out a breath, he dropped his hands and put them on his hips. Now what? Did he tell her? He frowned, was her taser still in his pack? He needed to make sure it was. Shaking his head, he looked at her boots outside the bathroom door, of course confiscating the three knives that he knew she had on her might be a good idea too. He had to tell her. Didn't he?

Shit. He'd marked a female without consent. The next thought popped into his head and his legs gave out, he dropped to a squat and rested his back against the dresser behind him. He'd marked Vesper Hughes's daughter. Lifting his hands, he rubbed them over his face and then held them over his mouth. His mate was an Alpha's daughter. How had fate fucked up this bad?

Dropping his hands, he looked at the bathroom door again. The water stopped. It was nothing against her, she was pretty spectacular, even in her slightly scary, out-of-control moments—but Vesper Hughes was going to have his balls for this. He stood up. Would he kick his mother and sister out of that clan? *Shit.*

Tripp reached for his phone, and it wasn't in his pocket. He glanced around the room and almost sighed in relief to see it sitting on the table. He needed to—what? He couldn't call Kenzo freaking out about this. He definitely couldn't call his mother and tell her he'd marked a female without consent, she'd have his balls for that alone. *Fuck.* When he told Amari that he'd marked her, she'd probably cut *off* his balls. He scowled at the door, he wasn't even sure she liked males, never mind having a mate. His body responded to the thought of her, and he looked down at the bulge in the front of his jeans, then rolled his eyes, okay, she liked them for *that*.

Blowing out a breath, he walked over to his phone and then turned around and paced away from it again. The only thing he knew right now was no matter what he was probably going to be ball-less at the outcome of this.

The door opened and she came out wearing only the other man's t-shirt. She looked soft and appealing dressed like that—except it was another man's shirt, his cat didn't like that at all. He cleared his throat when a growl started to roll from it. The worst part was he knew exactly what the loose-fitting material was hiding underneath and he had to jam his hands in his pockets to stop himself from going over to her.

Amari stopped and smiled at him, "you could have grabbed a towel." She turned around and went back in, then came out carrying one in her hand.

Tripp felt like he'd forgotten how to move or speak as she came right up to him and reached and started to dry off his hair. She smelled amazing now that the smell of fuel was gone. The floral-smelling soap and shampoo, mixed with her—*their* scents smelled fantastic. Oh yeah, he was so screwed now, he probably wasn't going to survive this. Reaching up, he put his hand over the towel and took over. "Thanks."

Dropping her hands, she turned and looked at the big man on the bed. *The bed.* There was only one bed. His body and cat went to the same place at the same moment, and he had to turn away from her and look like he had a purpose for doing so. Going over to his boots, he jammed his bare feet into the cold wet leather. Grabbing the jacket and then his phone, he motioned to the door, "I'm going to go scope out the area and see how many others are here."

"See if there's a diner or something close by," she motioned to the takeout garbage on the table, "I'm hungry." She gave him an adorable, cheeky grin and his insides felt like they were suddenly on fire.

"Uh, sure, burger?" He held onto the doorknob like it was going to jump out of his hand.

"Yes. Milk, a few cartons of milk too." She nodded her head and then turned and looked at the man again, "a quick bite and then we get him up and off the bed."

She stretched her arms over her head in a leisurely stretch and his eyes flicked to the hem of the shirt to see it rose high enough that he could see a small fraction of her bare ass underneath. Gritting his teeth together, he yanked open the door and stepped outside. The cool air on his wet body was like a slap in the face and he relished the feeling. Zipping the jacket up, he tucked his hands in the pockets and then looked around the parking lot to see if there was anything close by. It was the back of the building, so nothing there. There was only one other car in the lot, and he was sure the snow and cold weather were to thank for that. It made his task easier too. The fewer people around, the better.

As he rounded the corner, his phone buzzed in his hand. Pulling it out, he looked at it. Kenzo. He blinked, not even sure he could speak to him right now and make sense. *Shit.* He answered it, "Carson."

"You got him?"

Tripp stopped and stood there looking around, "yeah."

"Is he talking?"

There was a mom-and-pop burger joint across the street. "I had to tranq him, just waiting for him to wake up now."

"Where are you?"

He almost said standing outside, then realized what he was asking, "he had a motel room, so we're waiting it out there."

"Okay, good. Asher and York are on their way to you, but probably won't reach you until morning."

Tripp nodded, "should have some information by then." He was determined he was going to find out something from him now before he was neck-deep in shit.

"Is everything good with Amari?"

It's fan-fucking-tastic. His cat rolled through him briefly. "Uh, yeah."

Kenzo chuckled, "that sounded positive."

Tripp couldn't tell Kenzo how badly he'd screwed up. He shouldn't tell anyone. Marking a female with consent wasn't just frowned upon it was considered illegal. "How are the teams doing?" He needed to think about something else for a minute while he sorted this out.

"We'll be set up to move in as soon as it's dark. Multiple strikes again tonight."

Tripp nodded and wished he was there. "Good. I should have something out of him before dinner, I'll let you know."

He heard a door close, and the sound of a vehicle start. "What's going on, Tripp, your tone is so flat it's like you're sleepwalking or something."

He was wide awake. In fact, he may never close his eyes again for fear he would be stabbed in his sleep.

"I know Amari can try a man's patience and her father is not your favorite person, but she's solid to work with..."

"How do you know? Have you worked with her?" He blurted it out and winced at the slight growl in his voice.

"A few times."

Tripp scowled and stared at a car that drove by. His team leader had worked with his mate a few times. Were they alone? "Doing what?" What could he possibly need her for? He was the leader of the special operations team, he could call in anyone, why would it be Amari?

"Tracking poachers once and getting some of ours out of a tight spot—" he paused, "what the hell is going on, Tripp?"

Tripp closed his eyes and let his head drop, Asher and York might be picking his ass up when they got here, "she's my mate, Kenzo, and has no idea—" He lifted his head and turned to look at the corner, how was it she didn't know? "Can gas affect the ability to scent long term?" He'd known as soon as the water had washed away the offensive smell, how was it she didn't know? His cat sure as hell was throwing it out there when he bit her and every second since.

"Shit." That was all Kenzo said for a moment.

Tripp blinked, that was it? Just shit?

"If she inhaled it, I guess it would mess her up for a bit, burn the nostrils, but if she's shifted..."

"She has." He rubbed his hand back over his wet hair and felt how cold it was, even though he couldn't really feel it anywhere else.

Kenzo blew out a breath. He heard the engine shut off. "I didn't even think of you both being the same clan," he heard voices, but they were muffled. Were the teams getting ready to head out? "You're getting along though, right?"

The two of them in the shower flashed through his mind, they were definitely getting along—for now. "Yeah."

"When did you realize it?" Kenzo hissed out a breath, "never mind, I don't need to know that." He blew out another breath, it wasn't often his team leader seemed undecided, "you have to tell her, Tripp. Your cat is going to interfere and override you a lot, she needs to know..."

Tripp dropped his head down and kicked at the slush under his boot like some child that was avoiding looking at someone. "I fucking marked her, Ken." He mumbled it. What was the punishment for unconsented marking? He'd already had an outlaw status and worked his ass off to get out of that mess, now he could end up worse. What was worse than an outlaw?

"Oh," there was a pause, "oh, well, uh, you're still breathing, so that's-that's a good sign."

Never, in all the years he'd been working with him had he heard his fearless leader stumble for words. He snorted, "is it?" Sucking in a breath he blew it out, "it was without consent." He stated it clearly, owning up to it.

"I put that together, if she doesn't realize—well, fuck, Tripp, I have no idea."

Tripp blinked and then looked straight ahead, without seeing anything. "She might fucking stab me when I tell her."

Kenzo chortled, "that's a given—it's Amari, she's a man-eater."

The label made his cat still.

"Oh shit, her father..."

"Right. I've been in some deep shit before, but this is a clusterfuck like no other, boss." All the tension in his spine drained and he was surprised he didn't drop to the ground like a big gooey puddle.

"Okay," his tone was more Kenzo-like now, all business, "can you continue with your task? Do you want me to send someone else?"

Tripp shook his head, "I got it." He looked over his shoulder back toward the room, "and I don't know if I could let her leave right now either."

"Right, yeah, I've heard it's a big mindfuck when you find your mate."

Tripp snorted, "it's something."

"At some point, her sense of smell is going to return..." There was a sound like a tap on the glass and then the engine started again, "I won't even ask how you came to mark her, but I'm fitting the pieces together and telling you right now, you need to fight like hell to stay focused on this, Tripp, get the information out of that scum before Asher and York get there."

Tripp nodded, "I will. I might have to tie her up, so she doesn't kill him in the process though."

Kenzo blew out a long breath, "yeah, good luck with that, and uh, I know it may not feel like it right now, but congratulations on finding your mate."

It didn't feel like something he should celebrate just yet, "just, um, can you keep this between us for now?"

"Like I have a choice until you have her mark on you, no one else can know, bud—the only thing that's stopping me from reporting it is I know Amari and how trying she can be, plus the circumstances aren't exactly optimal."

Tripp watched the snowfall slowly, normally he loved the season change, but today he wasn't feeling it. "I don't think there is a scenario of any kind that would work with her..."

"Right, she's not really the type to fall for sweet-talking." He could hear the vehicle moving now, "keep me in the loop, okay? If shit's going to start falling on your head, I'll try to be a buffer for you."

"Like when her father wants to string me up and fillet me?"

Kenzo laughed, "you should know something," the line muted for a second, "shit, I have to go, our king is calling me."

Tripp nodded, "I'll message you later." He hung up the phone and then paused, he should know what? Shaking his head, he jammed the phone in his pocket and then started to march across the lot so he could go get her a burger and milk. He didn't need to know anything else right now, he had enough to figure out. His stomach rolled, and he should eat too—not that food was going to make any of this less volatile when she found out. He stopped as he stepped off the curb. *Shit.* He forgot to ask if the cleanup had found the campsite. Kenzo would have said if they hadn't, probably.

Growling, he started walking again, he needed to get his head in the game and put all this other stuff aside. His cat rolled through him to get his attention. "Don't even start, asshole, you should have given me a heads up before it got this far." Great, now he was vocally cussing at the other half of himself. At least he knew he wouldn't have to worry about her filing a complaint against him, that wasn't her style, she liked to handle things on her own. Was that better for him or worse? The image of the guy she bled out popped into his head. Definitely worse. *Mindfuck.* Oh yeah, he was there, and it was going to be like a goddamned maze finding his way out of this situation.

Chapter Twelve

Tripp leaned against the wall and watched the big man slowly come out of it. To get him sitting up in that chair had taken both of them and even then, it had been a struggle. The chair was barely visible now that he was in it. They'd had to use a rope to tie him upright and then bound his wrists. Amari had joked that Tripp's bag was magical because he had rope, wire, and ties and asked if he had a candy section in there too. Magic had nothing to do with it, he just liked to be prepared for all scenarios. Of course, accidental marking, there was nothing that could have prepared him for *that*.

A low growl came from the man, confirming that he was correct in identifying he was from a bear clan. That made Tripp feel a bit better that his sense of smell was still working. He was surprised because the whole time they were moving him, all he could smell was her and if he hadn't needed her help, he would have told her to go outside for his own peace of mind.

By the time he came back with food, his cat suddenly understood the severity of what had happened and was quiet and watchful now. Too little, too late, asshole was all Tripp could think—and he thought it on a loop every time he sensed his animal.

He glanced at the bathroom door and wondered what Amari was doing in there, the door was open but he couldn't see in it without moving, and right now he was *supposed* to be watching this guy as he woke up. The dart gun was in his hand, just in case, this idiot decided he didn't need his hands anymore and struggled against the wire wrapped around them.

The bathroom light went off and Amari came out and set her bag on the bed. She had put her jeans on, and for that he was thankful, the less skin of hers he had to caress with his eyes, the easier it should be to focus. The oversized shirt was now pulled to one side and knotted by her hip. When she turned and looked at him, he felt like he was punched in the gut. She'd done something with her hair that made it look like feathers in the breeze each time she moved her head. She smiled at him, an excited look on her face.

"Almost showtime."

She was wearing some kind of lipstick or something on her lips. No other makeup, just her pouty mouth was covered in pale pink shiny stuff. Tripp wanted to go over and taste the shit and that annoyed him off. He didn't need to be thinking about her mouth under his. Pushing away from the wall, he went over and picked up his coffee cup, and swallowed the last mouthful of the cold bitter liquid.

When he turned around, she was squatted down in front of the man, looking up at him.

"Wakey, wakey," she tapped him on the cheek with the palm of her hand, "open those eyes, asshole, I have better things to do than watching you sleep." She glanced over at Tripp and the look she gave him heated all the blood in his body at once.

Shit. Clearing his throat, he moved back to the corner, furthest from her so he wouldn't do something stupid, like tossing her on the bed, "stay clear in case I have to shoot him again."

The man moaned, and her attention was back on him. She moved back just enough that Tripp would have a clear shot if needed but was still bent down her face almost in his. "Yeah, the headache is intense isn't it, like your worst hangover *ever.*"

She sounded way too enthusiastic right now and that made him worry that she was going to go off the rails again. He glanced to see she didn't have her boots on, and from the small portion of the waist of her jeans that he could see, she wasn't wearing her belt either. It wasn't as reassuring as it should have been though, she'd already proven that she didn't need a weapon to do damage.

"That's it, swallow down that bile," she reached out and tapped his cheek again, "nice, right, and what about the taste? Nasty, huh?" When their prisoner lifted his head and squinted at her, she waved her hand, "remember me? Last time you saw me I was tied to a *fucking* tree." The poor sap in the chair stiffened. "Hey, I wouldn't struggle if I were you," she straightened up and made a point to look behind the chair, "that wire is tight and right across your wrists," she moved back into his view, "you could lose a hand and I'm pretty sure that shit doesn't grow back when you shift." She shrugged, "not that you're *ever* shifting again."

Tripp watched the expression on his face change when he realized how screwed he was. When he stilled, he hoped that meant he was going to behave, because he really didn't have time to wait for him to come out of it if he had to put him down again.

The man's eyes locked on her again and stupidly screamed retribution. *Oh, buddy, you aren't very smart at all.* Tripp couldn't help smirking.

"I'm Amari," she put her hand on her chest, "we weren't formally introduced, well, because I was unconscious with a bag over my head," she stood up and then motioned to Tripp, "and the sexy one in the corner is Tripp. We'll be your interrogators for today," she leaned down on her knees so she was level with his face again, "and if you're a good boy, you might see tomorrow," she shrugged and went over to the wallet on the dresser, and flipped it open. "Darrel, huh?" She dropped it back on the dresser and leaned back against it and crossed her arms over her chest.

Darrel looked at her for a second and then turned his dark eyes to look at him again. Tripp understood all too well the hatred in his eyes and lifted the dart gun so he could take note of that, just in case he was trying to formulate a plan to get himself out of this situation.

"Oh," Amari pushed away from the dresser and went into the bathroom. He heard the water turn on, then she came out carrying a glass, "I almost forgot how dry you get after the darts." She went over to him and grabbed his chin and jerked his head up, "open wide."

For whatever reason, Tripp thought she was actually going to give the man a drink. Instead, she tipped the glass and the water poured over his face. Maybe if he was lucky, a few drops landed in his mouth.

"Refreshed now?" She went over and put the glass on the dresser. "When you're feeling chatty, I'll pour some in your mouth." She nodded and then gave him a cold smile.

Tripp looked at Darrel, he looked even more pissed off than he had before, but was doing a good job sitting still so the wire didn't cut into him. At least he'd decided he wanted his hands. "I could watch her do this all day." It wasn't a lie; he could spend the entire day looking at her. *Focus.* His cat reminded him. He almost grinned, *now* his cat was in the game. Blowing out a breath, he pushed away from the wall and moved over to sit on the other chair across from him. "When is the pickup?"

"How much am I worth?"

Tripp turned to look at Amari, and she shrugged, "aren't you curious how much," she motioned her hand up and down her body, "this, is worth?"

Biting his tongue so he wouldn't say what was on his mind, he turned back to Darrel—who was completely focused on Amari and not him. "I guess you picked the wrong helpless female." His dark eyes finally moved back to him, "the little one," he frowned, "I forget his name, she bit off his ear while she was still tied to the tree." He didn't seem to care, "then when she wasn't, she bled him out," Tripp tapped the side of his neck where Amari had sunk her knife into that man. Turning his head, he glanced at her, "I'm sorry, darlin, what was it you said his blood tasted like?"

Amari moved just her eyes to look at him for a second, the look told him she was very entertained by him asking, "like candy."

Tripp nodded, "right, sweet like candy," he turned back to Darrel, "that's how the little guy's blood tasted." That got the man's attention, some of the hardness in his eyes changed to a mix of confusion, and the dawning of how much he'd underestimated the Alpha female was evident. "That," Tripp shook his head, "that wasn't her best move." He sat back and crossed his arms over his chest, "she took a taser to the other one's balls."

Darrel jerked his head to look at her and then right back to Tripp.

"That's right, she's very," Tripp rubbed his hand over his chin, "inventive with punishment." Dropping his hand, he tilted his head, "you could save yourself and just tell us what we need to know."

"If you think you're going to get out of this and go back to your vile choice of profession," Amari came over and stood a foot from him, looking down at him. Darrel lifted his chin to look at her, "there are two ways you're leaving here," she nodded her head slowly, "in cuffs with a few friends of ours or in a body bag," she shrugged, "your choice." She grinned, "one of the guys coming to pick you up is so broody, I just know he's got a lot of unprocessed baggage," she tapped her chest, "inside, so you know, he could just take it all out on you without warning." She smiled, "up to you."

Tripp watched Darrel as she turned around and went and sat on the bed, he just wasn't getting it. "Answer three questions and we'll get you something to drink and then leave you alone until your ride gets here." He wasn't about to tell him that wasn't happening until tomorrow. "When is the pickup, where, and who's the traitor inside the Alliance."

"Four questions," Amari said quietly, "how much am I worth?"

Tripp glanced at her and then back to Darrel, "what is a perfect female specimen going for?" He heard her laugh softly but couldn't let her distract him from this. It was already a struggle not to just sit here and look at her.

Darrel swallowed, it looked painful, his throat must be really dry, "I'm not telling you shit." His voice cracked as he talked.

Amari sighed in a loud dramatic way. "He has no sense of self-preservation, Tripp."

He nodded, still watching him, "I noticed." Leaning forward, he lifted the dart gun and pointed it at his face, "what do you think one of these would do," he bent his wrist and pressed it against the side of Darrel's head, "right in the temple?"

"Probably something bad," Amari stated, "they tell us not to hit anyone in the face with them."

Tripp nodded, "it wouldn't penetrate the skull, but the temple, it might pierce there."

"Nasal cavity." Amari turned and sat on the side of the bed, facing them, "it would definitely penetrate that."

Tripp moved the gun tip and then pressed it against the side of the bridge of Darrel's nose, forcing him to close the eye it was covering. "Right here?" He didn't turn to look at her, he wanted to see when this idiot realized his life depended on him talking.

"Yeah, don't you think that would work?"

Tripp nodded his head slowly, "I think it might." He sat back and moved the gun away, "they don't tell us what happens if we do make a successful headshot though," he watched the man look at the gun and then move his eyes slowly back to him. "Do you think it's strong enough to render someone a vegetable?" Tripp looked over to see Amari was very interested in this topic.

"We could find out and say it was an accident." She smirked.

Tripp frowned, "that wouldn't look good in my file."

"You always worry about what your file says?" She grinned at him this time.

"No," he smiled back at her, "not really." She leaned back on her hands and crossed her legs, then bounced her foot like she was bored. Tripp didn't mean to but still ended up looking at her from her toes to her face. The bite on her neck was visible and a sense of proprietary went through him when he looked at it. When he got to her eyes, they looked amused that he was taking the time to ogle her when they had work to do. He winked at her and then turned back to Darrel. "When is the meet to pick up Amari?" Darrel visibly clamped his mouth shut.

Amari leaned over and looked behind the chair. "You're doing a great job keeping your arms relaxed, Darrel, not even a single drop of blood." She actually sounded impressed and that pissed Tripp off, that she had any emotion for this man. Sitting up, she smiled at him, "I have an idea, Tripp."

He probably looked like an idiot staring at those lips and not answering immediately. "Oh?" His cat was closer to the surface and Tripp didn't know if it was because of her or the man she'd been taunting.

She stood up and went over to his bag and reached into the side pocket of it. She pulled out the wire they'd used on his wrists and spun around looking very animated, "what if," she bent down and reached under the bottom of the cuff of her jeans and pulled out a thick handle. He didn't see a blade. With the push of a button, it became a three-inch hawkbill knife.

Tripp raised one eyebrow, wondering if that was one of her boot knives or if she kept one in her cuff too. She was a walking, sexy little armory.

She paused to smile at him, "what if we use this," she held up the wire, "and wrap it around his balls," she cocked her head to the side, "I'm not sure how that works, really, I haven't done a close-up study," she glanced back at him and licked her lips and Tripp, being the sick bastard he was, suddenly pictured all the wrong things involving her lips and parts of him instead of the threat she was trying to illustrate to Darrel. "I'm thinking," she moved over to stand closer to the other man and waved the knife toward his crotch, "if he were to cough or try to move it might cut into them," she winced, "or off, I can't be sure."

Turning, he noted that she had Darrel's focus as he gave the knife and wire a wary look. "Either way it's the kind of pain that makes a man throw up." He said in an even voice. Darrel jerked his head to look back at him. His face was blanched, his eyes wide. *Oh yeah, now we've got your attention.* With slow moves, Tripp got up and motioned to him, "have at it, just try not to stain the carpet too much."

Amari nodded, "good point," she turned and moved quickly to the bathroom, then came back out with a towel. She pointed the knife at Darrel, "just sit real still though, I wouldn't want you to slice your own wrists." She dropped the towel on the floor under the chair, then squatted down in front of him.

Chapter Thirteen

Amari smiled at the phone and then looked at Tripp to see he was shaking his head.

"Wait. So—hang on. Back up," Blair murmured, "you were going to do what?"

"I don't think they asked for a group call to explain their methods," Calum said in an even voice.

"No, I know." Blair said quickly, "I just—I might throw up."

Amari put her hand over her mouth so she wouldn't laugh at him. "I wouldn't have done it," she pursed her lips, "I don't think."

"Please tell me you got the information. Otherwise, I'm going to go curl up in a corner somewhere and tremble in fear." Jesse sounded amused.

Amari looked up at Tripp and noticed he was giving her that look again, the one that said he'd rather pick her up and carry her somewhere else to do much more interesting things. "I'll let Tripp explain, it pisses me off and I might go back in and stab him." His look sobered.

"I would rather not pick up a body," Asher stated.

"Tripp?"

Tripp straightened at Kenzo's voice. He looked at the phone, "the pickup is for tomorrow morning, location unknown, they'll send a text an hour before." Tripp glanced at her for a second, then continued, "it's got to be close if they're only giving him an hour's notice."

"Do you want York and Asher to hang there and lend a hand?" Devin asked.

"No," he shook his head, "he told us too much, and shortly their whole network will know that he's missing, so we need him secure where they can't get to him."

"Okay," Devin paused, "Dad can't join in, so let's not keep us in suspense any longer."

She wasn't sure what he had texted Kenzo, but a half-hour later six of them were on a conference call. Amari exchanged a look with Tripp, the nerve in his jaw was pulsing. It made her feel slightly better that he was just as angry as she was. Although, he was hiding it a lot better than she was.

He ran his hand back through his hair to brush it out of his face, "the leak is still coming from inside."

"How?"

"Let him finish, Nate." Kenzo cut him off.

"He doesn't know who, just that they're part of Alliance security." Tripp rolled his shoulders like the tension was riding him heavily and she understood where it was coming from, right now she wanted to head to the Alliance headquarters and start stabbing people.

"The actual security team? Raymond is going to go ballistic." Kenzo said in a quiet voice.

"Are there any other details?" Calum's tone was quiet now.

Tripp shook his head, "all he knows," he glanced at her, a slight smirk on his face, "and I believe he would have told us if he knew more," Amari smirked back at him, "they're holding his family or a member of his family and if he wants them back alive, he has to help."

"They'll never come back alive." Kenzo hissed out a breath, "he probably won't live long when he stops sharing things."

"We have to talk to Raymond, he needs to know one of his is leading them right to ours," Jesse sounded angry and that was rare, usually he didn't get stirred up. "If they were able to get Amari…"

"No one is safe." Calum finished for him.

"I'll talk to Dad, I'm sure he'll want to call Raymond to come to see him and tell him in person," Devin paused, "can you check things on your end, Nate? See if you can find out how he's giving them tracking information?"

"Fallan and Dane are going to pitch a fit, they designed the new trackers, and if they've been compromised…"

"They knew right where to look," Tripp glanced down at her, "the wiring harness was pulled up, ripped out and the tracker was crushed on the ground."

"Shit." Nate started mumbling and she couldn't understand what he was saying. "All of them could be compromised then, the chips for the cleanup team, phone tracking, vehicles, all of it—"

"Are the phones still secure?" Devin asked.

It was as if everyone held their breath waiting for an answer. "Yes, they're solid. Unless they have one of the tech team's systems, they can't possibly tap into any calls. Every call is monitored," Tripp raised an eyebrow and then glared at the phone, "we don't hear what's said, we just monitor the signal and any interruptions, like if someone else is on it or trying to get in it…"

"Good to know," Kenzo said in a dry tone.

"They can't have access to everything or yesterday would have been a disaster and they'd be on us right now," Blair stated.

"I was just thinking that," Jesse added.

"What now?" Amari scowled at the phone. "Two-hour check-ins are pointless if they can follow us," she was so tired of this, "what about those we've transported? Rescued? Do they know where they have been moved to?" She was seething inside, "they'll know everyone we've sent to the Alliance holding," she waved her hand around, "what's to say the one helping them won't just let them back out again?" She paced away and then spun back around again, "are we supposed to just start doubting everyone we work with?" She hissed out a breath, "I'm pissed, Jesse, I'm so sick of this," she snarled at the phone, "if I get my hands on whoever—" She couldn't finish that train of thought.

"Amari." Jesse rarely used an authoritative tone, so as soon as she heard it, she looked back at the phone.

"Where are Deva and Calla, Jesse, are they safe?" Her heart pounded.

"They're fine. They're with us and the teams." He assured.

"Good." She put her hands on her hips and looked down at the ground, her cat was right there, wanting a piece of someone too.

"Hold on a sec," Tripp said.

She looked at him, he tilted his head and then searched her face. When he put his hand on her shoulder it felt like he was projecting calm to her. Her animal responded to it right away.

"Your cat has mine trying to claw its way out to kill whatever has upset you."

Amari's eyes widened and she looked at the phone.

"I muted us for a second."

She blew out a breath and nodded. "I'm just," she shook her head, "this is trash, this whole situation, Tripp…"

"I know." He ducked his head down so they were face to face, "listen, we're going to see this through," he motioned to the door a few feet from them, "then we'll track some more and take them down, regardless of who they are." He put his hand over his heart, "I swear."

Amari sucked in a shaky breath and then blew it out and nodded, "yeah. I'll cut them into tiny bite-size pieces."

He smirked, "atta girl. Focus it on the end result." He gave her a quick nod while searching her face to see if she was all right and held up the phone.

"I just need…"

He gave her a heated look, "we have company, or I'd oblige you with what would help settle you down. You can go for a run at dusk." He winked at her and then held his finger over the phone.

Amari's insides heated and she gave him a look, so he'd start the call again. As far as shutting her up, that worked. Now all she wanted to do was climb him and wrap her legs around him. She still wanted to stab people, just not as much.

"We're back," Tripp said while keeping his gaze on her.

"Anyone injured?" Kenzo asked.

"Not yet." She said and then rolled her head from side to side to try to keep a handle on her temper.

"I was saying," Nate said, "we need to check on the security team's families somehow and narrow down who it could be."

"I'll mention that to Dad when I talk to him," Devin said.

"This is bullshit guys," she said with a lot less hostility in her voice, "are we supposed to start watching everyone we work with?"

"The teams that are out, we can trust," Jesse told her, "If we couldn't half the ops would have failed."

Amari glanced to see Tripp still watching her, he nodded agreeing with her boss. "Just make sure all of them are in the loop, Jesse, no one goes anywhere alone and unarmed," she shook her head, "I even would have waited for my partner if I'd known they could follow us like that."

Jesse snorted, "I somehow doubt that. You would have just driven with a gun in your hand."

She smirked and then shrugged, "maybe."

"She's in good hands now, Jesse," Kenzo said, "Tripp will be her shadow."

Amari glanced at him again and he winked. Did he have to be so freaking sexy and appealing? She put her hand up and touched the bite on her neck, his eyes tracked her movement, she might even miss this when it was gone after she went for a run.

"I think they're just lucky only a couple of them ended up dead," Tripp said, sending her another heated look.

Amari had to force herself to look away from him, "just make sure the girls are carrying their tasers, Jesse."

Tripp raised an eyebrow at her.

"I'll pass it along."

"Are there any other shitstorms you want to share with us, Tripp?" Blair didn't sound amused.

Tripp shook his head, "that's it until we meet up with the one that thinks he's picking up his little Alpha female."

"I'd prefer him alive," Devin said, "there's no way anyone from the top is going to come to retrieve their new prize, so we need information from them."

Tripp gave her a questioning look, she shrugged, "we'll do everything possible to make sure they're still breathing."

Someone snorted and Amari wasn't sure who it was.

"Breathing and able to speak, if at all possible." Kenzo's clarified.

"Got it," Amari said, then looked at Tripp and rolled her eyes.

"We'll be there before morning," Asher said, "instead of stopping to rest, we're going to go straight through, he's going to be a hot commodity by tomorrow."

"I will give Raymond a heads up and make sure he keeps his arrival off the record." Devin didn't sound impressed. "I need to go, keep me up to date."

Amari paced away and played in the slush as the others left the call one after the other.

"Amari?"

She turned at Jesse's voice, "yeah?"

"I know you're used to doing your own thing, but until we have the ones that tried to purchase you in custody, please," he sighed, "please try to follow Tripp's lead."

She looked at Tripp to see he wasn't grinning or even close to it, points for him. "I'll behave, boss." She raised her hand in the air, "promise."

Jesse laughed softly, "I doubt that. Just get back to us in one piece, okay?"

"You know it." She smiled at the phone. Jesse and the co-ord team felt more like family than her family.

"Asher has a phone for you, message me after you get a location."

Amari nodded, "I will." She waited and he said nothing more.

"Tripp?"

Tripp jerked his head and looked at the phone at his team leader's voice. "Yeah."

"You two good?"

Tripp glanced at her and then nodded, "we're good."

"Focus and get that son of a bitch tomorrow."

"You got it, boss."

The line went quiet.

Blowing out a breath, she nodded her head slowly. She felt better on most levels. The girls on her team were safe, that was a relief. Now, if she could just figure out why her cat's emotions were all over the place, she'd be able to focus on getting this done. Probably because she hadn't killed anything in a few days. After what they went through, that might be it.

Chapter Fourteen

Tripp opened the door an inch and looked out it, then stepped back to let York come in. Right behind him was a man he'd seen around several times in the last few years, but he'd never spoken to him.

Before he could speak, Amari jumped off the bed and rushed over.

"Ash," she smiled at him, "is that for me?"

Asher held out the bag in his hand, "Zain got it to us before we left."

She took the bag and looked in it then grinned at him, "he got some of my stuff."

"He was waiting for them when they got back with your van."

She set the bag down and reached in it, "yes, clothes."

Tripp stood by the door and watched her take a few items out of the bag, his eyebrows raising when she pulled out a smooth gun case and another case that could only hold knives. What did she need more knives for? When she pulled out a package that crinkled, she turned and grinned at Asher, then hugged it to her chest.

"Z rocks." She held the package up.

Gummy bears? Her team director had sent her gummy bears.

"Here's your new phone." Asher held it out.

She already had the bag opened and jammed several of the bears in her mouth. Taking the phone, she grinned over at the man still tied to the chair, "told you I eat bears for breakfast." She smirked and then went and sat on the bed and tapped the screen on the phone.

Tripp watched Darrel look slowly from her to York, "please get me out of here."

York's eyebrows went up, then he looked over at Tripp, amusement in his eyes.

When he turned to Asher, he watched the expression on his face change to shock as he watched Amari. He turned to look at Tripp, and his gaze went right to his neck. *Shit.* He'd seen the bite. His eyes connected with Tripp's, and he could see the questions. Clearing his throat, Tripp went over and picked up Darrel's bag. "His wallet is in here; we're keeping the phone for the pickup location."

When he turned around York was untying Darrel. When he got to his back, he glanced over at him. "Wire?"

Tripp held the bag out to Asher, "keeps them from getting any ideas."

"I don't need it." Darrel said and looked from York to Amari, then back, "just get me out of here."

Amari looked up from the phone and smiled at him, "remember what I said, they'll hunt you down and carve you up," she shrugged, "or I will."

Darrel nodded and then watched York pull zip ties from his pocket. He nodded his head again but didn't say a word as York replaced the wire with the plastic ties.

Tripp put his hand over his mouth to cover the grin. Seeing how scared the large man was of Amari was not something he was ever going to forget.

"I'll get him loaded up." York went by Asher and out the door with him.

Asher swung Darrel's bag to his back and looked over at Amari, "are you sure you don't want us to hang back and lend a hand when you get the information for the meet-up?"

Amari popped a gummy into her mouth and shook her head, "I got special operations with me," she motioned to Tripp, "we're good."

Asher gave Tripp a slow once over, then nodded his head, "keep the team in the loop."

"Will do," she tilted her head and smirked, "were there bets?"

Asher's smile was slow, "Gia won, she said you'd get revenge on them."

"That's my girl." She motioned to the door, "just get him back before they know shit went South."

He nodded and turned toward the door.

Tripp opened it for him, then followed him out and closed it. He didn't know the man but could feel the hostility coming off him. York stood beside the van with the door open, but he was looking around and not at them.

Asher stepped off the curb and turned to look at him, "I don't know what's going on, but she better be fucking happy at the end of it."

Tripp crossed his arms over his chest. Did he attempt to explain it to him or just nod his head? "Her sense of smell was damaged when they poured gas on her," he glanced at the door, "we'll work it out." The look in his eyes didn't change, it was cold and reeked of vengeance, making Tripp wonder what he'd been through to put it there. "I'll make sure she's happy or die trying." It dawned on him as the words came out of his mouth that he meant it. He'd never felt like that about anyone in his life, aside from his mother and sister.

Asher snuffed out a breath as an animal would, "if she's not happy, she'll kill you herself." He inclined his head to him and then turned to get in the driver's side of the van.

Tripp watched them drive away. "Don't I know it." He whispered into the night. Inhaling a slow deep breath, he blew it out all at once and then turned to go back inside. She'd be going for a run now that their guest was gone, and then the real struggle would begin. His cat moved inside him. they were both in the same place, what if the female rejected them—then what? He had no idea but wondered if he should find some remote place and hide from her wrath.

Tripp reached over and pulled the curtain aside for the tenth time watching for her to come back. His cat wasn't happy their mate was out there alone. Both wanted to go for a run, but he wanted to wait and face what he already knew was coming. Rubbing his hand over his face, he got up. Marking a female without consent was all kinds of wrong, to begin with—doing it to Amari Hughes, every fiber of his being told him that was going to be all kinds of bad.

He went into the bathroom and flicked the light on and stood and looked in the mirror. He should shave some of this scruff off his face. Turning his head, he lifted his hair up and looked at it. He should shave the sides of his head again. Of course, neither was going to happen until he got back to his SUV where all his gear was.

Thinking about that brought him back to the care package Amari's teammate had sent her. Gummy bears. That was stopping. Now. If she required a fix of gummy bears, he'd be getting them from now on and not some other male. His cat stilled inside him. Tripp froze in reaction, then he heard the door to the room open. She was back.

He didn't get out of the bathroom before she came through the door and nudged him out of the way and leaned closer to the mirror. Tripp watched her reflection as she held her hair out of the way and looked at her neck. Yep, there it was for all to see, his mark. He should say something, he thought—then his back was slammed hard against the wall before he could open his mouth.

Amari held him in place with her forearm across his pecs. "What the hell is this, Tripp?" She used her other hand to pull her shirt collar down.

He looked down at her neck, "my mark."

She leaned into him, thudding him back against the wall again, then dropped her arm away. "I know *what* it is." She hissed out a breath and glared at him, "*why* is it there?"

A dozen words went through his mind, that he should say, but didn't.

She looked at his chest then back up at his face, a strange look in her eyes, then she leaned closer and inhaled deeply. He knew the moment she understood when her whole body stiffened.

At least she had the ability to smell now, was his first thought. His second or more his cat's thought was 'fix this'. He would have gladly obliged if he had a clue how.

Amari stepped back from him, "did you know?" She motioned to the tub, "before?"

Tripp shook his head, "all I could smell was the fuel."

"Shit." She turned away and put her hand through her hair and held it there.

He stood perfectly still, and his cat did the same, waiting. It was ingrained that a male be cautious with their mate before they were fully bonded. Tripp realized at that moment that he did want to be bound to this woman in front of him. No other type of female would ever accept his job or his ways. He jammed his hands in his pockets and looked down at the floor, trying to sort through *that* realization. He didn't know when he had accepted this. After the shock of their first few moments together on that mountain, he'd been intrigued and even admired her for not allowing precedence to dictate how she should be, but she was Hughes's, daughter…

For the third time since she'd come back, he found himself shoved into the wall, she gave him a hard look. "Don't expect me to mark you and be the happy little housewife you probably want—"

Tripp reached with slow movements and touched the side of her face, "do I strike you as the type of man that wants a woman that sits at home and smiles pretty when I come back from work?" She didn't brush his hand away and he took that as a small win.

"This is fucked, Tripp." The cold look she had been giving him softened slightly. "You were supposed to be a fun distraction."

He kept his teeth clamped together so he wouldn't say that's all he intended too. She may not want to be marked but telling a woman she was just supposed to be a quickie never ended well.

Amari released him and stepped back once more, he let his hand drop to his side. "I couldn't smell shit until just," she waved a hand at the door, "when I just shifted." She shook her head and then froze and looked back at him, "have you told anyone?"

He took a deep breath and exhaled quietly before he spoke, "Kenzo." He ran his hand over his head and brushed his hair out of his face, "I was freaking out, marking without consent isn't exactly something the Alliance is going to accept."

"Shit." She backed up and leaned against the counter, "what is he going to do?"

Tripp shook his head, "nothing. He's leaving it for us to work out."

Amari nodded her head slowly and then looked down at the floor, "good. I don't want you to lose your position on the team for something that," she waved her hand around and then looked at him, "well, it wasn't your fault."

The anxiety coming off her was almost smothering him. "If I'd known…"

"You would have turned me down?" There was something in her eyes, that he didn't have time to process, he knew enough about females to know that pausing too long in the middle of a volatile conversation never ended in his favor.

He took his time looking her up and down, a slight smirk on his face as he did. "No. I would have just kept my teeth away from you."

Her smile was slow but told him he'd given the correct answer, which also happened to be the truth. "I should have known," she said quietly, "my cat liked you."

He raised an eyebrow, "that's unusual?"

She shrugged, "yeah, she's never liked anyone I've hooked up with."

Tripp wasn't sure if it was his reaction or his cats, or both were on the same page, but he stepped across the room and cupped her jaw in his hand, "*not*," he looked at her lips, then back to her eyes, "a good idea to discuss other bedmates with me right now." He inhaled, his cat needing to take her scent into his body, "clear?" The scent of their combined signatures filled him, calming his animal down.

Amari's eyes were ultra-focused on him, the blue was being drowned in grey. "As crystal." She ground out between clenched teeth.

Tripp released her and stepped back before he picked her up and took that mouth that had been driving him to distraction since she'd walked out of the bathroom with that pink shit on her lips. He spun on his heel, "I'm going for a run. My phone is on the table, in case someone tries to reach me. His phone is right beside it." He grabbed his run pack on the way by the dresser and jammed his feet in his boots. He didn't care if it was minus forty out, he wasn't pausing long enough to get his jacket. He needed to put some distance between them. Grabbing her and tossing her on the bed was all he wanted to do right now and that wasn't going to give her time to process this.

He walked to the end of the motel and headed down through the ditch, not even caring if anyone was watching him. Tripp had always struggled with his temper but hadn't seen that coming at all. Of course, he knew she'd been with other males, that was a given. It wasn't like he'd never been with a woman before either. Hissing out a breath, he gave his head a shake, this was going to get crazy—and right now in his shifter world it was the worst possible timing ever. The last thing he needed when they were so close to ending the atrocities of the Tomas family was a mate to worry about. Yet, there was no way he was walking away or regretting his mark on her neck. It was a complete mindfuck and he needed to get back to work and get his brain focused on something else. Killing was the first thing that popped into his head. He started jogging, he needed to get out of sight faster and shift—go burn this whatever was wrong with him off.

Chapter Fifteen

Amari turned her head and looked out the window so she wouldn't look at him again. She wanted to be mad at him, but she couldn't put all the blame on him as hard as she tried. Neither of them could smell anything at that point and she was the one to tell him to use his teeth. A shiver of heat traveled through her at that thought. If she could, she'd kill that jerk all over again for pouring the gas on her—it was his fault she was mated, or half-mated. She scowled at the glass, what did that even mean? Half mated. She was good and truly marked, but he wasn't—what now?

Her cat wasn't any help right now, she was acting all weird like she was thrilled their mate had put his mark on her but at the same time, she was anxious and constantly prodding Amari to reciprocate and sink her teeth into his neck. She glanced over at him, more specifically at his neck, and for a brief second thought about her mouth against it. Clearing her throat, she looked out the windshield. "How are we going to do this?"

"I'll have to wait until I have eyes on," he reached over and turned off the radio, "and hopefully they're alone."

"I can't believe we forgot to ask Darrel if they knew each other by sight."

"Yeah, I don't know about you, but after he told us how they were getting the information I was too preoccupied with wanting to kill something to think clearly."

She looked over to see him looking at her, did he have to be so good-looking? She straightened in her seat and leaned down to get a bottle of water, anything to keep her hands occupied so she wouldn't reach over and touch him. Her cat was right there wanting to be closer to him. Is this how mating was? Constantly wanting to jump each other. How did they ever get anything done? "It would make sense that he'd bring backup, right?" She opened the water, while she watched him out of the corner of her eye, "I mean, an Alpha female is a pretty big deal." She took a drink.

"That makes sense, except if he wants to see Darrel." She watched him bring up the GPS on the jeep and check the route again, "a few more minutes."

"How fucked are we if he's already there?"

Tripp snorted softly, "pretty fucked."

Capping the water, she leaned forward and looked at the map, "if we turn just up here and come around it from behind, we can get a look before we drive right into it."

He slowed down and hovered his hand over the screen, "that could work."

When he turned off the main road, she looked out the window and then the windshield, "if you let me out, my cat can book it take a look..."

His head snapped to look at her, a hard expression on his face.

"I can get there and back faster than taking the road," she pointed out the window, "that hill over there should be high enough up and I can see if they are there and alone." She watched the muscle in his cheek pulse, "come on, special operations, have a little faith in how good I am."

"Shit. I don't like it, but it's the best plan."

Amari grinned, "I didn't like being taken, but it is what it is."

Raising an eyebrow, he looked back over at her, "if you scent anything that's off, you high tail it right back to me."

Amari put her hand over her heart and smirked, "on my honor."

He sneered at her, but still slowed down to stop.

Amari leaned down to grab her run pack when his hand stopped her.

"The pack stays here," he held her look with a steady one, "I don't know what toys you have in it and can't take a chance you'll go off the rails and eviscerate him if he's there."

Her smile was slow, no one she knew would ever have the balls to say that to her. "Me?" She unclipped her seatbelt. "I'm harmless."

He grinned, "uh-huh and I'm a boy scout."

Amari laughed, "okay, the pack stays." She looked at the map and then pointed, "I'll meet you here, and don't worry I have a very good sense of direction, in all forms." She opened the door and hopped out. Taking her jacket off, she tossed it in on the seat and then held his look as she kicked out of her boots and set them in. It was so wrong, that she was going to strip down in front of him and enjoy watching his reaction. Things were dire, they had to get this person coming to pick her up, and countless lives could be saved with the information they might have—yet she was loving how he looked only at her eyes and didn't let his eyes wander. The look she was giving him, dared him to look. When she dropped her jeans onto the seat, she stood there, hands on her hips, watching him.

He took a deep breath and then she watched his eyes move slowly down over her, then leisurely make their way back up to her eyes, "retribution is going to be sweet, darlin."

"It always is." She shut the door and shifted.

However distracted she was right now, her cat was on task and took off into the trees along the road. Amari focused on the direction she was running, checking the scents around them as they went. The light snowfall had mostly melted into the ground, which enhanced every smell of nature. It also made anything that didn't belong easier to pick up. Her cat found nothing out of the ordinary or manmade, that was a good sign.

She hit the top of the hill in what she was sure had to be record time. Stopping, she turned and watched in the trees in the direction Tripp would be driving, she could make out the disruption of the exhaust in the air. Her cat swung her head in the other direction. *Don't blame me, we're in this mess because of you. The only time in our lives it mattered that you put the brakes on, and you didn't. Now we're mated and stuck in this clusterfuck, dear kitty.*

Her cat let her know she was unimpressed before she allowed Amari to take control and get them to the top where they could see the meet location. It was open with trees surrounding it, but a good spot, hard to set up an ambush. That was a plus. Before she hightailed it back to the jeep, she checked along the road coming in from the other direction, there was no sign of a vehicle as far as she could see.

Happy enough with that, she turned and headed down the hill to meet up with Tripp again. It wasn't like she'd ever thought of what her mate might be like or pined for one like some females did. Her heart was shut off from mushy emotions like that as if a piece of her was missing from birth. Amari couldn't miss what she'd never known, and it helped her do what she had to do to help others and survive this unsafe world they lived in.

She slid down the hill toward the road, her only goal was to get to the spot before Tripp did. Mate or not, she couldn't just hand it to him. She jumped and cleared a snow-covered boulder jutting out from the earth and landed without issue to continue to zig-zag down it.

Her father lecturing her flashed through her mind, one of his endless ones about feminine behavior and being worthy of a mate. Like that had anything to do with the body fate selected for you. Aggravation of thinking about him renewed her speed as the ground started to level off. She wondered what his thoughts would be knowing her mate was one of the members of the special ops—that no proud Alpha liked to acknowledge even existed because they were so off the charts and unmanageable. Yet they were wholly necessary to do the things others couldn't or wouldn't.

If she could decide what the hell she was doing about this mating fiasco, and the decision was in Tripp's favor, she might drag her borderline terrorist mate to meet dear old dad. It was about time she settled a few things with him. Problem was, she couldn't think of him without violent inclinations filling her.

Skidding across the road, she managed to stop right in the middle of it, and sit just as Tripp jumped on the brakes, sending the Jeep skidding sideways on the narrow road. She caught the amused look on his face, and then got up and walked to the door.

Tripp leaned over and popped the door open. "Come on, Kitty cat, get your clothes on." He smirked.

She stretched up and landed her front paws on the seat and tried to give him a hard look, but her cat betrayed her and gave him a soft come hither one instead.

Tripp stood up and looked down at her, "I don't like this."

Amari rested her hands on her knees and looked up at him, "it's the best plan and you know it." She wiggled her hands, "come on."

Tripp heaved out a breath and squatted down again, "twice, we've used you as bait."

She looked at him, amusement in her eyes, "next abduction can be all about you."

He couldn't help smiling at her, "promise?"

"On my honor." She smiled.

The playful look she was giving him made him want to kiss her, and more. *No time for that.* "Try to look defeated." He smiled, "or keep your head down."

Amari lifted an eyebrow at him and leaned back against the tree, "if they know anything about me, they're going to know I'm not going to be cooperative."

"Are you ever?" He tilted his head, "cooperative?" Tripp leaned over and adjusted the collar of her jacket, then did it up. "Can't have him seeing that right off."

She realized he was covering the bite mark. She hadn't thought of that. Taking a mated female would be useless on all fronts. "What are you going to tell him if he asks about Darrel?"

"Just leave it to me, okay? We need him to turn his back to me."

"And if there's more than one?" She hoped she'd at least get to take a swing at someone today.

"We'll deal with it," he jerked his chin toward the tree, "put your arms back."

She reached behind her and felt him tug the rope that was around one wrist, pulling her arm further back. He wrapped it around the other wrist and then placed it in her hand.

"Just try to look like you're tied to the tree until I can see if there are any others with him that have been dropped off before he gets here."

She nodded as he stood up, "wait, pull up the back of my jacket."

With an amused look, he bent down and did as she requested, "can't block access to your knife."

"How did you know?"

He stood up and shrugged, "Kenzo warned me."

Amari laughed softly, "yeah he would know, he was almost on the wrong end of one once," she gave him a quick look, "sneaking up on me isn't a good idea."

"No, it is not." Tripp stood there looking down at her and then sighed loud before he squatted back down. Grasping her chin lightly, he tilted her head up, "no stupid chances, okay?" He leaned down and kissed her mouth hard, then released her and stood up. "Vehicle coming."

Amari watched him walk away and then scowled, wondering if he'd only kissed her to disarm her plan. How was she supposed to think about maiming some jerk when all she could think about was kissing him?

Closing her eyes, she took a deep breath and blew it out. *Focus. You can be his little kitty cat later.* She opened her eyes, stunned at her cat's thoughts. "We're going to have to have a talk later." She meant it for her animal, but he glanced over at her where he was leaning against the jeep, you too, she thought, and then looked at the road to watch for the vehicle.

Chapter Sixteen

Tripp watched the truck pull up beside his SUV and stop. He didn't see a passenger, just one male in the driver's seat. The man took his time looking at him and then around the area. He wasn't stupid Tripp thought, checking out the lay of the land before exposing himself. He didn't want to spook him, so he stood still, and kept his arm at his side, the dart gun visible.

The door opened and he got out, first thing he noticed was he was dressed in decent clothes. His pants looked like they'd been pressed and without a single wrinkle, and his jacket was smooth, with no marks on it anywhere Tripp could see. Being a delivery person must pay well. His boots were new, with not a scuff on them. He was clean-shaven, even his black hair was styled with an immaculately straight part. He wasn't a huge man, but he'd be a challenge in a fight.

"Are you Darrel?" He asked, still standing by the door.

Tripp shook his head and then motioned to the trees, "call of nature, he'll be back in a minute."

The man bobbed his head and closed the door. In his hand was a cloth bag and that made Tripp edgy, not knowing what was in the bag.

The man stepped clear of the truck and then looked over at Amari. "Pretty little thing." He said.

Tripp glanced at her to make sure she was sticking with the plan. "Do you do this a lot?" Tripp motioned to her with the hand holding the dart gun. "Pick up?"

Shaking his head, the man moved over closer to Amari, but still not far enough that Tripp wouldn't be able to get a shot in without him seeing him move to take it.

"Not often." He dropped the bag to the ground and pulled his jacket together. Tripp caught the outline of a gun holster as he did. *Shit.* "I only collect those Mr. Tomas wants in his personal collection."

Personal collection? Like she was some doll or something… A low growl came from Amari, and he couldn't even get mad about it because he'd had to swallow his own.

The man grinned, "she's feisty, he'll like that." His face sobered as if he wasn't as pleased about it as he let on.

Tripp moved closer, scenting the air as he went, he couldn't get a fix on what clan this fool was from and that was always a concern. "I wouldn't get too close," he paused when the man glanced over at him, "one of the guys got a little too close and she bit off half his ear."

Eyebrows raised the guy looked at him and then slowly back to her, "that's great." He sounded entertained. "That she fights back. Hopefully not too much."

Tripp sent Amari a look while he was staring at her, she had that look on her face, the one that made him want to brace for whatever was going to happen.

"So many of the females are so docile it's a bore to Mr. Tomas."

The fool needed to stop talking or he was going to lose body parts and not from Tripp's doing. "She's anything but boring."

Nodding his head, the man glanced down at the bag, "aren't you going to count it?"

The bag had money in it? "Not my job."

He shrugged, "fair enough." He motioned to the gun in Tripp's hand, "how long does one of those last? I've got an hour's drive until I meet up with the plane, after that she'll be in a cage."

A cage? A fucking cage like a pet. He tried to keep his face free of emotion, but it was hard to do. Tripp turned to look at Amari, hoping she didn't do anything to blow it until he could see if this idiot was willing to share more. "Animals don't like plane travel much."

He shrugged, "it's a short flight, they'll have a collar for her to make sure she doesn't shift."

With a shrug he hoped didn't appear as stiff as it felt, he aimed the gun at Amari, "it should keep her out long enough to reach the plane."

The man looked elated, "I'm really looking forward to seeing her shift." He grinned at him, "a cougar, right?"

"That's what they tell me." They needed this one's phone and any information he had in that head of his. He looked at Amari to see she was glaring at him and not the idiot. The look was easy to decipher, she was telling him to shoot him before she did something they'd both regret.

"Damn, look at that hatred. Good for you." There was something in this guy's tone that set off alarms for Tripp.

Amari jerked her head back to glower at the errand boy. Her look promised retribution.

"Oh, there he is." Tripp looked at the trees on the other side of him, so the man would turn too. When he did, he aimed at his back and squeezed the trigger. The man dropped to the ground before Tripp could think about adding a second one.

"Took you long enough." Amari jumped to her feet and went over to him; she squatted down and took a deep breath. "Tripp."

Tripp went over and picked up the bag and opened it. "Yeah?" There was a nice bundle of cash in it, and Amari would finally get her answer about how much she was worth.

"He's a half-breed." She whispered it.

"What?" He went over quickly and bent down to check the man's pulse. He had no idea if the dose in the dart would stop a one-forms heart, never mind one with mixed genes. There was a pulse and it felt strong enough. "Shit." Dropping the bag, he stood up and pulled out his phone, "Flip him over off his face."

She rolled him over as he dialed Kenzo's number. There was no time for covert text messages. "He's got a gun under his jacket."

"Yeah?" That was how his boss answered the call.

"Will a tranq harm a half-breed?" There was no time for polite greetings.

"We've never had a half-breed to try them on, but one-forms can only handle one shot." There was a door closing and Tripp could hear boots moving fast on the floor, "the contact is a half-breed?"

Tripp nodded and watch Amari check his pockets, "yeah and he only does pickups for those that are intended for Tomas' personal collection."

"Holy hell. Hang on." He heard muffled voices as Kenzo covered the mouthpiece.

"His ID lists some place in Chicago, with a *suite* address. He's not a low-level gopher." Amari looked up at him, "have we hit the jackpot?"

Tripp nodded, "seems like."

"Tripp." Kenzo was back.

"Yeah?"

"Get your location chipped, *now*." Kenzo's tone alone told him it was urgent.

"On it." He went quickly over to the jeep and opened the door to get to his bag. "He was driving for an hour then loading her in a plane."

"You're on speaker." Kenzo said quickly and Tripp could hear hushed voices in the back, "give me the chip number, Illias is going to get a location."

Tripp pulled the case out that protected the trackers from getting wet. He opened it with one hand and pulled one out, "seven, zero, zero, nine, Charlie." He read the number as he walked back to the body on the ground. When he reached him, Amari got up and headed over to the truck, and opened the door. "Putting it on him," Tripp told whoever was listening as he activated it.

"What firepower do you have on you?"

Tripp tucked the chip into the man's pocket and then glanced back at the van, "a couple of handguns." He checked his pulse just to make sure he was still alive. "His address is Chicago." He stood up and looked down at him, "he's dressed like some high-paid bodyguard, but his vibes were off." Amari was digging in a bag in the truck, it looked like it was new and had never been used. "Boss, they're going to notice if he goes off the grid."

"That's my thought too." Kenzo said in a distracted way, "got your location, get him loaded in whatever you're driving."

"Leave his truck?" Amari came over to him, he tapped the speaker and handed her the phone.

"Leave his truck. You need to be moving until we can get to you."

Tripp held her look for a second and saw that she understood the urgency of it, "give me a direction to move in."

"We're figuring that out now, finding the closest chopper." There were muffled voices again.

Amari pressed the phone into her chest, "I'll drive, you can keep watch."

Tripp nodded and bent down to pick him up. Adrenalin helped him heft the deadweight up into his arms. "Get the door." He started for the Jeep, "then grab some ties."

She hurried over and had the door open by the time he reached them.

"Tripp?"

He glanced at the phone, not recognizing the voice. "Yeah?"

"Do you have any of the mylar blankets with you?"

Tripp grunted as he got the upper body into the backseat. "Uh, unknown. I left most of my gear in my SUV." He looked over his shoulder at Amari, "take a look in my gear."

She gave him a blank look, "what am I looking for?"

"A foil blanket, Amari."

She glared at the phone, "and why do we need this, Illias?" She went around the Jeep and opened the other door.

"He might look like a privileged errand boy, but he's still a half-breed and I think Aiden Tomas would want to keep tabs on him."

Tripp shoved his legs in the Jeep and leaned in the open door, "you think he has a tracker on him?"

"It's a possibility. Take our chip off him and set it in your vehicle then cover as much of his body as possible. If you have more than one use them all."

Amari handed him zip ties across the seat. He took them and tipped the unconscious man forward.

"That will block the signal?" Amari was opening and closing the pockets of his bag.

"Not completely." Illias mumbled something, "if you're close to a tower, it's going to still ping off it, but it should scramble enough that the periodic hits will make it hard for them to zero in on your exact location, especially if you're on the move." Someone said something in the background, "it works like…"

Amari glared at the phone, "I don't need the details, Illias, just get someone headed to us," she pulled out two of the small packs that held the blankets, "this is the catch of the week."

"I'm sending a route to your phone, Amari."

Tripp secured his hands, then his feet for good measure. He'd never encountered a half-breed before, so he didn't know how strong they were. The only thing he did know was they couldn't shift fully, or that's what he'd heard, he didn't know it for certain. Using wire was out of the question, not knowing how fast he healed. "What about the plane he's supposed to meet?" He looked up the mountain, "there can't be too many places for one to land around here."

"We'll be sending someone else for that," Kenzo answered.

Tripp took the one blanket and wrapped it around the man, right up to his chin, then shoved him forward again and tucked it behind him. With the second one, he started at the back. This was bad timing as far as the teams went, he knew they were lined up to breach other locations. "Once this one is taken off our hands..."

"Not happening," Kenzo said. "We are not equipped to overtake a plane."

Amari shoved his bag back into the back of the jeep and closed the door. She came around carrying the phone in her hand, "can the plane be tracked or something."

Someone laughed, "of course, it can." Illias sounded amused.

"We've got a chopper headed your way now."

Tripp felt better. A chopper made it a lot harder to intercept. "Where are we on that other situation with security?"

"We're working on it. The circle of trust is much smaller now." Kenzo told him.

Tripp turned around and went over to the truck he'd been driving. "Is it a rental?" He looked back at Amari, she was right behind him, still holding the phone up, she nodded. "I'm not going to track the truck."

"Get anything that was his out of it and get moving, Tripp," Kenzo told him.

"We'll be moving in less than five."

Chapter Seventeen

Amari looked at the gas gauge and then in the mirror for the tenth time. Their catch of the day was still out cold. Had she been out that long? She didn't think so. Her shifter metabolism burned faster, but this poor sap in the back seat had a lot of normal DNA in him.

She looked over at Tripp, "we need to get gas soon. How much further?" Her nerves were tight, they'd been driving for a little over an hour and Tomas' people would come looking soon.

Tripp grabbed her phone from the cup holder and looked at it. He hadn't talked much the entire drive. He tapped the screen and looked at it, "it's around here."

Amari leaned forward in the seat and looked around. "There is nothing here." She glared out the windshield. Trees and fields as far as she could see. "Are they just going to land anywhere?"

"Wouldn't be the first time." He set the phone down and looked back out the window. His gun hadn't left his hand the entire drive. "They have to know something is up by now."

A moan from behind her had her eyes flicking to the mirror. "Errand boy is coming to."

Tripp turned in his seat so he could look. "Morning sunshine," he sounded happy, "welcome to the first day of your new life."

"What's happening?" He sounded groggy and out of it and she got it, that feeling of mud in your head and the throbbing pain made it hard to focus.

"We've arranged a fun ride for you, just sit tight." Tripp leaned forward and looked to the sky.

"You have to let me go. He'll find you and kill you."

Amari looked at his reflection, he looked scared, and her gut was telling her it wasn't because of this situation. "Don't worry about us, worry about saving your own skin and remembering every little detail of your life." She slowed so she could watch him and not drive them off the road. He gave his head a shake, trying to clear the fog. She winced, remembering the pain that went with even the slightest movement.

"No. You don't understand." He coughed and she slowed more afraid he was going to throw up and she'd wear it.

"We understand that your boss thinks he rules our world, but he's learning that he's wrong." Tripp put up his hand, "slow down, there's a chopper."

Amari gripped the wheel tight and took her foot off the gas, "is it one of ours?"

Tripp made a deep rumbling sound, "good question." He grabbed his phone and tapped the screen. Putting his window down, he leaned out it and looked at the sky. He put the phone against his ear, "yeah, we have a chopper, is it ours?" He nodded, "got it." He patted his hand on the dash, "stop here." He kept the phone to his ear.

"My brother won't stop looking for me. Aiden doesn't like to lose…"

Amari slammed on the brakes and turned in her seat before the Jeep was stopped. "Your *brother*?"

"Hold on," Tripp lowered the phone, "you're brother is Aiden Tomas?"

The scared man nodded, "half brother."

"Shit," Tripp opened the door and got out quickly, "tell them to get down—" he nodded, "you heard?"

Amari slammed the Jeep into park, and opened her door, reaching down beside the seat, she picked up the leather case her gun was in. Releasing the clasp, she pulled the small revolver free and got out. Tripp was watching the chopper come in, she wasn't concerned with what was coming from the sky, she stepped away from the vehicle and started turning in a slow circle. Her heart was racing, her cat was in full alert mode. Aiden Tomas had a half-breed brother. Catch of the day didn't cut it, this was the catch of a lifetime. She heard the helicopter clear the trees but continued to scan the area around them. She could hear Tripp talking on the phone but couldn't make out what he was saying. "Come on. Get on the ground." She whispered needing the machine to land as she turned to check the area in front of the Jeep.

Movement on her right had her glance that way, Tripp was opening the back door and three guys were running across the field. Two of them were carrying rifles and her heart settled a bit. She did a double-take, the one not carrying a visible weapon was Raymond Hardy, the director of Alliance Security. He glanced her way and gave her a quick once over, then nodded his head to her. He was a big son of a bitch and was probably one of the few people in her world that actually scared her. He had to be at least six foot seven and she'd never been able to conclude what clan he was from and was sure she didn't want to know because whatever animal was inside him had to be a beast once it was out. He didn't waste words, just went over to the Jeep and looked in the backseat. A slow, not pleasant smile formed on his hard face, and it sent a shiver through her. She almost pitied Aiden Tomas' brother now. Almost.

He leaned in the door and reached out toward the man, she caught the glint of something in his hand, and then the bound captive slumped in the seat. She expected him to step back and let one of his men get him out, but he just leaned in the door and in a few short seconds was standing up with the man slung over his shoulder. That cinched it, not only was he the scariest man she'd ever seen, but he was hella strong.

"Get moving." He said loud enough she could hear him over the chopper whirling.

Tripp nodded and slammed the back door.

Amari moved back to get in and watched him run across the field with the man flopping around over his shoulder. She jolted and got back in the Jeep and shut the door. With the gun still gripped in one hand, she put the vehicle into drive and watched as Tripp got in and closed the door. Gun still in hand, she white-knuckled the steering wheel and stepped on the gas.

Tripp watched out the window in the direction of the chopper, but she didn't pause to even look that way. When Raymond Hardy said to get moving, you moved. The helicopter buzzed over them and then the sound started to fade.

"Fuck me." Tripp huffed out a breath like he'd been holding it.

Amari nodded, "Aiden Tomas' half-brother." She kept her eyes on the road, "find me a direction."

"We need to get my SUV and ditch this Jeep." He leaned over and tapped the screen on the GPS.

Amari focused on trying to settle her breathing down, she needed to keep them on the road and if she didn't relax a little that was going to be hard to do. Her phone ringing startled her, she looked down at it and then remembered the gun in her hand.

Tripp leaned down and picked it up and tapped it. Then reached over and carefully took the gun from her hand.

"Is it true?"

She recognized Devin Addison's voice on the phone.

"He said he was Aiden Tomas' half-brother?"

Amari nodded. "He did."

"Rayne is losing it." He didn't sound like a prince right now, he sounded like a pissed-off, concerned mate.

"Does she know him?" Amari had heard that at one point Rayne was engaged to Aiden Tomas, she'd never gotten more details than that, but had always wondered how the hell that had happened. How did a shifter, one that was the fated princess of all clans end up with the very man that was making their lives a living hell?

"She just looked at the photos of his ID Tripp sent and yeah, she's seen him before."

Amari blinked and then glanced at Tripp, he looked like he had the same epiphany she just had. "He has to know everything." She said it even though it was an obvious statement.

"That's what we hope." Devin didn't sound any calmer.

"Are they taking him back to headquarters?" Tripp leaned forward and pointed at the GPS screen, she glanced at it to see he wanted her to turn right shortly. She nodded.

"No. Undisclosed location. Only Raymond and his three guys will know." Someone said something in the background, "none of them have any family, so they're in the clear."

Amari nodded, "good."

"We're heading back to my SUV and then we'll dump the Jeep," Tripp said.

She slowed down and turned, then pointed to the gas gauge and looked at Tripp, he nodded.

"Check in when you're there." The voices in the background got louder. "We're going earlier tonight, so Illias will be busy, contact Zain instead."

Amari nodded, "Okay. Be safe."

"Safe has nothing to do with it now," Devin growled and then the line went quiet.

"Shit." Tripp set her phone down and turned in his seat to look behind them.

She held her breath until he turned back around and settled in his seat. "Yeah."

"Things are going to get crazier from here." He said in a distracted way.

Amari nodded and glanced at the GPS screen, "we need to get back to the teams and help." She turned her head to see him nodding.

"I was just thinking the same thing." He turned and looked behind them again. His phone rang and he answered it without looking at it, "Carson."

She held her breath hoping something hadn't gone wrong. "Mom?"

Amari looked over to see he was surprised by the call. His whole stance changed. She didn't know that others were giving out the new numbers since the breach of their information. She had only made Zain give hers to the rest of the co-ord team.

"Really? How was she?" He was smiling now.

A twinge of jealousy hit her; she wished a call from her mother made her smile like that. Not that her mother ever called her. How long had it been since she'd spoken to her? A year? Could be longer, she wasn't sure.

"I can't wait to run with her." He nodded.

Snapping her head back, she watched the road. Now was not the time to think about her family, she needed to stay on task and get them to—she glanced at the gas gauge again, a gas station first and foremost.

"Uh, I can't say right now, things are a bit hectic with work—but as soon as I get some downtime, you'll see me."

Hectic? That was an understatement. She smirked, if Aiden Tomas' brother gave up details, things were going to explode as far as the teams went and shut down the insanity that they all lived with. Her end goal was to see families reunited, children being able to go to school, and gatherings, without the constant fear that they were going to be taken or worse. She wasn't sure where that would leave her when life returned to normal, but she'd find a purpose, that she was sure of.

"I will. I love you too." Tripp hung up and sat there looking at his phone. She wanted to ask him about the call, but didn't want to start talking about family, what did she have to add to a conversation like that? "My sister's first shift." He said in a light tone.

She glanced at him, "really? That's great." She jerked her eyes back to the road, "did it go well?" He had a little sister?

Her chest tightened, she had no idea if her younger sister had shifted yet or not. How old was she now, twenty-one, two? If it hadn't already happened, it would be soon.

"Yeah, mom wasn't sure she was going to come back." He chuckled.

"I get it." She smiled despite the heavy feeling in her chest, "my first time I would have run for days if my body had let me."

"Yeah." He sucked in a slow breath, "seems like forever ago now."

Amari nodded, "yeah it does." The silence was filled with memories and a lot of things she just wished she could forget. She'd decided long ago that hoping to go back in time and erase them was never going to be a reality. She cleared her throat, so the emotions wouldn't be audible, without those past events, she wouldn't be who she was today. She liked who she was, even if most others didn't. "Gas needs to happen soon."

Tripp leaned over and looked at the dash. Her cat picked up on his scent when Amari breathed it in and was practically rolling around inside her like a kitten would in catnip. She gripped the steering wheel tighter, now was not the time for that you skanky creature. She bit her lip so she wouldn't grin. He was leaning over-focused on the GPS screen.

Knowing he had a little sister and that his mother made him smile, changed the way she saw him. He was still wild and crazy, which were good traits in her book, but the tone he'd used while speaking to his mother—it got to her. He wasn't a jerk like most other men, the ones that once they were grown didn't need a mother or show respect.

This mate stuff was making her emotions a liability. She knew she couldn't ignore it; his cat had claimed hers, and she got that, but right now her goals in life did not include a mate. She didn't know how it was going to work after they got back to the teams. Obviously, some things had changed, and she'd have to see him sometime, but her plan was to go their separate ways and ride this out and see what happened. Her cat made her feelings on *that*, painfully clear, making Amari tense at the almost tangible smack.

"You good?"

She blinked and glanced at him, "yeah. Anxious cat issues."

He snorted, "they have no problems expressing their feelings and opinions."

She grinned, "even when their feelings are irrelevant." He looked at her, searching her face until she turned back to the road.

"Five minutes and we can duck down into this little town."

She nodded and looked at the bleak gas gauge, "hope it's downhill, we might be coasting in."

Chapter Eighteen

Tripp glanced at her again, she was too quiet, and it was driving him crazy. He glared at the road. Sure, she was watching for any tails or movement along the road, but she had to be thinking about something while she was doing that—but what? It was going to be dusk in an hour and he wanted to be in his own vehicle by then.

His cat was more paranoid than he was. *Your own fault*, he relayed internally. *You marked her without consent and now have to sit there and wonder how that's going to end.* How was it going to end? Obviously, she was going with him back to the teams, she had no vehicle and wasn't traveling alone. *Mine.* He would have laughed if it wouldn't make him look a little crazy. Squeezing the steering wheel, he inhaled a slow deep breath, then regretted it. Her scent was amazing it made him think of a river rushing down a mountain, wild and free.

"Tripp."

He turned to look at her. When she glanced at him, her sexy eyes were heavy with a secret. His body responded with a 'hello gorgeous' reaction. Just what he didn't need right now—

"Can you pull over up here?"

It was whispered. Not urgent. Her tone set his guts on fire. He nodded and looked for somewhere not in the wide-open area to stop. Maybe she needed a quick pit stop? He spotted a few trees close to the road and figured that would be good enough.

As he pulled under them, she kicked off her boots and was working her arms out of her jacket. It was really not a good time to go for a run. Was everything just hitting her now? He'd seen it before, people panicked after an event. Jamming the jeep into park, he turned to explain that to her when she pulled her shirt over her head. He opened his mouth to tell her that, but nothing came out. He closed it before he drooled like a moron. Her skin was pale, and he knew how soft it was. The cool air hardened her nipples and he had to squeeze the shifter in a death grip to keep from reaching over to her. She unbuckled her belt and then tipped her seat back and slip the jeans off.

Tripp couldn't have moved if his life had depended on it. His body was rock hard, throbbing and his cat was quiet and watchful when she pulled her feet free of the denim. She turned to look at him, her eyes told him a run was the very last thing on her mind. Inhaling slowly, he brought the scent of her need into his body.

Holding her look, he reached and took the gun from the holster at his side and set it on the dash. The smile that formed on her mouth was slow as she got to her knees and stretched over the gear shift, leaning into him. Now his cat was hesitant, waiting for her to make the first move. She reached over and dropped his seat to lay back and then crawled over the shifter and straddled him. Tripp's whole body was on fire, he needed to lose the clothes, or he was going to die from a heat stroke.

As he wrestled his arms out of the coat sleeves, she ripped open his pants and reached inside. Tripp clenched his teeth together, trying to get his shirt off without tearing it apart. Her hand stroked him and squeezed. He could barely remember how to breathe through the heavenly feeling of her hand wrapped around him.

Lifting his hips, he shoved his pants down to his thighs. She didn't pause, just released him, and mounted him, shoving him deep inside her. He glanced to see her eyes closed and that was the only part of this entire scene that bothered him. Reaching up, he grasped the side of her head, then closed his fingers to take a handful of hair. Her eyes opened and he felt like the luckiest man on the planet. Her eyes were filled with fire, and he was sure they were going to consume him. This woman did nothing halfway. Pulling her head down gently, he lifted his head and claimed those pouty lips. He took the taste of her into his mouth and swallowed her moan as she rocked her body up and down his. Pulling his mouth away, he watched her eyes, "there's only one *must*, babe, eyes open so you know who's inside you."

She hissed out a breath as she dropped onto him again but didn't break eye contact with him. Satisfied she got his meaning; he released her head and gripped her hips to help her.

He didn't know where this sudden need had come from, but he was more than willing to help her. She was so hot and wet that it felt like he was being burned alive by lava. Clenching his teeth together to keep a reign on his control, he discovered his mouth was half full of sharp teeth. His cat wanted to repeat the same damn mistake as the last time.

Amari's breathing was increasing with each movement and the hitch in it as he filled her was chipping away at his restraint—

The sound of a vehicle registered with the blood rushing through his head. Leaning up, he grabbed his gun and switched it to his other hand, holding it near the window.

Amari's rhythm didn't pause, but she lifted her chin to look out the back window.

He watched her face instead of doing what a sane person would do and stop this to ensure they were safe. He'd been with thrill-seekers before, but they always copped out at the last second. Nothing, not even danger was going to stop her. She was so perfect for him, it was unbelievable. She moaned but kept her eyes on the road. When her face was illuminated by the lights of the vehicle, Tripp lifted the gun to rest just under the window. He was going to be really pissed if they were interrupted. He hoped for a second it wasn't some family out for a drive, because they were going to see a sort of wildlife they definitely weren't expecting.

Amari's muscles clenched around him, and he had to focus to keep his grip on the gun. He tasted blood as his teeth cut into his tongue.

The car rushed by them, not even slowing in the slightest. Amari dropped her head down; her legs were shaking, and he was beyond caring what was happening outside this vehicle. He grabbed her hips and prevented her from impaling herself on him again, prolonging the edge she was so close to crashing over.

Her eyes flicked to look at him, pleading to let her finish. He could feel the cold metal in his left hand digging into her flesh and she didn't care in any way. She was the most gorgeous creature he'd ever seen. *Mine,* he thought in unison with his cat.

He was suddenly regretting the confined space of a steering wheel and no room to maneuver. Lifting his head, he licked over one hard nipple, causing her body to quiver in response. Sucking it into his mouth, against sharp teeth, rewarded him with her moaning. He slammed her down onto his body, making her whine a sound more animal than woman and her body began to milk him. When she started to go lax, he lifted his face from her breast and licked along her neck, she was no longer helping to move her body, so he did it for her. He was so close now but determined he was taking her with him. With his tongue, he found his mark on her and licked over it. She hissed out a breath, her body clenching around him.

Tripp let his cat come closer to the surface and emitted a low growl that made her body react immediately. He dropped the gun and heard it hit the floor, as he bit into his mark and held her flesh in his mouth. She began helping him move her fast, their bodies connecting harder, driving her over the edge again. He followed her this time with an orgasm that bordered on violent.

Licking over the bite, he braced for the backlash from it happening again.

She collapsed on top of him. "Are we going to have to muzzle you during sex?" Her breathing was fast and hot against his skin.

Tripp grinned and kissed the bite mark. "Obstructing my mouth would be disappointing," he blew out a breath, trying to settle his breathing down, "for both of us."

She pushed herself up, her hands braced on his chest, and looked at his mouth. "We'll see about that next time." Her smile was slow but was reflected in her eyes, "that," she slowly lifted herself off him, "was great." Leaning down, she kissed him briefly, "I was so tense."

At least she was thinking about the next time. Raising one eyebrow he dropped his hands away from her as she moved off him and back over the gear shift. "Any time you need to relax, I'm here to help."

When she was back in the passenger seat, she looked over at him, her gaze moving down him slowly, "you should drive before I invite you over here."

Drive. *Shit.* He'd actually forgotten everything. "We need to get moving." Lifting his hips, he pulled his pants back up, then popped the seat into the upright position. "I'm not going to feel at ease until I have all my gear again." Reaching down, he felt around for the gun, thinking that was a first for him, sex with a gun in his hand. He gave her a quick glance and knew there were going to be a lot of firsts with her, and he couldn't wait for each and every one of them.

"How much longer until we're there?" She worked the jeans back on in the confined space.

He took his time, his eyes caressing over the exposed skin on her body before answering. "Forty-five minutes at most."

"Good."

He tried not to look at her breasts as she pulled the shirt over her head. He failed and his body hardened. Clearing his throat, he turned back to look out the windshield. *Put in drive, step on the gas.* He reminded his lust-filled brain.

Chapter Nineteen

The next fifteen minutes were filled with an awkward silence. His cat was behaving like a gloating asshole, and he couldn't think of a way to convey his thoughts on why they shouldn't be having a victory party yet, at least nothing that he could do while she was sitting right beside him. Yes, she was good and truly marked, but the last time he checked, her cat had not reciprocated with a bite of her own. Was it the cat holding back or the woman?

It needed to be discussed, now, when they were alone. "We should," he looked over to see that he had her attention, "talk about things."

Her eyes moved to search his face for a second. "I'm not big on sappy conversations."

Tripp smirked and looked back at the road. "Well, it can't always be stab-now-talk-later."

Amari laughed softly, "don't I know it." When she blew out a breath, he had to wonder what she'd been thinking about and if she'd been considering the fact that they were mates too. "So," he felt her eyes on him, "how does this work?"

Sending her a quick surprised look, he shook his head, "being as I've never been mated before," he gave the steering wheel a squeeze, then turned to watch where he was going, "I have no idea."

"You haven't thought this through?"

He decided that mentioning she was the one that accosted him first to frolic in the shower, was a bad idea. "Been a little busy." He glanced down at his phone wondering how the teams were doing and if Tomas' brother was truly secured in an unknown location.

"Yeah. The past few days have been full of surprises." She chuckled, "I hate surprises."

Tripp smiled, but kept his eyes looking straight ahead, "not all of them have been bad ones."

"Easy for you to say, you weren't knocked out while you were driving."

He moved just his eyes and looked at the open window. Reaching over, he pressed the button to put it up all the way. "True."

"What happens when we're back to the teams?" She shifted in the seat, so she was turned toward him, "with us?"

Taking a breath, he paused, all he could smell was sex. The air inside the jeep reeked of it. "That's not really my call at this point," he gave her a quick look, "is it?"

Amari shook her head and looked down at her hand. "I guess it isn't."

He forced himself to look straight ahead. Tripp wanted to reach his SUV before dark, so he could give it a once over and disable the tracking unit.

"I don't know, Tripp. My cat is acting like a scatterbrained twit the past few days."

He clenched his jaw so he wouldn't speak and stay something stupid, like 'you don't say.'

"I just," she shifted in the seat and looked behind them, "finding my mate has never been on my list." She turned back, "know what I mean?"

Tripp nodded, "I do." It was the truth. He was happy with his life or had been until a few days ago when he'd been sent to find a missing Alpha female. *That*—how the hell did he explain the situation with her father? In all the possible outcomes, that didn't end well. Every angle of this, once they got back to other people was going to be a shit show. "I don't want to sound like a dick," she looked back at him, "but shit is going to get real when we're back with the teams."

"I can't wait for the action."

He shook his head, "that's not what I'm talking about."

Her brows furrowed, "what?"

Tripp inhaled slowly, then turned back to watch the road. "Every shifter within a five-mile radius is going to know."

"That we got naked together?" She sounded amused.

He shrugged, "that too, but no, I'm talking about a very visible bite on your neck, and," he brushed the hair back from his neck, "the absence of one on my neck."

"Oh." She blew out a breath, "I didn't think of that." Amari cleared her throat, "Listen, no one needs to know I didn't consent before—"

"You know as well as I do that's not going to fly. You carry my scent now and I don't have yours."

"Yeah," she turned to look out the windshield again.

"Honestly," he glanced over to see a serious focus look on her face, "I don't know how I'm going to react when you're around the others."

"What do you mean?" Concerned eyes connected with his.

"You near other males."

She snorted, "you don't have to…"

"I got pissed off because one of them sent you gummy bears." He growled.

She turned, amusement on her face, then it faded, "it was just Zain."

"My cat doesn't seem to care." Tripp wasn't trying to upset her, just needed to give her the facts to avoid issues later. If that was possible.

Chapter Twenty

Amari sat back in her seat and was silent for a minute. "We're going to have to work something out, Tripp—I will *not* be sidelined by anyone." She leaned over so he could see her face without turning his head. "I'm going to do my part to take out Tomas and everyone that's helping him. The day they get him, I *will* be there."

He looked at her for a second, her focus was stone-cold and unmoving. She flopped back into her seat, letting him know that was all she was saying on that. He lifted his gaze to watch where he was driving, slowing down so he wouldn't miss the turn. It was a good excuse to give him a moment to think of how to explain to her that there were some things you couldn't curb your animal from doing, not that he was an expert on it—because, until her, he thought he was always in control of his animal, with absolute certainty. He slowed more so the tires were crawling over the uneven ground. He saw his SUV. This wasn't right. "Amari, that's not where I left it."

She leaned closer to the window and looked at the vehicle. "Maybe it had to be moved for someone to land."

"They land on the other side of those trees." He knew that for a fact because he'd walked in slow motion through them while giving himself a pep talk to get on the plane.

"Park back a bit, keep the lights aimed at it."

Tripp nodded because he'd been thinking the same thing. *Fuck.* Had they gotten here before them? The tracker, if they were dialed in on all the vehicles, could have known exactly where he was the whole time. He put it into park and pulled his gun out. There would be no tranqs this time.

Amari reached down and got hers free from the case, she looked nowhere but out the windows.

"You should stay here…"

"Bite me." Leaning down, she loosened her boots.

Smart idea, in case she needed to shift. Tripp nodded, there was no way he could protect her if she refused to listen. Something told him it would always be that way with her. "Climb over and come out my door."

"Yeah." Her voice was steady, which didn't surprise him at all now, she was cool in tense situations where emotions had no place.

Tripp opened the door, keeping his eyes on the tress. It was the only place someone could be the rest was open and visible. He stepped out, using the door as a shield. He didn't need to wait for her, she cleared the shifter and was out the door, behind him.

"I'll cover behind us." She whispered it and put her hand on his back.

They moved as one, out from the protection of the Jeep. He kept his gun up, his eyes scanning the area as he listened for any movement. Amari didn't make a sound behind him, which shouldn't have surprised him, but it still did. Her hand was still on the small of his back, so she could move when he did. It was like they'd been doing this together for years. Inhaling, he quickly processed the scents around them. There was only one body signature close by. Friend or foe, he couldn't be sure.

"Simmer down." A deep male voice came from the trees. "We're on the same side."

He adjusted his direction and aimed the way it came from. He felt Amari turn so she could see that way too. He couldn't see anyone.

"Glad you're okay, Hughes."

Amari stiffened, "Tait?"

"Yeah." A tall man with long blond hair stepped out of the trees. How he'd managed to not be seen, Tripp has no idea.

"It's okay, he's one of ours. From the surveillance team." She moved to stand beside him. "What are you doing here?"

Tripp lowered the gun, but he wasn't holstering it until both he and his cat knew this was one of theirs.

"A few of us were sent this way when you missed check-ins. To see if there was a base around here." He looked at Tripp and made it obvious he was checking him out. "Zander is watching for planes, and I came back here to disable the tracker in your ride." He motioned his head toward Tripp's SUV. "She's all fueled and ready to go."

Amari went over and opened the passenger's door of the Jeep, reaching in she got out the leather case for her gun and put it away. "You guys going to follow that plane?"

He shook his head, "no, just tag it."

"We need to dump this Jeep." Amari grabbed her pack out of it and closed the door.

"I'll deal with it. There's a nice ravine a few miles West."

Tripp gave him a quick look and turned back to the Jeep. The only surveillance member he knew was Uri. He'd seen some of them in passing and there was this creepiness to them that put him on edge. His cat seemed okay with his presence. He glanced at Amari smiling at the other man. Jamming his piece back in the holster, he stepped back to the open door and reached in to grab his phone. As long as she kept her distance from him, Tripp wouldn't be forced to do something stupid that would result in her stabbing him. Grabbing his bag and pack, he slammed the Jeep door and turned to his SUV.

At least the tracker was disabled. Amari opened up the back and set her backpack in it.

Turning to bid the creepy man goodbye, he paused when a phone rang.

"Yeah."

He glanced through the door to see Amari answer hers.

She smiled, "Hey, Z, I was just going to let you know we're at the—" she frowned, "what?" If her brows went any lower, her eyes would be closed. "Fuck. How?"

Tripp sent her a questioning look.

"Hang on." She tapped the phone screen and then tossed it on the seat, "it's on speaker."

"Well, that saves me contacting Tripp then."

"Why are you contacting me?" Tripp leaned back against the open door and watched Amari. She had her hands on top of her head and looked like she was going to explode. "What's going on?" Had something happened with the teams?

"Change of plans," Zain-the-male-that-sent-Amari-gummy-bears said. "You two aren't heading to the teams right away."

Tripp turned his attention to the phone. "You have something else we need to do?"

"Uh, yeah." Zain was much quieter now. "I don't know how or who, but Amari's father found out she'd been taken." He cursed softly, "Jesse and I didn't share it outside the teams, but he still found out."

"And?" He looked at Amari who was standing there with her hands on her hips looking at the ground.

"He's demanding she be brought home."

Tripp looked at the phone and then back to Amari, "he couldn't call her and tell her himself?"

"He doesn't have my number." She said in a low tone.

Tripp opened his mouth and then snapped it shut. He'd given his mom and sister his number. Maybe she hadn't had time since she got the new phone.

"I've been ordered to never give out her number."

"By who?" Tripp was surprised. Her own father couldn't call her?

"Me." Amari picked up the phone and looked like she wanted to squeeze it until it shattered into pieces in her hand. "This can't wait?"

"No. Even our king has said it's best if you make a quick appearance and then get back to work."

"Shit." She blew out a breath. "We were heading back to the teams."

"I know. Jesse said to tell you there will be plenty of fun to be had once you do this and get down there."

"Shit." Her whole aura went cold.

"Sorry." Zain said quietly, "I tried."

"I know you did. Thanks. Tell Jesse I'll talk to him later."

"Got it." There was a ring in the background, "gotta go, we got relocates all over the map right now."

"Yeah." She tapped the phone screen and then tossed it on the dash.

"On that happy note, I'm out." Tait walked by him and went toward the Jeep. He stopped behind the SUV and looked at Amari, "if it helps, Hughes, your abduction has landed us some big prizes."

Amari snorted, "happy to help, Tait."

He turned and looked at Tripp, then inclined his head and got in the Jeep without further comment.

"Is it just me or is there something a bit off about the members of the surveillance team?" It was a sad attempt at changing the heavy mood. He got in and looked at the steering wheel. He'd missed his ride with its comfortable seats and dark windows.

Amari got in and closed her door, "have you met the rest of us? Name one member of any of the teams that seems normal."

Tripp inhaled slowly as he thought, exhaling, he shrugged, "okay, you got me there." He grinned and turned the key.

Amari leaned over and tapped the GPS unit's screen a little harder than necessary. He watched her put in her clan address.

Putting it in drive, he turned it around and headed back down the path to the road. "Don't stab me, but I have questions."

She sat back in her seat, "I wouldn't stab you, you're driving, and your rig is too nice to wreck by crashing it." She looked far too amused after saying that. He couldn't be sure but thought she actually meant what she said.

"Don't hurt your brain over thinking that, Tripp." The smile was gone. "Ask your questions." The expression in her eyes was far away like she was reliving something.

"Your father isn't allowed to have your number?"

"Right." She turned and looked out the window. The anxiety coming off her was strong enough that his cat was even concerned now.

"Okay." He glanced at the GPS and debated on telling her that he didn't need directions to her clan. "Why?" He knew he was pushing it, but if he was going to break the order of never stepping foot on the Hughes clan land again, he needed to know why. He watched her out of the corner of his eye, and she didn't turn to look at him.

"I call my mother from time to time."

That wasn't much of an answer. "But you don't speak to your father—" little pieces were clicking together in his head, "why?"

She sighed loud and long, then reached down and loosen her boots and kicked them off. "I guess I should warn you this visit will be hostile," she shifted in the seat and put one foot up on the dash, "if you knew my father, you'd get it…"

"I do know your father." He turned to see the surprise on her face.

"Oh, so then you know he's an asshole."

Tripp grinned. "I do." He was so shocked by the direction this conversation was going, he decided to keep the details of his knowledge of the man to himself for now.

"All right then," she dropped her foot back down and leaned against the door, looking at him this time. "He banished me from the clan years ago."

An Alpha banished his own daughter? He'd never heard of that. "What the hell? Why?"

She sighed, "I saved my little sister."

Tripp looked at her, then quickly back to the road before he did wreck his ride on one of these corners. "From what?"

"Being taken, or killed," she shrugged, "we'll never know for sure, but he had a gun and was watching her through the scope of his rifle."

"Who?" He slowed down enough that he could focus on the road and still look over at her.

"I didn't know about Tomas and all of that at the time, I don't even know if my father knew about it," she looked down at her hands, "but, a one-form man was stalking my sister, so I took him out."

"In cat form?" He wanted to stop the vehicle and put it in park while they talked about this, but he also wanted to get the hell out of this area where Tomas' people would soon be swarming to look for his brother.

"No." She said it quietly and then looked out the window.

She'd killed a one-form. His chest felt tight. That was really high on the list of things *never* to be done.

"He smelled of different clans, but he definitely wasn't one of us. After I found out about Tomas it all made sense, you know? That taking her during puberty—"

"Yeah, it does." He cut her off because of the emotion in her voice. "Your father didn't get that? The Alliance didn't investigate?"

"I don't know. I was banished before anyone found out and I don't know what happened after that." She blew out a breath, "Shepard Addison tracked me down and found me a place to go and helped me get more training to help the Alliance."

Tripp white-knuckled the steering wheel. Asshole Hughes had banished his own daughter for saving his other daughter. "How long ago was this?"

"Five, six years now I guess." The flat tone was back in her voice.

The tone made him feel better, it probably shouldn't have, but it did, mostly for his sake because if she'd gotten any more upset by it, someone was going to pay with their blood. Vesper fucking Hughes was on the top of the list for prime sacrifice. Five or six years ago? She would have barely been through her first shift. *Fuck.* He didn't know when he'd become such as sappy moron, but if she could share that with him, then he owed her some truth too. He hit the brakes and slid to the side of the road. Slamming it into park, he turned and looked at her. "I know your father is an asshole because I'm not allowed to step foot on your clan's land ever again." He watched the questions form on her face, "my mother and sister are part of that clan, but if I want to see them, we have to meet somewhere else."

"Carson." She said it softly with recognition in her voice. "You're *that* guy."

Tripp smirked and then sobered, "well, if you mean that guy that dared to call out your father for his bullshit, then yeah, I'm him."

"I remember that." Tilting her head, she looked at him for a moment, "You're from a clan in the South? I don't remember the details."

Tripp rolled his shoulders, and those all too familiar knots were back, "my father was part of an Alliance security detail, he died protecting a clan from rogues." He looked past her for a second out the window and had to clamp down on his own emotions, "mom didn't want to stay there after that, so we headed cross country to stay where she had family." He cleared his throat, "it was a rough go, we had to stay off the radar of other clans, and other Alliance security details, but I got them there, then your father refused to allow us into the clan."

Amari nodded her head slowly, "that's right, I know your mom," her expression blanked, "knew your mom, I helped her and," she squeezed her eyes closed for a second, "Ginny?" She opened them. He nodded at the mention of his sister's name. "I helped them get settled in."

He hadn't known that part, his mother never mentioned the Alpha's daughter in any of their many talks in the months following that. "I didn't know that." He gave her a quick look, "so you haven't always been out of control?"

She grinned, "oh, I have been, much to Daddy's heartbreak." She rolled her eyes.

Tripp wanted to reach out and pull her closer, apologize for a father that had done such a stupid thing to her, but the vibes coming off her right now were clearly growling 'don't get too close'. "Thanks for helping them. Kenzo and Calum whisked me away from there so fast, I didn't even get to say goodbye."

"That explains how you ended up on one of the teams."

"Does it?"

"You survived Kenzo and Calum, so they probably took you under their wing and trained you up."

Tripp leaned back against the door and looked at her, "I didn't require much training."

"Me either." Her smile was slow but real.

He shrugged, "so you'll understand when I drop you off at the entrance to your father's land then?"

She snorted, "Oh, you're coming with me, driving right on by the markers at full speed all the way to his doorstep."

"I'm what?" He shook his head, "I have orders that the king signed…"

"*Fuck* the orders." She waved her hand around and picked up her phone, "there's always a way around those." She paused and looked at him, "drive, we mustn't keep Daddy waiting."

Tripp stared at her for a second, then turned back in his seat. Putting it in drive, he glanced in the mirror and then pulled out onto the road. What was she up to and was it going to get him killed? He glanced over at her to see her raise the phone to her ear. She was *way* too happy looking right now.

"Mother." She said softly, "I'm fine. Not a scratch." She nodded, and he looked back to the road. "No, no nothing like that." She chortled, which sounded odd coming from her, "rumors are always exaggerated, you know that."

Tripp glanced over to see her looking at him, something dangerous in her eyes and his cat responded to it instantly, as did the lower part of his body. Damn, he was definitely in trouble here.

"Mmhmm, we're heading that way now." The tone she was using was not an Amari tone, if that was even a thing, "yes, I'm still with the brave man that rescued me." She grinned at him.

Oh shit, she was going to get him killed and the sick bastard that he was—he was actually getting turned on by her scheming.

"It's all right that he comes with me, right," she huffed out a breath, "I'm just so-so scared now."

Tripp's head snapped and he looked at her again, she had the biggest shit-eating grin on her face. *Damn.*

"Yes. Tell Father we'll be there tomorrow." She nodded, "I will. Me too." She tapped the phone and then smiled at him. "My mother can't wait to meet the man that rescued me from some horrible fate." She slumped back and put her hand over her chest.

"You're going to get me killed." He couldn't help smiling back at her.

She winked at him, "I'll protect you," she shrugged, "and what is he going to do in front of the others, have you arrested? The man that saved me?" She chuckled, "I don't think so."

Shit. He should warn Kenzo something bad might be in the air. As entertained as she was with this jab at her father, he knew there was no way that Vesper Hughes was going to be all-forgiving suddenly. "We should, uh, give our team leaders a heads up."

"That I've been summoned by my father?" She shrugged, "I'm sure they already know."

"No, that I'm going with you."

Turning in the seat, so she could look at him, she waved her hand around. "You really think my father will outdo his past bullshit because you're driving me there to see him?"

Tripp looked back at the road and let a few seconds pass before he answered, "I think it's very possible."

Amari sighed, "*fuck*, you're right." She motioned around them, "we don't know if they're in the middle of an op right now or what though."

It was a good point, darkness was close. "Yeah. Grab my phone and bring up Kenzo and type one two three and send it to him."

"What does that mean?" She leaned over and pulled his phone out of the holder.

"It's just our way of saying call me when you're not in it."

"You guys couldn't just type, call me?" She sounded amused.

"Never know where one of us will be and if we still have our phone on us." He shrugged.

"I guess." She put the phone back in the holder. "Okay, Mister Bond, message sent." She laughed softly.

Chapter Twenty-One

They'd been driving for almost an hour now, and for the most part, were silent. She wasn't sure if the tension was from digesting information or the fact that they still hadn't heard from Kenzo. Was everything going okay for the teams? She hated not being in the loop of information. She looked over to see Tripp ultra-focused on the road, his grip on the steering wheel wasn't as relaxed as he was attempting to make it look, and his knuckles were white. "Was tonight a big op?"

He glanced at her for a millisecond and then back to the road, "I don't have details, just that they'd stepped it up."

"Maybe they split the teams to hit more at once." She hoped it was something like that and everything had gone okay.

"It's possible. Things are going to get messy now that we have Tomas' brother."

She nodded, "wonder how that's going."

"Guess we'll find out when we're back with them to help."

She debated for a moment on calling Zain, but if things were happening, he'd be busy helping coordinate people around, and then Tripp's phone lit up.

He motioned to it, "it's all you." He grinned, "you can tell him you're trying to get me killed."

Amari smiled and leaned down and answered the call, then tapped speaker.

"Tripp?"

Tripp looked down at the phone, a serious expression on his face, "boss, what's wrong?"

Eyebrows raised she looked from him to the phone. How did he know by just his name that something was wrong?

"A few injuries, nothing serious." There were voices in the background, "injuries that *shouldn't* have happened with these *trained* individuals."

Amari looked to see the expression on his face that said someone was in shit. "Everyone's all right?"

There was a pause, "they will be." He mumbled something she couldn't make out, "if it weren't for that Noah fellow, it would be a hell of a lot worse." There were car doors closing in the background, "I just told Calum if there's ever an opening on our team, I want Noah."

Tripp grinned, "the man has skills?"

Kenzo snorted, "I can't even describe what the man has."

"The breaches went well?" Amari stared at the phone.

"They were successful, although Kaid just told me if we were going to continue at this pace, he needs more people on his crew." Kenzo chuckled.

Amari grinned, more members for clean-up was a good thing, it meant they were getting somewhere with stopping Tomas and the others involved.

"I take you got the message from your father, Amari."

She rolled her eyes, "I did. We're heading that way now."

"We tried, but there wasn't even anything we could do, even our king tried, sorry."

She shrugged, "it's fine." She turned to look at Tripp and grinned, "Tripp has been invited by my mother."

"What?"

Tripp blew out a breath, "what she means to say is her mother invited the man that rescued her, but she has no idea who that man is."

"Did you explain?" Kenzo sounded like he was out of breath.

"Oh, I did. She called her mother after I did."

"Fuck. What are you trying to do, Amari?"

She smirked, "it took me being abducted for my father to allow me back on the land, so fuck him. Tripp is coming with me, and it can be a twofer—the two people he dislikes the most," she shrugged, "maybe that vein in his forehead with rupture, and he'll bleed out." She held the surprised look Tripp gave her, then slowly turned her head and looked back at the phone.

"Shit." Kenzo growled low and then blew out a loud breath into the phone, "what about the situation between the two of you—is that resolved?"

Amari smirked at the roundabout way he worded it. "We haven't really discussed it, Kenzo."

She looked over to see Tripp run his hand over his head, brushing the hair back.

"No disrespect, Amari, but you're taking a man forbidden to go there onto your father's land with his mark on you, but none on him."

She shrugged, "it was consensual, I told him to use his teeth and he did."

Tripp looked over at her, his expression was stuck somewhere between shock and amusement.

"You guys are going to give me grey hair." He muttered something else, but she couldn't make it out.

Amari put her hand over her mouth so she wouldn't laugh out loud. Kenzo Dean was from the snow leopard clan, so his hair was already a mix of white and dark grey shades.

"Sorry, boss," Tripp said with a big smile on his face.

"No, you're not. Asshole. Hang on." She could hear him walking on pavement or cement and had to wonder if they were still at one of the sites. "When will you get there?"

"Tomorrow, after lunch."

The phone was muffled, so she couldn't make out anyone that was talking. "I don't know who, but someone will be there with you two." Kenzo sounded annoyed, "we have a few smash hits to do in this area, so try not to get yourself killed before someone representing the Alliance is there."

"I'll do my best." Tripp's tone was quiet, she looked over to see him smiling though. "Good luck with the smash hits, and hey, look at it this way if I do end up dead, you have room for Noah."

"Asshole." The line went silent.

"Kenzo seems edgy tonight." She turned and smiled at him.

"Yeah," Tripp smirked, "wonder what that's about."

"He's really sending someone to save your ass?"

Tripp shrugged and looked back at the road, "sounds like it."

"Lucky you, to be that special." She shifted so she was more comfortable in the seat.

"I won't be so lucky when he's right in my face when I see him again."

Amari nodded, "probably not."

He motioned to the dash, "another hour and I thought we could stop and go for a run and grab a bite to eat."

A run sounded good right now, the idea of seeing her father again after all these years wasn't something she was looking forward to. He was in for a surprise though; she was no longer the hesitant young girl she had been when he'd sent her packing.

She looked out the window, packing, that was a joke, she'd had time to grab some clothes and a few of her things before she was escorted off the land. She hadn't even gotten to say goodbye to her mother or sister. She sneered at the glass, her own brother had been with those that escorted her, so she'd seen him and was pretty sure her last words to him were something like 'see you around, asshole.'

Her brother, Bauer, was a typical next-in-line Alpha, with all the attitude that a position of privilege brought with it. She wondered if he'd changed at all or gotten worse. She'd met others that came from Alpha families, and they weren't complete jackasses, like Gia and the prince, Devin, he was as down to earth as they got. Why was it her family had to be the type where it went to their head? She remembered a few things Gia had said about her father and siblings, that made her feel a little better, maybe it wasn't *only* hers.

In her own opinion, those worthy of leading should, not because of a birthright, but then that would put the entire Alliance and king in question. Shepard Addison, she had no issues with at all, he'd saved her. From what she knew about working with his son, he would be a fair ruler as well.

Alpha's though, that system needed to be re-examined and the worthy should hold that position. Who would she talk to about that? She rolled her eyes at the darkness outside, because one woman's jaded opinion would be taken seriously.

Turning, she looked at Tripp, he seemed as thoughtful as she was, "where do you live if not with your family?"

He didn't look away from the road, "Mae took me as one of her clan, so I could work with the team." She watched him take a deep breath and then exhale, "when Kenzo and Calum dragged me away from your father's land, I thought I was done." He shifted around in the seat and then looked more relaxed with one hand on the wheel instead of gripping it hard with both, "I cooperated," he smirked at her, "mostly. So, Mom and Ginny would have clan protection."

Amari needed something to take her mind off her life but was interested in his history too. "How did you go from being forced off the land to working on the biggest bad team we have?"

He looked at her for a second, a serious expression on his face, then turned back to watch where he was driving. "It's kind of a blur, actually." He was quiet for a few moments, "Kenzo stayed with me at some camp," he reached and adjusted the brightness of the dash lights, so they weren't as bright, "I didn't know at the time it was a training site for the special operations team." He brushed his hair back from his face and then glanced at her briefly, "when Calum returned a few days later, Mae was with him, and I was offered a position in her clan if I agreed to train to help the Alliance." He shrugged, "apparently I impressed them by getting the three of us here undetected and onto your father's land without anyone knowing."

Amari grinned, "he wasn't happy." She kicked her boot off and pulled one leg up onto the seat, "I remember that much."

Tripp turned to look at her, amusement in his eyes, "no he wasn't."

"Calum must have pleaded your case to Shepard Addison," she knew all about that, "he's good that way."

"Is that what happened with you?" he held her look for a second and then turned back to the road, "when your father banished you?"

"Eventually." She hugged her knee to her chest and watched out the windshield, "I was on my own for about six months before I came across other clan members." She remembered how cold that time had been, and surviving through the winter, she'd spent most of it in cat form to stay warm. He was quiet, not pushing her to talk about it, but she wanted to share it with him. Only a few people knew her story and they had saved her from a life that could have ended much differently. "I figured," she shrugged, "well, once I settled down and didn't want to burn my father's house to the ground," she glanced over to see him smirking, but looking into the night and not at her, "I figured that guy I'd killed, you know, that he had other clan scents on him and his gear—so I thought it must be a thing and not some one-off, right?" She turned back to watch the path cut by the lights in front of them. "I spent a few months lurking around the outer perimeters of other clans, watching to see if any others were targeting our kind showed up."

"Did they?"

She knew he was watching her but didn't look over at him. "Yeah." In the dark she looked down at her hands like she expected to see blood on them, "more than one." She said without shame.

"Did they live to stalk others?" His voice was quiet.

Amari shook her head and turned to watch the dark out the window. "No. They were maimed by a rogue mountain lion and left to rot." She paused to see if he had anything to say about that. When nothing but silence filled the vehicle, she looked over at him, "I kept some of their stuff, evidence of what they were doing—*intending* on doing. I went to Cecil's clan to plead my case and contact the Alliance." Dropping her leg, she reached back and got a bottle of water from between the seats. "I thought for sure I was an outlaw at that point, that my father would have reported what I'd done."

"It was a ballsy move," he said quietly, "taking that chance."

She opened the bottle and took a drink, "I know, but they needed to know what was going on."

"You probably saved a lot of lives," he looked at her, "taking care of those hunters."

She held his look for a moment, there was no shock or surprise in his eyes, no judgment either. "That's what Shepard Addison told me when Calum came to retrieve me and take me to see him."

Tripp smirked, "ever noticed Calum seems to be everywhere at once?"

Amari smiled, happy for the break from the serious talk, "I have."

He watched her for a few seconds and then looked away. "You're brave. It couldn't have been easy out there on your own." He reached over and touched her hand, "I'm sorry you had to go through that."

It was stupid that a brief touch from him meant so much to her, but it did, and she couldn't pinpoint why. She looked at the hand he had touched, "I'm not, I might have been pissed at the time, but I like who I am now. If that hadn't happened, I wouldn't have gotten this far."

He moved his head in agreement as he watched the road. "I get that. Sometimes you have to dredge through the sludge to reach a better location." He glanced at her with amusement in his eyes, "I guess you're not going to thank your father for it though."

Her smile was quick to form, "Never." She sobered quickly, "I know I overstepped, I get that now, but what he did without hesitation, that wasn't right."

"He's good at that. Quick judgment." He reached over and took her hand and brought it to his mouth and kissed it. "I don't mind that I'm playing a big part in your revenge." He squeezed it gently before releasing it, "hopefully Ken gets someone there, so I don't end up dead." He put both hands on the wheel and she watched them flex, "because if your old man starts on me this time, it's not going to end well."

Amari could feel the aggression rolling off him and didn't blame him at all. He'd brought his mother and sister all the way there only to end up separated from them because of her father. "Don't worry, he'll be too preoccupied with my presence to even notice yours."

Tripp snorted, "upsetting you in any way isn't going to end well for him either."

There was nothing she could say to that. Looking out in front of the vehicle, she had to wonder what she was going to feel when she saw her father again after all this time. The last time she'd seen him her heart felt like it had shattered into a thousand pieces. The cold look in his eyes meant for her was something she didn't think a parent could feel when they looked at their child. She'd saved her sister's life and had been repaid with harsh words and a life of lonely existence.

Chapter Twenty-Two

Tripp looked over at her again, she hadn't spoken since he'd switched back to driving. When they agreed to drive through the night, he'd relinquished the wheel to grab a short nap. They'd stopped and gone for a quick run to fill their bellies; she had seemed out of sorts at that point.

After his short nap, he'd messaged Ken with an earlier arrival time and, he looked at the clock on the dash, a few more hours and this would be done and over with and they could both get back to the teams and help.

"Tripp."

He glanced over at her, "yeah?"

"Tripp. What the hell kind of name is that? Did you have a nice *trip*? Be careful, you'll *trip* and fall…"

"I don't know, *Amari*, where my folks got the name from, but it's mine, so I'm keeping it." His cat felt like he was standing ready for something. What was going on?

"I don't like people." She looked back out the window. "I like being alone, my skin starts to crawl if I'm stuck with someone in my face all the time."

He turned back to watch where he was driving, "am I in your face?" Where was she going with this? And where had it come from?

"No. You're driving."

Waves of hostility were pouring off her. "Right. So, why are you telling me this?" Few words. Basic questions. That was a safe plan.

"Because you bit me."

"You kind of told me to."

She made a scoffing sound, "that's beside the point—I can't be held responsible for what I say in the middle of good—great sex."

Tripp looked at her, to see her scowl back at him.

"You know what I mean." She yanked her jacket away from her neck, "that's why I'm telling you this, because of this bite," she dropped her hand back to her lap, "you're going to be in my face."

He counted to ten inside his head, hoping in that time he'd figure out what was going on. "That clears it up." Squeezing the steering wheel, he forced himself to watch out the windshield. "I don't like people either. Three people in a room are two too many."

"Exactly." She sighed loud and long. "Do you have a home?"

He frowned at the road, "Yes. Well, no, not really. Mae lets me use a small house just off the clan land when I'm around." He inhaled slowly, trying to convey to his tense cat that he was figuring it out. He was trying to. "Do you have a home?"

She snorted. "Not now. Those assholes made me crash it."

"You lived in your van?"

"Yeah? What?" Her tone was abrupt. "It was perfect. Everything I wanted was in it and I never got sick of the scenery."

Tripp nodded, that made sense to him. "I can respect that." Was she worried about her gear? They would have saved it for her.

"*Stop* being so nice. I'm being a bitch to you and you're sitting there taking it."

Because I have no idea what the hell is happening. "You'd prefer I didn't?" His animal was currently prowling in circles inside him.

"No. Yes."

Tripp glanced at her, then back to the road to make the corner. "Do you need to go for a brisk walk or run? I can stop."

"No. What's a run going to fix." Her voice was louder now.

"I don't know," he said slowly, "because I'm not sure what's broken right now."

"*Nothing.* Nothing is broken." She spat the words. "You think I'm broken?"

His brain felt like it might detonate any second now. "Noo." He knew it was a stupid question as it came out of his mouth, "are you?"

"How would I know?" Her tone was filled with defeat now. "I mean, if I were I'd be the last one to see it, right? What a dumb question." The hostility was back.

The mental whiplash was bad, his cat was unsure and when that happened blood was usually spilled. He slowed and then pulled off the road. It was a bad place to stop, in the wide-open, high points all around them, but he needed to get to the bottom of whatever in hell was going on.

"Why are you stopping?" Now she sounded annoyed.

He gave her a wary look, "because if you're trying to pick a fight with me, I thought I'd give you my undivided attention."

"I'm not trying to pick a fight." She crossed her arms over her chest and stared out the windshield.

"No? You don't like my name or people. I bit you thus, I'm in your face…"

"That's not picking a fight?"

He took a deep breath and exhaled slowly. "Okay, what is it then?"

"Why are you being like this?" She glared at him, "Uh." Yanking the handle, she opened the door and got out.

Tripp sat there and watched her walk down into the ditch and keep going. Groaning, he jerked the gear shift into park and then pulled the keys out of the ignition. She was still walking. "Shit." He got out and jogged after her. "Where are you going?"

Amari stopped and stood there, her back to him. "Nowhere."

He glanced around, checking the air to make sure they were alone. "The speed you're moving, you'll get there in no time." His cat agreed with his assessment that there was no one nearby. "What's wrong?"

She turned around, "nothing."

He stared at her, not even sure what to do.

"I'm fine."

"Uh-huh." Tripp had learned one thing in this world, no woman *ever* used that word and meant it.

"What? I am." She huffed out a breath, "and why do you even care?"

Tripp nodded his head slowly, "well, for starters," he waved a hand between them, "there's enough anxiety coming off you that it's starting to feel like a tidal wave." She just continued to stand there and look at him. "Second, my cat is currently trying to come out through my skin without the assist of a shift."

"Fuck." She turned on her heel and walked away.

"Amari, babe—" he started after her.

She stopped and spun around and glared at him, "*don't* call me that. It makes it personal and intimate."

He stopped and put his hands on his hips, "and you want cold and removed."

"Yes. No." She turned her back to him.

"Amari," he moved with quick steps to stand in front of her before she took off again, bending his knees so he could see her face, he looked at her, "talk to me." He wanted to shoot something. Sooth her. Hold her...

"I don't want to go back there." She said it almost in a whisper.

She didn't need to tell him where, he knew and he wanted to go there about as much as he wanted to cut off one of his hands. "Neither do I." He knew it was going to be a shit show.

"Then let's not." She crossed her arms over her chest and nodded.

"I don't think that's an option." Was it? The king hadn't been able to do anything about her father demanding her to come back, so…

"*He* gave up his rights to summon me when he banished me."

Tripp wanted to touch her, but with the mash of emotions pouring off her, even his cat thought that was a bad idea. "I know." He kept his tone soft. She was practically vibrating out of her skin, and he couldn't be sure if it was going to turn into a teary moment or a blood bath. "Look," he touched her chin with the tip of his finger to hold her attention, "you're not the scared kid he sent away." He gave her a small grin, "far from it." His cat nudged him, telling him to continue, "hell, I'm not the same man he dealt with either." Her sexy eyes were locked on his now and he couldn't chance her being distracted by memories right now. "He's going to regret it."

She drew in a slow breath and then nodded her head, "that's true. I didn't know what to do then…"

He dropped his hand away. "I don't see that being an issue now." He smirked.

The anxiety lessened right away. "You're right. I'm not afraid of him." Her voice was more normal now. "He has no power over me now."

Tripp wanted to breathe a sigh of relief but wasn't falling for what might be a false moment. "That's right. You'll get to see your sister again." He had no idea if she had in all these years, but little sisters were good at pulling on heartstrings and helping you keep your focus—he should know, he'd do *anything* for Ginny.

She was nodding slowly. "Let's do this."

Tripp wasn't sure if it was from his words or the internal conversation she had to be having. Whatever it was, he needed to stay calm and keep it together, they'd soon be in her father's territory, and he needed her to help him watch their backs.

He moved closer, lifting her chin again, his cat remained watchful, trying to sus out if this was a bad move or not. Tripp didn't care, he needed to be close to her, even if it was just for a minute. Lowering his head, he kissed her mouth softly, a brief connection. "Let's get there, get this over with and move on like it never happened."

Her breathing hitched and he stood there waiting for a shift of emotions again. She licked those sexy lips of hers and he couldn't help watching the movement. Now, was *not* the time for that, he reminded himself, then leaned down to take her mouth anyway.

Amari's arms snaked around his neck as she returned his kiss. His cat should have been happy that she was thoroughly distracted and sending out vibes that were no longer confusing, but he wasn't. He objected completely to their bodies fitting together so perfectly that it was like they were cut from the same pattern by fate.

When she grasped his hair in her hand, Tripp's body was entering the 'oh yeah' state, but his brain instantly sent out a message that said, 'not the time.' Tearing his mouth from hers, he looked down at her lust-filled eyes. "As much as I want to, we can't go in there reeking of sex, it will not set the tone in our favor."

"Nothing we do or don't do will make it favorable for us." Her voice was rasping.

He brushed the hair back from her face and thought for a second, he could happily spend hours just looking at her. "We should go." His mouth said it despite his own thoughts and his body's objections.

Her hand slowly released the grip on his hair. He could smell her desire, but logic also won with her. "Let's get this over with." She dropped her hands away from him and stepped back. Her sexy eyes moved over his face, then she turned and headed back to the road.

Blowing out a breath, he ran his hand through his hair and watched her for a second. Alpha Hughes better watch his step, he thought, because he would do anything for that woman, even the stupid things he shouldn't.

Chapter Twenty-Three

Amari still couldn't believe her little meltdown. That was so unlike her. She wasn't some wishy-washy, drama queen like that had her spinning a half-hour ago. She looked over to see Tripp was relaxed and didn't even seem like he cared about the shit they were about to wade into. Rolling her head from side to side, she tried to relax the tense muscles. She had been a bitch, saying some of that to him and she regretted it, even though it had rolled right off him as if he knew she didn't mean any of it. The fact that they were both quiet, without that awkward silence vibe happening told her he was just as much a loner as she was, and that was a good thing, right?

His phone ringing startled both of them. He answered it quickly. "Carson."

"Tripp, it's Mae."

Amari looked at the phone, she didn't really know Mae but had nothing but respect for a female leading a clan. They were few and far between.

"Shep just told me what's going on." There was a short pause, "I don't suppose I can talk you out of it?"

Amari looked to see him glance at her. "No. Amari wants me there." He winked at her.

"I see. Am I on speaker?"

"Yes, you are." He looked amused, not solemn like most would be when their Alpha called them.

"Amari, I'm sure Tripp has explained the circumstances of the last time he saw your father."

Amari sat straighter, she wasn't her Alpha, but respect was still due. "Yes, he has." She glanced to see his expression held no judgment. "I'm sure Alpha Hughes will be too distracted by my being there to notice Tripp. He banished me years ago, I've never been back."

There was a long pause. "I see. I knew you were no longer part of his clan, but I wasn't aware of the circumstances, I'm sorry."

Amari shrugged; wasn't her fault her father was a posturing control freak. "Your boy will be fine, Mae, there's going to be someone else there to keep things under control."

"Who is going to be there?"

Amari smirked, "we're not sure, Tripp's team leader, Kenzo Dean said someone from the Alliance would be there with us."

"I'd still like something more concrete, for both of your sakes." There were voices in the background, "Amari, I would like to extend a formal invitation for you to be one of my clan members."

Amari jerked forward in her seat and looked at the phone and then at Tripp, he didn't look shocked or surprised.

"We'll have to forego any sort of ceremony until you can be here. All I need from you right now is your agreement and then the Alliance laws of clan protocol make sure that your father has no right to reprimand you without my consent." She cleared her throat, "that applies to both of you, in case you've forgotten, Tripp."

"I haven't." He glanced over at her; a questioning look on his face. "There's something else you should be aware of, Mae."

Amari realized what he was asking and shrugged, too distracted by the possibility of belonging to a pack again. The bite on her neck was never going away, so it wasn't like it was going to be a big secret.

"What's that?"

Tripp reached over and took her hand, squeezing it so it wasn't balled up with tension. "Amari and I are mates." He lifted her hand and kissed it softly. "It's not a done deal as of yet, but I'm hoping she'll decide I'm worth the trouble and accept me." He gave her a big-toothed grin.

Amari couldn't help but smile briefly back at him.

"That is wonderful news, congratulations, the both of you."

"I just thought you should know because if Alpha Hughes starts on her, it's within my right…"

"I know, but I trust you to control yourself as much as you're able, Tripp." There was an authoritative tone in her words this time. "Amari, while I know Tripp has a few interesting traits, I do hope you'll decide to accept him, he's one of the most dedicated men I know," she sounded proud and it caused a lump in Amari's throat, "but, I'm sure you know this already."

Amari cleared her throat and looked down at their clasped hands. "He's very good at his job." It was the best she could come up with and not let the shaky emotions be heard in her voice. To be part of a clan again after all this time—she started speaking before her emotions won the battle inside her. "I will accept your invitation to be part of the Martin clan and will endeavor to do my part to ensure the community thrives and bring honor to you."

"Spoken only the way an Alpha's child could. Welcome to the clan, Amari." The voices in the background were louder, she had probably put them on speaker so someone could witness her oath. "Tripp, the house is yours, we'll clear out all the clutter for the next time you're here. A newly mated couple needs a place of their own."

Amari pulled her hand free from his. A clan, a home, what was going on?

"Thanks, Mae." He gave her a wary look, "I don't know how often we'll be around with everything that's happening…"

"I heard and it's about damn time we ended the tyranny that's forced us all to hide." The voices in the background grew louder, then became muffled.

Amari liked her attitude; she could see them getting along well in the future. *Future.* In a few days' time, her whole entire world was changed.

"I'm going to have to go, Tripp, we've just had a birth in the clan, and I want to check in on the family."

She tried to think if her father had ever done that and couldn't recall a time he'd announced something like that. Her mother, she'd go see the new mom, she was sure of that.

"Congratulate the parents for me," Tripp said it so easily, it made her feel awkward.

"That's wonderful news." She offered in a quiet voice.

"Try to keep things bloodless when you get to the Hughes clan, both of you."

Amari smirked at the way she said it like it was something she had to ask of Tripp often.

"We will try." He said as he looked over at her, amusement in his eyes.

"Once again, welcome, Amari, we're damn lucky to have you as part of our clan."

"I will try to make you proud to have me." The lump was back in her throat again.

"Call me when you're done with Hughes, Tripp."

"Absolutely, Mae."

The line went quiet.

"I guess she doesn't realize there are ways to kill someone without blood being spilled."

Amari looked over and appreciated his attempt at humor. Blowing out a breath, she looked at the phone once more, like she wasn't sure that had just happened.

"Welcome to the clan," Tripp said in a more serious tone.

"I never," she looked away and out the window, "thought I'd be part of a clan again."

"Mae is one of the good ones," he put her window down a few inches like he knew she needed fresh air, "I've met a lot that shouldn't be leading anything."

Amari nodded, "yeah me too. Most of them, though put their people first and go above and beyond."

"Guess we both have a home now."

A mate. A clan. A Home. None of them was something she thought she'd want—ever, but now some of it was sounding like it might be worth the hell she'd gone through.

"Hey."

She looked over to see him holding out his hand to her, she looked at it and then at the man that was supposed to be paying attention to where he was driving, but was watching her instead, she took it before he crashed his pretty ride.

"We'll get through this, all of it, together." Lifting their hands, he kissed hers.

She couldn't handle any sappy moments right now; she was barely hanging on as it was. "You're very oral, Tripp," she lifted their hands as if to illustrate.

His grin was slow and sinful, "darlin, you have *no* idea."

She felt her cheeks heat and her blood warm. "Don't start, you already said we weren't allowed to go in there smelling like sex."

Tripp squeezed her hand, then released it to adjust himself, "my body has other ideas."

Amari inhaled and there was no missing the pheromones from his cat filling the interior of the vehicle. She looked out the window and then glanced at the GPS like she needed confirmation of where they were. "We could stop—"

"I would like nothing more than to stop this truck and lay you down right now, but we need to get this over with so we can move on with the rest of our lives…"

"And get back to the teams." She sucked in a breath and crossed her arms over her chest. Back to work would be the best thing right now.

"I can honestly say the last thing on my mind right now is that group." He glanced at her and gave her a player's smile.

Something to look forward to, and it wasn't the teams for once. "Fine, keep driving, let's get this done with." She needed the confrontation with her father right now while she processed that she was part of a clan again. She still didn't know what she was going to do about being a mate, but just the idea that she had the purpose of belonging to a clan made her want to cry and laugh at the same time. She hated this new wishy-washy feature in her personality and some yelling and glaring at her father should purge it from her well enough.

Chapter Twenty- Four

Tripp stopped in the middle of the road and sat there. The bumper of his vehicle was a foot away from the invisible line to her father's clan territory. He knew every inch of this boundary; he'd run in many times over the years. Turning, he looked over to see recognition on her face. "Ready for this?"

Amari shook her head but motioned toward the windshield. "Let's get it done." Her expression was hard, but her words didn't reflect as much conviction.

Nodding, he pressed the gas again. The only problem with upping their arrival time to the middle of the day was more people would be out and chances of this turning into something bigger was almost certain.

"We're not going inside his house or office. He can come out to us." Her tone was cold, and he couldn't find fault with that, not after what she'd been through the last time she was here—the last time he was here.

"That works for me." It did too, without the confines of walls, his cat wouldn't become restless and distracting. He rolled his eyes like anything was going to distract him from the tense she-cat beside him.

He slowed and turned the corner that led to the large grouping of houses. He didn't even know which one was his mother's, he hadn't been allowed to stay long enough to...

"That's your mom's—or was when I was still here."

Turning his head, he looked to where she was pointing. He slowed so the vehicle was rolling slowly by it. It was a decent-looking place, with a nice yard, his mom would like that. There weren't a lot of houses this far out, so that would please her too, she liked her peace and quiet.

Just as he was going to step on the gas, the door opened, and two young women came out. The one he recognized immediately and then felt the guilt move through him, it was his sister, Ginny and she had changed a lot. It had been longer than he thought since he'd carved out time to meet up with them.

"She's grown so much."

He was about to agree and then realized by the wistful tone in her voice, she wasn't talking about Ginny. The other woman had golden blonde hair and from here looked a lot like his mate. "Is that your sister?"

"Yeah." She turned more in the seat and looked out the window. "I can't believe it. She's beautiful."

Tripp opened his mouth to say just like her sister but decided no words were probably better right now. "Do you want to say hello?"

She looked at him, apprehension on her face. "I don't know."

Tripp glanced by her to see they were headed to them. "Too late." He motioned with his chin for her to look. They were less than ten feet from the vehicle now, both had wary looks on their faces.

Amari reached in slow motion and pushed the button to put the window down. He heard her take a deep breath slowly. "Chantal." That was it, just her name.

"Mar?" The young woman's eyes widened. Her mouth opened and then she rushed to the window. "What are you doing here?" She whispered it, then looked around.

"I was summoned."

Tripp smirked at his sister when she caught up and looked in at him, her eyes almost popping out of her head. He cleared his throat. "Get in, you can accompany us to the Alpha's house."

The back door opened, and his sister climbed in without hesitation. She leaned between the seats, almost on top of him, getting right in his face. "What are you doing here? Are you crazy? Tripp, you need to turn this around and get off the land right now."

The door slammed. "Neither of you should be here," Chantal said with panic in her voice. She hissed out a breath, then reached around the seat and grabbed Amari. "I'm so glad you're okay, but you have to go." She released her and sat back, a stunned look on her face.

Amari shifted in her seat and looked at them. "I was summoned, and Mom said to bring the man that rescued me."

Ginny looked at him, "you?"

Tripp nodded, then shrugged, "I think I rescued her captors more than her." He caught the smirk on Amari's face before she sobered again.

"Does Mom know *who* you're bringing?" Chantal looked from her sister to him.

Tripp shook his head, "I don't think names were mentioned."

Ginny flopped back against the seat and put her hand over her mouth for a second. Dropping she looked at him, "Mom is going to have a heart attack."

Tripp shook his head, "I'm sure it will be fine." He lifted one shoulder and then let it drop and turned back around in his seat. Stepping on the gas, he drove cautiously down the road, not sure if there would be kids hanging around.

"Why did Dad summon you?" Chantal's voice was nothing like her sister's, it was soft and gentle, then again, she hadn't been through what her sister had.

"I don't know, the message was relayed." Amari was almost sitting in her seat backward now, not looking anywhere but the sister she hadn't seen in years. "I can't believe how much you've grown."

He glanced in the mirror to see Chantal roll her eyes.

"That happens." She said with a smirk.

Tripp smiled, there was a little sass in her after all.

"This is going to be intense," Ginny said.

Tripp nodded, "probably." He met her look in the mirror, "I didn't know you two were friends."

"We have a lot in common." Ginny said, then leaned forward between the seats, "outlawed siblings."

Tripp grinned. "Oh, there's more than that." He glanced over to see Amari looking at him, indecision on her face. He wouldn't say it though, that was for her to share. Her shoulders slumped and he knew she'd decided. Shifting, Amari pulled her jacket aside, so the bite was visible.

"No way." Ginny was almost in the front seat too. "You guys are mates?"

Tripp bumped her with his arm, "driving here." He got a better grip on the steering wheel.

"Well," Amari shifted in the seat, "we're half-mated at the moment."

"What? Is that even a thing?" Chantal gasped, "he's not claimed, oh my god, Mar, that's—*so* bad…"

Amari chuckled, "it's a long story, and things have been a bit crazy…"

"We ask any of the co-ord teams and others that work for the Alliance about the both of you," Ginny said with a proud look on her face.

Tripp winced, "oh?"

Ginny nodded, "yeah, you're both these badasses that no one messes with."

Amari glanced at him and then at her sister, "you ask about me?"

"Of course, I ask about you. I tell Mom everything I hear too. We're both very proud." Her voice was a little shaky, which wasn't surprising the mix of emotions trapped in here with them was getting a little more than he could handle.

"What do Bauer and Dad say?"

He didn't like the hesitation in her voice and wanted to reach over and take her hand, to assure her that he was right here with her but wasn't sure if the show of affection would be well received right now.

"They don't ask, I don't offer," Chantal said in a quiet voice.

Tripp looked straight ahead, he could see the building at the end of the street and knew it had to be the Alphas. He needed to mentally prepare himself and his cat for what came next. "You ladies should make yourself scarce."

"Oh, I'm not missing this." Ginny leaned forward again, "you should meet outside though."

"That's the plan." He slowed the vehicle and then pulled past the building, so he had a few seconds to look around before the man in every one of his nightmares was in his face.

"We'll go in and get him, Mom too," Chantal said. "The more around, the better."

Tripp looked over to see Amari adjusting her belt. "Don't suppose you'd leave your belt and boot toys here?"

She glanced at him and then looked right at the gun strapped to his leg, "are you leaving that?"

He shook his head.

"Then, neither am I."

Tripp put it into park and then turned it off. He looked out the window to see if there were any Alliance vehicles there. There wasn't. Picking up his phone, he opened it to send a message to Kenzo to let him know they were here. He did that quickly. Before he could put it in his pocket, it rang. He answered it but didn't get a chance to speak before his boss did.

"They'll be there in ten minutes. Keep your mouth shut and attitude on lockdown for *ten* minutes, Tripp."

He smirked. "I can do ten minutes."

"I hope so. Call me when you're leaving the place."

Tripp looked in the side mirror to make sure no one was approaching them. "Will do." He hung up and put it in his pocket. "Ten minutes." He told Amari.

"Well, I'm not sitting in the car waiting."

He never imagined she would.

"We'll go get him." Chantal opened the door and both sisters climbed out on the same side of the vehicle. Ginny had her phone against her ear, no doubt telling their mother that he was there.

When Amari turned to get out, he touched her arm. When her eyes connected with his, he could see the doubt there behind the anger. "You've got this."

She inhaled slowly and nodded, "I wanted to talk to him for the first year—since then," she looked out the window, "he doesn't matter now."

Leaning over before she could bail, he kissed her cheek lightly. "I've got your back. Know that." He whispered and then leaned away and opened the door. Getting out he took off his jacket and tossed it back in. It was cool, snow was on the way at some point, but the jacket was gone so he had the freedom to move. He looked through the open door to see Amari was taking hers off as well. The atmosphere between them right now had the same vibes they went through just before an op. Turning, he looked to see their sisters coming out, both had a look that told Tripp this might end up being an op with their lives hanging in the balance.

Blowing out a breath, he looked over to see his mate's expression harden, any emotions that weren't required to do this were completely pushed to the back. Closing the door, he walked around the front and over to her. He glanced to see his mark was very visible and raised one eyebrow, "I'm not sure if you're showing that off to brag about the amazing catch or to distract from any other discussions." He winked at her.

Amari smirked very fleetingly. "Guess you'll never know for sure."

He couldn't help the grin on his face. She was something, his mate, and right now he hoped he lived longer than today so he could get to know more about her.

Chapter Twenty-Five

This wasn't going to be like any other family reunion that Tripp had ever witnessed. He knew there would be no hugs, tears, or thankful words spoken. He stood beside her, keeping just enough space between them that if she needed him, he was close, but also giving her room to move. Twice he went to rest his hand on his sidearm and then crossed his arms over his chest so he wouldn't look like he had plans to shoot anyone. He didn't want to; well, he was about sixty-five percent sure he didn't want to shoot the man that he'd plotted revenge against for these many years.

Amari stood facing the house, the toes of her boots an inch behind where the walkway to it started. She didn't even want to step onto the property. The entire area was her father's clan, but this, his residence, was a personal space, and Tripp respected her decision. He also hoped he could keep things as impersonal as possible. The last time he'd seen the man, he'd said some things that weren't pleasant and were also still how he felt about him today. This time, he was focused on the man's daughter. Sure, he'd been an asshole to Tripp, but what he'd done to his own child was lower than low.

Chantal and Ginny stood off to the side of the walkway, anxious looks on their faces. He wanted to go over and assure them that it was going to be all right, but to do that he'd have to leave Amari and that he couldn't bring himself to do that.

The door opened and a woman came out, her mother hadn't changed at all since he'd last seen her. She was taller than Amari, her hair a darker blonde, but her daughter's eyes were the same as hers. She came down the steps quickly, as a mother would rush to their child, but then stopped a few feet away, assessing her banished child from head to toe.

"Mom," Amari whispered it with a tone that sounded like disbelief, that she was actually seeing her.

"You're beautiful." Her mother's tone was just as faint. She glanced at him, and the loving look faded.

"Tripp is the one that found me." Amari's voice was back to normal now.

He watched the woman's eyes round as recognition filled them. "You should have said something..."

"Does it matter? Really?" That was the tone Tripp expected from Amari, hard and filled with sarcasm. "I was collared to a tree covered in gasoline when he got there..."

The Alpha's wife gasped, then stepped forward, "you're right, it doesn't matter." She reached out and touched Amari's shoulders and smiled down at her. For a moment, Tripp thought it might just be all right, and then her expression changed again as she breathed in their scents.

Straightening her arms, she looked at Amari's neck and then at Tripp, before giving her child a surprised look. "You're mates." She whispered it with awe, a smile so brief on her lips it could have been her wincing, he wasn't sure. "Your father is...."

"Coming out the door." Tripp watched the man he loathed come down the steps and move in their direction. He always wondered if over the years he'd remembered that expression wrong, but as he looked at him now, he knew he hadn't. There was no relief on the man's face, that his daughter was alive and well, in fact, there was nothing there that told Tripp he was at all pleased by that fact.

"I'm right here, Amari. There won't be a repeat of the last time." Her mother whispered then released her and stepped to the side, but still stayed close enough that she could have just reached out and touched the child she hadn't seen in years.

Tripp watched the man look Amari over like she was some nuisance he didn't have time for.

"Vesper, Amari just told me how dire her situation was when she was found," Tripp could hear a hint of desperation in her voice, "this is the man that saved her. I asked her to bring him."

There was no need for introductions as Alpha asshole Hughes stopped walking and looked right at him. That look, the one that told Tripp he was lower than an insect was right there on the man's face for all to see. Yeah, he'd remembered that expression all right.

"Did you know who *he* was?"

Tripp caught a flash of something that could have been love or close to it as the Alpha looked at his mate, but it was so brief, he couldn't be certain.

"Does it matter?" She responded and, at that moment, Tripp knew where Amari had gotten her bite from. Of course, the circumstances of her life had hardened her more than her mother, but it was still there. "They had our *daughter* collared to a tree and had poured gasoline on her," she made a jerky motion to Tripp, "*who* he is bears no meaning on it at all."

Vesper Hughes looked at his mate for a moment, a softer expression on his face, and just for a second Tripp thought maybe the man did have a heart, but when he turned back to his daughter the distant look was back. The man must be frozen inside. The compassion had only been for his mate and not his child.

"I always knew your traipsing around like that was going to yield you trouble."

Why Tripp had thought this man was capable of compassion, he had no idea. His eldest daughter could very well be dead right now and he seemed more annoyed that she was alive than anything else. Tripp felt Amari tense and didn't have to look at her to know she was bracing to clue him in. The air was suddenly heavier. If she had been nervous or anxious at all, that was now gone. In its place was something that went beyond anger, something colder than loathsomeness.

"Dad." A man with the same shade of blond hair as Amari came down the walkway. His eyes matched the Alpha's but there was no mistaking this was her brother, the next Alpha of the clan. "Amari, we're just glad you're all right." He stopped to stand beside his father and smiled at her. Tripp watched his eyes flick to look at her neck, but the smile on his face didn't falter. He decided he might have to like Asshole Hughes' son for knowing when to keep his mouth shut.

Vesper glanced at his son and then back to Amari, a removed look on his face. "Of course." He motioned a hand to Tripp, "this is who rescued her, Bauer. Your mother invited him onto *our* lands."

Bauer looked at Tripp, and after a few breaths time recognition lit his eyes. "Thank you." There was no forgiveness in his eyes, but he spoke the words with sincerity. "Special operations, right? I called Raymond Hardy for a full account."

Tripp inclined his head, "that's right." The tense vibes were so thick right now, he had to tell his cat to stand down and let him handle this.

Bauer nodded again, then stepped past the point his Alpha sire stood and extended his hand.

Tripp definitely liked the man now, he broke clan protocol and moved ahead of father asshole to shake the hand of the one that brought his sister out of a messy situation. Tripp clasped his hand.

"Thanks." The shake was brief but still monumental. He released his hand and stepped back. "From all accounts," he looked down at his sister, "I'm sure they had their hands full with you." There was something resembling pride in his eyes as he looked at her. "I check up on you from time to time." He smirked, "and some of the things I've heard are," he glanced to his mother, "are interesting." He finished and then sobered.

"I was unaware you did this." His father said in a low tone.

Bauer shrugged, "she's still my sister." His posture relaxed making him appear less like his stiff male parent, who Tripp noticed was a slightly redder shade in the face now.

"Her," Vesper motioned to her like she was not relevant to him, "escapades do not redeem her crime."

"My *crime?*"

The way she ground out the word set Tripp on alert. He may not have known her long, but in the short time together he had come to understand any abrupt change in her tones usually led to blood—or death.

"I saved Chantal from," she growled low, "you don't even want to know what captives go through at the hands of Aiden Tomas, *Father.*"

Vesper's look hardened further, "I'm aware of some of the details in some instances."

"*Some instances?* If you could see the women and children," she hissed out a breath, "even the state of the men we pull out of his vile houses, you would throw up and then cry like a little baby," Tripp reached over and touched her arm, trying to calm her. His cat was going crazy from the hostile emotion coming off her. She glanced at him, and the rage cleared briefly as she recognized him. Huffing out a breath, she shook off his hand but made no move to eviscerate the man in front of her. "The men that are forced to *serve* the Tomas family have collars around their necks, Father—they aren't allowed to shift."

Tripp could feel the animosity rolling off her and for a brief second thought of stepping in and stopping it. Amari was owed this reckoning and unless it got out of hand, he was going to let her have it.

She took a step forward, closing the distance to her sire. "They're covered in scars, neck raw—" she sucked in a breath and stared up at the man, looking for a reaction. There was no visible sign that her father cared one way or the other. Amari growled low, "if I hadn't done what I did, do you know what would have happened to her," she pointed to her sister, "*father?*"

Tripp caught her brother putting his hand on his mother's arm to stop her from interfering.

"They take them before they can shift so they can *breed* them with males of the same clan. So they can barter and trade them all over the globe as little trophies for the sick one-forms private collections and elite club attractions."

Tripp heard someone gasp but couldn't look away in case Amari jumped on her father, who still looked completely unmoved.

"Which is exactly why your days of running around like a vigilante are over." The Alpha stated in a tone that set Tripp's cat off even further.

"*What?*" Amari waved her hand toward him, "you have *no* say in what I do."

"I am your father and Alpha." The words were clipped and loud.

"You. Are. *Nothing.* Nothing to me. I waited months for you to realize you had condemned your own daughter to near starvation and hypothermia—

Tripp glanced at her; she'd left out that part of her trials.

Amari sucked in a breath, and then her spine stiffened. "You are nothing to me now." Her voice was steadier, the volume still just as loud as the one the Alpha had used. "I am no longer of this clan." She enunciated each word so there would be no confusion about what she said.

"Amari?" Her mother gave her a concerned look.

Vesper Hughes' eyes hardened further, Tripp was amazed they didn't shatter and fall from his face, they were that cold. "I know you didn't pay attention to clan law, *but* you do not get to…

"I am now a part of the Martin clan," she looked at Tripp and he knew exactly what she was going to say. He began chanting inside his head, *'don't, don't do it'*, "just like my mate."

She did it. Oh shit. The hostility in the air was now peaking at DEFCON 2 and Tripp braced for trouble as her father's gaze locked on the bite mark on his daughter's neck. When those icy eyes moved to look at him, they changed to pure hot animosity.

"You marked my daughter, but I don't see any such indicator on you that says it was *with* consent." He spat each word at him like it tasted bad in his mouth. "Bauer, we're going to need the authorities here. *Now.*"

Amari moved fast, her hand reaching behind her, and Tripp knew a blade was about to be brought into this little scene. He grabbed the hand behind her back in a firm grip and used his other arm to pull her back against his chest. "That won't be necessary, darlin." He whispered. She was tense in his arms but relinquished the hold on the hidden handle in her belt. "I assure you," he glanced from Bauer to his father, "it was quite consensual. Saving all our kind has gotten in the way of ceremony lately." It was complete bullshit, and he knew it, but in his head, he wanted to believe under different circumstances things would have ended in a happily-ever-after moment— because that shit happened *never* in his life.

Amari's breathing slowed; her cat was closer. He could feel her muscles harden against him like a cat would when it was preparing to spring at prey. Tripp had to cool this down or he was going to be dealing with an angry cat and not just the woman his arm was wrapped around. His cat was also just under the surface and felt like a supervisor looking over his shoulder waiting to see if he fucked this up.

The Alpha glared at him.

His son looked from his father to Tripp, then to Amari. "Dad..."

Whatever he was going to say was drowned out by the loud echo of a helicopter dropping down out of the sky and buzzing over them.

Thank fuck, was the only thing Tripp could think at this point. He didn't know who Kenzo had rallied, but he hoped they were big and mean because they were going to need to be to diffuse this garbage situation.

He felt Amari relax in his hold and released her to allow space between them so they could turn to watch the helicopter set down in the middle of the ornate park in the center of the clan village. Ballsy, in a good way, they knew how to make an entrance.

As soon as the high-pitched whirl slowed, he recognized Konner Flores in the pilot seat as he turned and spoke to the passengers. *That* was the kind of backup he needed; a fellow warrior that also happened to be good with diplomatic dealings. Tripp didn't have the patience for diplomacy, he'd rather just shoot everyone present that annoyed him and go climb back in his ride and leave. All of his team knew that on any op, it was better if he left the talking to one of them, too often words fueled his rage.

No one moved as Konner hopped out and ducked down to run around to the other side of the chopper. He opened the door and a big red-headed man got out. In his hand was a shotgun. Tripp knew he wasn't Alliance security, not unless their uniform policy had changed to jeans, scruffy work boots, and a t-shirt. He didn't know who he was, but his whole aura screamed, 'don't fuck with me' and Tripp was just fine with that sort of attitude.

Konner held his hand out and a blonde woman climbed down. A petite redheaded woman followed her.

"Rayne," Amari whispered.

Hot damn. Kenzo had done better than an Alliance rep, he'd sent the princess to save his ass. He leaned closer to her, "who's that with her?"

"Other than Konner, I have *no* idea." She glanced up at him, "but the big guy screams huge cat just looking at him."

Tripp shrugged, "huge cat with a shotgun works for me." He turned back and watched as Konner and the women approached them. The armed man stopped and stayed halfway between the chopper and where they stood. He scanned the area once and then watched the tiny woman accompanying the princess as she approached them. The look in his eyes screamed 'that's my mate' and Tripp understood the situation could get volatile without warning now. He met the man's eyes over their heads and when he inclined his to him, Tripp almost heaved a sigh of relief knowing the big guy had his back in this.

Instinct had him move closer to Amari, too many unknown variables were in play now. When she held her hands to her side and started to lower her head to the princess, he jolted, having forgotten protocol completely.

The lovely woman, now a few feet from them gave her head a slight shake and held Amari's look. She didn't want them to acknowledge her status. That surprised him, but didn't, not after he'd heard her mate on the calls, and realized neither thought they belonged on a pedestal.

"Amari." She smiled at her and then looked at him, "and you must be Tripp." She inclined her head but made no move to come closer to either of them. "Sorry I'm late, this plan was tossed together rather quickly." She smiled. In that smile, Tripp saw the salvation of the Alliance and the entire shifter community, he couldn't say why, it was just a feeling that came over him.

Konner came up behind her and nodded to Tripp, then did the same to Amari before he acknowledged the Alpha standing there fuming. "Alpha Hughes," he glanced to her mother, "'mam."

"Oh," Rayne motioned to the woman beside her, "this is Kelsey," she glanced to the shotgun-wielding man, "and her mate, Gage. As you know," she looked from Tripp to Amari, completely ignoring Alpha asshole, "things are a bit hectic right now, so Devin wasn't able to come. His seconds came in his place, well one of them," she huffed out a breath, "Konner is filling in for Calum because he's, um, *busy*."

Tripp frowned, why did she say busy like that? Wait, Calum was one of the prince's seconds? So many pieces clicked into place inside his head he almost vocalized it like an epiphany. He glanced at Gage and was met with a look that said he'd rather be elsewhere doing something else. On that, they were of like mind.

Kelsey smiled at Amari and then Tripp, it was one of those contagious ones that you couldn't help returning. She glanced over at Chantal and Ginny and then nodded to Amari's mother before turning to look at Vesper Hughes. "I'm sorry, I must have missed you paying your respects to our princess while I was still buzzing from my first helicopter ride." Just like that she went from a cute little redhead to a fierce 'you have one chance to comply' woman.

Tripp had to clamp his teeth together to keep from grinning when the Alpha's expression turned to shock.

"I'm—I apologize." He looked at Rayne and then lowered his head.

Her mother did the same. "I'm sorry, Princess, I was a little taken aback by the helicopter landing in the circle.

Rayne smiled at that and touched Amari's mother's head lightly so she would straighten, "yes," she glanced at Konner, "I told him I didn't want to have to run from some field." She winced, "I'm glad flower season is over."

Amari's mother nodded, "it's fine." She motioned to the house, "would you like to come in for coffee or-or tea?"

Rayne smiled, "I would love coffee, but unfortunately I don't think we are here for long."

Vesper finally realized he wasn't going to receive acceptance from the princess and straightened up. He cleared his throat, "I didn't know you were coming. Is this business?" He looked so uncomfortable Tripp wanted to do a jig—*if* he had any idea how to do one.

"I've been sent to speed up Tripp and Amari's delay." She looked at Tripp, "with Calum out of the operations for a bit, we need you," she looked at Amari, "*both,* back with the teams."

A look of concern appeared on Amari's face, "is Calum all right?"

Rayne smirked, "oh he's fine, it's Shae's first," she glanced at Tripp and then at Vesper and she shrugged.

"Oh." Amari blew out a breath. "Talk about bad timing."

Kelsey grinned, "you have no idea, Shae was so mad about it."

Tripp looked anywhere but at the women, he wasn't really feeling a conversation about a woman's cycle. He turned to Konner, who lifted an eyebrow at him and flicked his eyes to look at Amari's neck before asking the question with his expression. Tripp lifted both shoulders and let them drop, basically telling him it was a long story.

"Is there time for Tripp to at least see his mom?" Amari touched his arm, bringing his attention back to her. "He doesn't get to see her often."

He couldn't believe in all of this, she was thinking about him and asking that.

Rayne smiled, "I'm sure a short visit won't make or break the schedule." She looked up at Konner, "I'm going to go meet the newborn twins from Konner's clan and then head back to try to be helpful to the teams."

Tripp glanced to see Vesper Hughes standing there looking like he might burst a few blood vessels, he was pissed. "I think we're about done here anyway." He reached over and took Amari's hand in his and then looked past the Alpha to the two sisters standing back in the background. "Maybe our sisters could come down and have a coffee with my mom?" He looked down at Amari.

She gave him a surprised look. "I'd like that." She turned and looked at her mother, "Mom, would you like to join us? It's been so long since I've seen you, I'd like to spend a little time with you."

"Dad." Bauer gave Amari a tender look before turning to his father, "we should really get back and finish going over that."

His father cleared his throat and then nodded in a stiff way. "It was a pleasure to meet you, Princess, please come back any time you like."

Rayne offered him a cordial smile, not the one with the warmth that had rocked Tripp. "I'll mention that to Devin, he has plans to visit all Alphas in the Alliance once things settle down." Her smile widened, "we've been discussing changes with Shep, so," she clasped her hands together, "some exciting changes will be coming soon."

Bauer stepped around his father and hugged Amari briefly, "call me. Chan will give you my number."

Amari nodded, her eyes glistening with unshed tears. "Yeah."

"Wait." Tripp stepped away from Amari and looked at the red-faced Alpha male. "You owe your daughter an apology."

The expression on his face screamed, 'not in this lifetime."

"I agree," Rayne stated in a steady tone.

Alpha Hughes looked from the princess to Tripp and then back to her again. He inclined his head, maybe an inch before turning to look at his daughter. The hatred was plain in his eyes and Tripp couldn't figure out how a father could look at their own child with that look. There was obviously something broken inside that man.

"I apologize, Amari." He said it barely above a whisper.

Tripp glanced at his mate and looked at the expression on her face. It meant nothing to her. If anything, she looked a little sad as she studied this man before her. Taking a deep breath, she exhaled slowly and then turned her back to her father in the clearest form of shunning him that spoke volumes to everyone watching.

The Alpha scowled at her back, but before he could speak, his son took a firm grip on his elbow and turned toward the house.

No one moved or spoke as Bauer got his unwelcome father back into the house. The girls moved over closer, both looking unsure of how to proceed in front of Rayne. Before he could figure out if he should introduce them, she went over to them.

Rayne looked at Ginny and grinned, "I love your shoes, we have to talk about those. I'm Rayne."

"Ginny. Pleased to meet you."

Rayne looked over at Tripp, "you must be Tripp's sister?"

She nodded.

"And you with that gorgeous shade of blonde have to be Amari's."

Chantal held out her hand, "Chantal. It's an honor to meet you."

"Same." Rayne turned and looked at Gage. "You can probably relax, Gage."

He shrugged and shouldered the shotgun, then walked over with an easy stride. "I heard coffee mentioned." The scary vibes were gone from the giant of a man.

"Gage, I think we need a chopper." Kelsey smiled at him.

"Not a chance, you're scary enough on the ground." He laughed, then leaned down and kissed the top of her head.

Rayne smiled, "coffee." She looked at Ginny, "maybe you could show us where?"

Ginny motioned to the other side of where the helicopter was parked, "Mom is over there."

Tripp turned around to see his mother standing beside a small car. He smiled and then reached into his pocket and took out his keys and tossed them to Konner, "want to grab my ride and bring everyone down?"

Konner caught the keys. "Happy to."

"We'll go down with my mom." He said to Rayne.

Rayne came back over and stood beside Amari's mother, "I'm sorry, I didn't catch your name."

"Camille."

Rayne smiled, "what a lovely name. Camille, please join us for coffee." Her look turned to something he could only call clinical. "I'd like to discuss some of the changes coming to the Alliance clans and get another woman's take on it."

Camille looked surprised but nodded.

Tripp squeezed Amari's hand and then leaned down to whisper in her ear, "you were saying about female leaders?" He straightened up and received a big smile from those pouty lips.

"About damn time." She said softly.

"Come meet my mom." He tugged on her hand. He glanced at Konner, "guess we're even now? I came to your rescue, you to mine."

Konner grinned, "isn't that what we do?"

Tripp shrugged, "occasionally." With that he started across the street to where his mother stood smiling at him, dragging Amari along with him. This hadn't gone at all the way he thought and for the first time in a very long time, he thought maybe his life was finally going to start heading in a new, not all-bad direction.

Chapter Twenty-Six

Amari still couldn't believe she'd seen her family. She looked at her phone. She had their numbers now and could talk to them. Bauer was cooler than she remembered. He'd changed over the years, for the better.

"You must be excited about the new ideas Rayne was talking about."

Amari looked over at him. "I'm just processing, you know? Seeing my sister and Mom," she smirked, "even my brother isn't the jerk he used to be."

"Sounded like he's been keeping tabs on you."

"Yeah, that's weird. All we used to do was fight and now—"

"He cares about you."

She nodded, not sure how to express how she felt about that. Her cat was being weird right now and she couldn't figure out why. She got that way sometimes when she wanted to go for a run, but this was something else. She glanced back at him, hoping to distract herself. "Your mom is pretty cool."

He grinned, "Yeah, she's great." Tripp looked at her for a second, "I'm glad our sisters are friends and can watch each other's backs."

She nodded, "yeah, hopefully, they both manage to stay out of trouble."

"Unlike their siblings?" He leaned forward and looked at the sky, "check out those clouds."

She moved forward and looked up. The sky was darkening with full heavy clouds. "Guess a storm is inbound."

Tripp put the window down and she watched him lean closer and take a deep breath. He straightened up and glanced at her, "snow."

That explained her cats off behavior, they were built for snow, but those memories from years earlier always came back in bad storms. "Think we can outrun it and get across the border before it hits?"

"I don't know. It's moving in the same direction we are."

"Should we stop and gas up and grab some extra supplies, just in case?"

He nodded and leaned over and reached for the GPS screen, "that's a good idea."

Amari tapped her hand on her knee. They didn't need any more delays. The teams had a lot to do, and she had been away from them too long.

"Is internet enabled on your phone?" He glanced at her, "most of the new ones don't have access for safety."

She grabbed her phone out of the cupholder. "I'll check." She tapped the screen and went to open the browser—there wasn't one. "I'm going to say no. There's not even a browser installed."

"Shit. I wanted to check on this storm and see how much area it's going to cover."

"I'll call Zain when we stop, but we need to figure out where first." She looked in the back of the vehicle. "Do you have a storm kit?"

"A storm kit? I have mylar blankets and warm socks."

She snorted, "clearly you've never been stuck in a winter storm before."

"Okay, what do we need for a storm kit?"

"Candles, those little tea light ones are the best, a coffee can and it has to be metal, not those cardboard ones." She thought for a second, "we have protein covered—do you have a flashlight? Oh, and plastic bags, like garbage bags to keep you dry." She always carried that. Always. Of course, with her gear stored somewhere from her wrecked van, she wasn't prepared for a storm for the first time since she'd been out there homeless and on her own.

"I understand everything, but the coffee can and candles."

"For warmth, you put the candle in a can, it's not widespread heat, but it helps a lot."

"Okay, I'll get candles, bags, and a can of coffee, or a metal container of some sort." He gave her one of his sexy smiles and for a moment she thought getting stuck in the storm with him wouldn't be all bad.

That thought brought her back to this mate issue they seemed to have. She'd already announced they were mates to her family, and she'd noticed Rayne and the others checking out their necks at some point. She was going to have to address it and make a decision. Her cat stirred and let her know that a decision wasn't in the equation. They were mates.

"There's a gas station and store about twenty minutes from here. We'll make a quick stop then," he looked at the sky, "try to outrun this."

By the time they reached the store, the clouds had opened, and the snow was coming down so hard there was close to no visibility. Tripp yanked his hat on and looked at her, "call your guy and see how long this is going to last."

Amari watched him set up the gas pump and then picked up her phone. Zain answered on the fourth ring, which was unusual it took that long, she was sure he sat with the phone in his hand twenty-four hours a day. "Z—"

"Hang on, Amari, I'm going to have to put you on hold for a second, shit is crazy here."

The line went quiet. She lowered the phone and looked at it. That was a first too. Putting it on speaker, she set it on the dash, turned, and looked into the back seat.

Tripp opened the back door and stuck his head in. He gave her a questioning look.

"I'm on hold."

The snow was caked on his hat already. "Put these seats down and take stock of our water and everything—we'll make sure we have enough to weather this storm if we have to." When she nodded, he closed the door.

Kicking off her boots, she climbed into the back seat. At least she knew now what had her cat so anxious, this wasn't going to be a light snowfall.

She had both seats laying down and the supplies from the back sorted on them by the time Tripp opened the door and added three bags to it. She paused and watched him brush off some of the snow and then climb in the front seat. Zain still hadn't come back on the phone.

Tripp took off his hat and shook it onto the floor. "In the blue bag in the cargo area are a few blankets." He turned to look at her, "there's a small grocery store a few miles up, do we need anything from it?"

Amari looked at the items in front of her. "We should have enough water to get us through. Some fruit and snacks other than protein and jerky would be nice." Opening the bags, she looked to see what he'd bought. Gummy bears were the first thing she saw. When she looked up, he sat there looking at her. "Drive, they might close early with this storm." She smiled; he'd bought her gummy bears. It was stupid, she knew that, but the idea that he had thought about her meant more than she could ever say out loud.

"Sorry about that," Zain said loudly. "We're dealing with a shit storm here."

Amari moved and grabbed her phone. "We're dealing with a blizzard here, Z. A heads up would have been nice."

"I'm supposed to be a weatherman now? I don't have time to send out weather reports—not with shit hitting the fan everywhere right now."

Amari frowned, then motioned for Tripp to drive. "Because of the storm?" She didn't like how panicked he sounded. Z was always a little bit of a drama queen, but he normally didn't lose it over anything unless it was important.

"The team's endeavors have come to a screeching halt, which has pissed everyone off, especially with you two nabbing a blood relative of Tomas—we're all afraid if we pause, they'll move everyone, and we'll have to start over."

Amari scowled at the windshield; she didn't know how Tripp was seeing where he was going. "The storm can't last that long—"

"The storm is not the only issue."

Dropping her feet to rest between the front seats, she leaned on the back of Tripp's and held the phone where he could hear and still focus on driving. "Break it down for us, Z."

"Shit—okay, we have Rayne stuck at the Sanctuary, thank god they made it back before the storm—so, Devin's pissed his mate is *that* far away." He sucked in a breath, "Calum and Shaelan are out for, we can't say how long. Obviously, Konner is stuck at home too, choppers can't fly in this crap, which by the way is supposed to last two days."

Tripp blew out a breath and leaned closer to the windshield. Two days of forced downtime never sat well with any of them that liked to keep moving. Or needed to keep moving, like herself and obviously Tripp.

"Asher and Foster, along with York and Jett, I don't even know who that is, are stranded doing transports to four different clans from people rescued in the last ops, because the camp—I'm sorry, *Arcadia* and the other facilities are full," Zain blew out a long breath, "Gia and Deacon have their own shit show right now with new clan members and an almost finished residence for them, but not finished enough. We have another female, Sloane, I think her name is, out for the duration of her *time* and headquarters is a fucking mess—secrets and hush-hush rotations of guards or team members watching your *prize* catch. Trying to keep things looking like it's biz as usual so our rat here doesn't tip anyone off—" when he sucked in another breath, she shook her head.

"Calm down, Z…"

"What? *Shit.* Hang on, guys." She could hear other voices in the room with Zain now.

Amari looked out the back window to see there was no visibility and then climbed over the seat and dropped down to sit. Tripp was focusing on the road they may or may not be driving on. There were no lanes, no markers to even tell where the ended and the ditch began, the wipers were going full speed trying to keep the windshield clear, but they were failing.

"Amari, where are you guys now?"

She glanced at Tripp again, he didn't look away from the windshield.

"Two," he chuffed, "three hours from the border. Hard to tell when I don't know where the road is."

"Okay, let me look," there were footsteps on hard tile, "coming from the Hughes clan—" he spoke slowly like he was dragging his fingers over a map.

"Do you know where the Harmon clan territory is?"

Tripp gave her a quick look and shook his head.

"I do." She said quickly.

"Okay. Okay, that could work."

"*What* could work, Z?"

He blew out a breath into the phone—

Tripp turned into what she thought might be a parking lot. How he'd found it in this storm she had no idea.

"We have a mother and her two teen daughters lost in the storm—a very upset mate and father along with an Alpha preventing him from going out searching without backup—the storm hit there before it moved across the map."

"Shit." She said softly.

"I know you can track anything, anywhere, Amari *and* I've heard nothing but the praises of Tripp Carson sung lately," he huffed out a quick breath, "can you guys go help? We literally have no way of getting anyone else there."

She looked over at Tripp when he stopped and put it into park.

"How long have they been gone?" He wiped his hair back from his face.

"Two hours, they were out on a nature walk when this hit," Zain answered in a voice that sounded like he rolled his eyes as he said it.

Tripped reached down and grabbed his run pack and opened it. "Show me," he handed her a folded waterproof map.

Amari set the phone on the dash and opened the map. Skimming her finger along it, she spotted the area the clan was in and tapped her finger on the plastic.

Tripp blew out a breath. "We're looking at least an hour out in this." He glanced out the window.

"It will be getting dark shortly after that," she added.

He nodded and then looked at the phone. "Do the daughters shift?"

"No," Zain answered. "They're thirteen and fifteen."

Amari grimaced, picturing the mother out there with two girls in what Amari thought of as the drama phase of their lives.

"Okay," Tripp nodded, "tell the Alpha we're on our way and for *everyone* to sit tight. We don't need a dozen people lost in this."

Zain blew out a relieved breath. "Will do."

"Call me when you get there, Amari, Jesse will be pacing even more than he already is."

Amari nodded and watched Tripp check the map and then reach for the GPS. "Okay, Z."

She hung up the phone and then climbed back into the back to check that he'd gotten candles and garbage bags. A trek in the storm wasn't something she thought they'd be doing.

"Your fruit is going to have to wait, darlin."

She paused to see him looking at her, "I know."

"What kind of clan is the Harmon clan?"

"Bobcat."

He nodded his head slowly and she could see him thinking it through. "Alpha is smart not letting Dad run out into the storm."

She frowned.

"This amount of snow and a breed that size…"

"Ah," she nodded, "yeah we'll manage in the deep snow better."

"Give me a kiss, darlin, this is going to be a tense trip," he smirked at her, already reaching for her.

Amari let Tripp pull her closer, "but you get to rush in and be the savior again. Twice in one week." She smirked.

He gave her a playful look, "it's what I do, babe." He cupped the back of her head and gave her a slow, thorough kiss that she felt all the way to her soul. When he pulled his lips from hers, his eyes locked on hers, "I was hoping to get stuck alone with you in this storm."

Her smile was slow, "if we get there, and find them, we could still get a day stranded somewhere before we head back to the teams."

"Being stranded never sounded so damn good." Releasing her, he jerked his chin toward the bags, "get those in the totes and then get buckled in, I'm going to need another pair of feline eyes to help me find the road."

Chapter Twenty-Seven

After emptying and repacking his bag with blankets and supplies they'd set out into the storm. The wind was strong and made visibility impossible. He hoped once they got down off the ridge, it would be easier to navigate. Their animals' coats and big paws were built for weather like this, so at least they weren't cold.

The worried-out-of-his-mind mate and father had given them a quick rundown of the land, and the general direction his females usually went. He had headed out and tried to find them, but in the blowing snow had lost his bearings and barely made it back. He was lucky he did, Tripp was struggling to get through it. He'd never seen one of this clan after shifting, but they weren't exceptionally tall on two legs, he'd noticed. That wasn't always a sure way of telling their animal size though. Any smaller than his animal's size and it would be really hard to navigate. His cat was large, probably weighed in around two-twenty.

He looked at the tail end of his mate that he was having to work hard keeping up with her right now as she zig-zag down into the valley. He hoped it was the valley and not the ravine they were warned about. Carrying the bag on his back was throwing off his balance and his speed, but at least his cat was working with him. He wasn't sure if it was because of the lost women out there in trouble, or from his mate barreling through the snowstorm ahead of him without an ounce of caution.

She came to a skidding stop and then glanced back at him. He knew she wasn't just standing there waiting for him. He caught up and stopped as quickly as she did. The ground dropped off in front of them. With the swirling snow, he couldn't make out how far down it went or the terrain—if there was any.

She looked at him again and even with her eyes in the form of her cat, he could see she was debating on going down the quick way. Tripp crouched down and moved toward the edge slowly, so the pack wouldn't tip him over it. He couldn't make out more than flashes of rock the snow hadn't covered yet. Backing away, he turned to her, with his shoulder he nudged her back from the edge and then looked toward the trees he could see the outline of. It would take longer to get down, but at least the ground didn't drop off into the unknown.

She made a low meow noise, which was the equivalent of no. He bumped against her again, hoping she was just messing with him. His cat was less than impressed that she was even considering it. If he wasn't wearing the heavy bag, it wouldn't be so bad, but he was, so it was out of the question. Her safety was more important than anything.

Amari turned and looked at the trees and then back at him, for the briefest second ever he thought she was going to go to the trees and head down that way, but then she bumped his shoulder in a playful way and leaped over the edge. Tripp's heart seized in his chest, he dropped down and tried to see her, the wind chose then to pick up and he couldn't see a damn thing.

He could take off the pack and follow her, but then when they did find the others, they would have no supplies—or clothes. With a loud shriek, he hoped reached her despite the wind, he let her know how unhappy he was with her move. He took off toward the trees. If one hair on her body was damaged in any way, he was going to be beyond pissed, and then he was going to—do something stupid he shouldn't—but had no idea what at this point.

Tripp skirted around a tree and jumped down off the ridge as he surveyed the area to try to determine the fastest way down without dying. His animal prevailed with more calm than he felt and poured on some reserved speed. Tripp wasn't sure if it was better to let his animal lead right now, but he couldn't shake the image of her lying on the ground injured. He was going to bite her when he found her, that much he knew.

His cat took a sharp turn, and the pack slid a bit to the side. Cursing in his head, he focused to help the animal keep balanced. His cat was stone-cold determined at this moment and wasn't taking any shit from him, their mate was down there somewhere, *and* three lost females.

His cat suddenly crouched, and they were sliding down an incline. Tripp was trying to figure out how he was managing it when he realized it was because it was the first snowstorm of the season and the grass and growth underneath weren't frozen, making it slick enough that his cat was basically skiing down into the valley.

The visibility was better as they reached the bottom. Now he was on board with his animal's plan and asserted himself, so he was back in charge. Tripp took off toward the area the father had told him they liked to walk. Scenting the air with each breath he inhaled, he hoped he could find his mate. It was faint and hard to pick up her trail, but his cat confirmed they were heading in the right direction. There was no scent of blood in the air, so he hoped that meant she wasn't hurt. He should have felt relief, and he may have on some deep level if he could think beyond the anger that fueled him. Normally Tripp had it under control, but he couldn't get beyond it this time. As soon as they got those women back to their clan, he was going to have to have a serious discussion with his mate about her reckless behavior. It stopped now; no excuses would be accepted.

Amari glanced behind her checking again for Tripp. Regret was a new feeling for her, but she was deep in right now. She shouldn't have taken off like she had and left him up there, knowing he couldn't follow with the extra weight. Her cat, who was normally on board for all kinds of adventure was doing something Amari had never felt, not in a very long time... concern. She was worried that he wouldn't get down here and find her.

Huffing out a breath, she came to a sliding stop and turned around. Visibility was better down here, but it still wasn't perfect. She scanned the entire scope of her vision, looking for him.

Swinging her head, she checked that she could still smell the floral scent, the kind that didn't come from nature. One of the girls missing was wearing some kind of perfume or spray and it was like a neon sign. It was getting fainter, which worried her, that their body temperature was dropping and not giving off the odor as much.

Checking once more for Tripp, she forced her cat to turn back in the other direction. He was a capable man; he would be just fine. Amari was annoyed that she was having to do this right now when every second counted. Once she found those lost and got them back to their warm home, she was going to have to do some soul-searching. She needed to decide if she wanted to do this for the rest of her life. *Care* about someone this way. She wasn't the cold heart others thought her to be. In truth it was quite the opposite, she felt too much. Feelings were a liability; she'd learned that one the hard way. It was okay to care or be concerned, but it was best to keep it on the inside. If she let it show, others would doubt her, and think she was too emotional to do the things she needed to do. She had a small circle of friends she would go to any lengths for, her team—now, she needed to figure out where Tripp fit in with that. Could he fit in with that? She couldn't be sure right now.

No time for this. Her cat interrupted. Her creature was much better at keeping emotions on lockdown.

With a growl, she swung her head to look straight ahead and lowered it so she could scan the ground for any evidence of someone walking this way. The new snowfall would make it hard, there would be no covered impressions in the snow, but a bent branch, or trampled plant was a pretty good indicator.

Her cat stopped unannounced and lifted her head. Amari inhaled, then wondered why then the sounds came to her. Someone was singing. She listened, blocking out every other sound, make that two singing. Mom was a smart one, distracting them by having them sing. It was also like ringing a bell and saying, 'here we are.' With slow steps, she let her cat find the direction it was coming from and then took off that way.

She would have run right past them if it hadn't been for the singing. Mom had them hunkered down under a small outcropping on the rock face, trees blocking it from view. Amari went through the trees and then stopped when a low warning growl came from the mother squatting in front of her two girls.

Amari sat right there and lifted her head high, hoping Mom would see that she was wearing a run pack and wasn't some hungry mountain lion looking for a snack.

"It has a pack on, Mom." One of the girls said quietly.

The mother straightened and then her shoulders slumped in relief. "I don't know who you are or why you're here, but I'm really glad to see you." She offered an empty smile.

Amari assessed quickly that they were uninjured, just cold, and scared. She continued to sit in the same spot, so Tripp would be able to find her, she could do nothing to help them when he had all the supplies. She looked over her shoulder to see if she could spot him.

"Are you waiting for others?" One of the girls asked. "See, Mom, Dad sent someone to find us."

"Yeah, you can stop worrying he's lost now."

Amari didn't have to look back to see which one had spoken, that bored sarcastic tone could only come from the older of the two children. Teens, she really didn't understand them at all.

She watched Tripp clear the trees and slide to a stop. His sides were heaving from the run, but his eyes locked on her, not the ones they were supposed to be looking for. Amari didn't need words to know he was pissed with her stunt and if he could speak right now, he'd be telling her she was a bad, bad kitty.

She got up and gave him room to move into the tiny space.

"They have a backpack. Tell me you brought mittens." The younger of the two girls said.

Tripp hunkered down and looked at the mom. With cautious movements, she shuffled over to him and stretched out an arm to release the clasp at his side. They may be here to rescue them, but she was still wary of the larger, strangers being near her children. Pulling the pack free from his head, she moved back and opened it quickly.

Tripp gave Amari another 'we're going to talk about this later' look and then went back out through the trees.

Amari decided she was better off staying in cat form at that point. She didn't need to be airing her issues in front of these females with her mate. She paused in thought at that. *Her mate.* Snapping her head back around, she looked to see the mother wrapping a blanket around the two girls. When she pulled out a packet with one of the mylar blankets in it, she gave her a confused look.

"Wrap them over the warm blankets." Tripp crawled into the space and nudged Amari as he went by her.

Amari noted, he was in some sort of track pants and t-shirt, and that black beanie. She'd never considered keeping a pair for those times when she needed to shift back and forth. She lay down and watched as he pulled other items out of the bag.

"I'm Tripp," he motioned with his head, "that's Amari, we're from the Alliance."

"They called the Alliance?" The mom sounded surprised.

"We were in the neighborhood." He shrugged it off like it was no biggie that they'd driven through a storm to get here as quickly as they could manage. He held out a bottle of water to the oldest girl, "hydrate, it helps."

She nodded and took the bottle from him.

Amari watched him pull out the can and then a candle. "This is my mate's brilliant idea," he glanced at her, a faint smile on his face, "let's warm up those hands."

"I never would have thought of something like that." Mom said as he lit the candle and set the can closer to them. She looked over at Amari, "thank you, for finding us."

"Once you're warmed up, we're going to head back to the village." Tripp offered the youngest a protein bar, "this storm is going to last a couple of days, so even if we have to make a few stops along the way, it's better that we do it now and not tomorrow."

The mother nodded, but her expression was filled with worry. "It will be easier with the two of you leading the way."

Tripp only nodded to that and then set a garbage bag on the ground and sat down. He leaned back and rested his hand on Amari's hip like this was something they did all the time. She looked at his hand and then to his face, his eyes said a serious discussion was imminent, and his mouth twitched with a smirk as he chewed on some jerky. She dropped her head onto her paws and looked away from him. The last thing she needed was someone to harp on her over everything thing she did, if that was what this mate stuff was all about, his talk was going to go in a totally different direction than he planned.

Chapter Twenty-Eight

Tripp jammed the last of his gear in the bag and did it up. He glanced at the door again to see the snow was still coming down. Sighing, he looked at his phone, Kenzo had told him to hang on and hadn't returned yet. Amari hadn't returned either. She'd been ushered off to the home of those they'd found while he'd elected to get things back in order with his gear. He was so aggravated right now; he didn't know which way was up.

"Sorry about that, quick strategy session."

Grabbing the phone, Tripp took it off the speaker and put it to his ear. He leaned against the workbench and stared at the door, "ops canned?"

"Temporarily, but if we can't move in this weather, neither can they. The cities are basically shut down during weather like this, so that's in our favor."

This wasn't what he wanted to hear; they were so close to hitting the jackpot as far as finding Tomas' people. This was personal, his father had died because of the Tomas family. His loss wasn't directly connected, but the rogues wouldn't have been rogues if it weren't for them trying to hide their females from the Tomas family. Until they got all his movers and shakers, they would never stop him.

"We're regrouping and hoping to pull off a few more, despite the weather. I want you to head to us, as best as you can in this."

Tripp nodded, "it will be slow, but we'll get there." He watched Amari come back into the garage. She was wearing a bright red, puffy jacket and matching toque, both caked with snow. She looked like an ad you'd see on a billboard for a winter vacation destination. Shaking his head, he raised an eyebrow in question to which she shrugged and then came over and held out a piece of jerky. From the smell of it, he knew it wasn't some prepacked product. His stomach growled, reminding him he hadn't eaten any real food in a while. Taking it from her hand, he took a bite and then tracked her every move. She set a bag in the front seat.

"There's going to be a short break in the weather, maybe an hour, then it's going to be bad—according to the weather radar."

He'd almost forgotten Kenzo was on the phone. Blinking to tear his gaze from her, he looked outside to see how heavy the snowfall was, it looked like a solid white blanket. "When's the break starting?"

"Half hour, if this app is right."

"We'll cover as much ground as we can."

"If it gets bad, Tripp, find somewhere to hole up until it passes."

"What kind of timeline are we looking at for the new ops?" Amari was doing what he could only call housekeeping on the inside of his ride. Wiping off the dash, the door—

"It's going to take us a few days to get enough bodies back here to do anything substantial."

Tripp nodded, that worked for him—he still had to deal with his mate. He had no plans to walk into an op with his head scrambled and emotions all over the place. It was a good way to get dead if his focus wasn't on point.

Amari took off the hat and jacket and put them in the back seat. She turned around and tilted her head in question.

"We'll be heading out in five." He told his leader in a quiet voice.

"Keep me updated on your progress. We have members stranded in the North; they can't move a foot right now. The fewer trying to travel in this, the better."

Tripp was glad they'd already been heading South before this had hit. He watched Amari put her belt back on and then adjust her boots. "We'll be careful." He needed to hang up, the longer he stood there watching her, the more his anger flared again, the image of her lying broken at the bottom of that ravine playing in his head on a loop.

"Check in later." The line went quiet.

Tripp tucked the phone in his back pocket.

"They packed us a picnic." She motioned to the bag on her seat. "Guess it will be an indoor one." Leaning on the door, she looked outside.

Food was the last thing he was thinking about right now. "We'll eat once we're on the road. The storm is supposed to pause for a short break, so I want to get as far as we can before then."

Her expression changed to a more focused one. "What's the status of the ops?"

"Snafu currently, but they're hoping to get something together in a few days."

Amari smirked, "Snaf what?"

Tripp blinked, "uh, situation normal all…"

"Got it. Snafu, I like that." She grinned. "Okay, so the game plan is to try to get to them before winter wonderland takes over?"

He nodded, almost willing to forgive her for scaring the hell out of him earlier when she smiled at him like that. The image of her lying broken and unmoving at the bottom of the ravine flashed through his mind and later he'd try to figure out if it had been prompted by his animal or his mind.

Amari put her hands on her hips. "Well, let's get the lecture over with so we can get on the road."

"Lecture?" Tripp grit his teeth, "you think I'm going to lecture you?"

She lifted one shoulder and let it drop, "yeah, I caught the looks from you when we found them."

Tripp jammed his hands in his pockets so he wouldn't go over and shake her. "That look didn't mean I was going to lecture you."

She cocked one eyebrow at him, "no?" Another half shrug, "what then?"

Jerking his hands out of his pocket, he took four long strides toward her and then clamped down on his temper, "you were reckless." The growl in his tone was his animal letting them both know he was close and wanted in on this discussion.

She snorted softly, "and?" She scowled at him, "your S.O., I thought they got off on that?"

Tripp opened his mouth and then shut it so fast his teeth clacked together. She wasn't entirely wrong. "Not when other lives are at stake." He ground his teeth briefly, trying to force his mind to find the words to explain it to her. "Those women needed us to find them."

"We did." She crossed her arms over her chest and glared back at him.

"You had no idea what was hidden by the snow and wind when you jumped over the edge."

She shrugged again and he had to bite back a growl, "I managed."

Something inside him broke loose and he couldn't stand here and try to discuss this like a rational person a second longer. Two strides had him right up in her face, his hand spanning her throat to get her attention. "You knew I couldn't follow," he ground out through his teeth, "that I wouldn't have your back if you ran into a problem."

Amari inhaled slowly, holding his look steady, she made no move to try to break his grip on her neck. "I knew you'd get down to me in no time."

"That's not the point, Amari."

At the mention of her name, her pupils dilated ever slightly, "what is the point, Tripp?"

Her voice wasn't shaking, her tone was even and that annoyed him more than anything else. The fact that she wasn't on the offensive as he held her back against the open door. She just stood there, unaffected by it. "We're mates." His voice was softer, his emotions close to tipping to somewhere he didn't want to go. "If anything had happened…"

"So, I'm supposed to tippy-toe around forever now because I have a mate?"

Was she? Would he have to? He had no idea where any of this shit led to, none at all. "You're not alone now." It dawned on him that he wasn't either.

"Yeah, I got that." She sounded bored.

How could she not care that his hand was wrapped around her throat? His animal stirred, coming closer to the surface.

"Either fucking kiss me, Tripp, or let me go before I hurt you." She pushed her knee between his legs and rubbed it against him.

His body responded immediately and not in a defensive way. He was one sick bastard, and she was his equal in all ways. He flexed his hand around her throat as he leaned down and crushed her mouth under his.

"Oh good, I was afraid you'd already left."

They jumped apart and turned to see the youngest of the girls they'd found standing behind them. She was wrapped in a blanket and not even wearing a jacket.

Tripp cleared his throat and jammed his hands into his pockets. "We're heading out in a minute." The kid either had the best or worst timing, he couldn't be sure.

She smiled up at him and then came over and hugged him tightly. "Thank you." She released him and pivoted to do the same to Amari, "I forgot to say thank you."

Amari looked uncomfortable with the hug. "No problem." She crossed her arms over her chest as soon as the child moved away.

"I want to be like you." The girl looked up at Amari, her eyes drowning in adoration, "when I'm bigger." She smiled, "I want to help people."

The frosty exterior Amari had melted right before his eyes as she reached over and touched the side of the girl's head, "work hard and don't take any sh—guff from the boys, okay?"

The girl nodded. "Okay." She jerked her head to look at Tripp, then back to Amari, "I want my mate to be just like him."

Amari smirked and looked him up and down, "that's a good goal to have." She looked down at her and winked, "now get back in the house and stay there until this storm is gone."

The girl's head bobbed up and down. "Have a safe trip." She hopped a few steps and then ran out into the snow.

Tripp shoved his hair back from his face and cleared his throat, "We better get moving."

Amari held his look for a moment, there was something in her eyes he couldn't figure out. She turned her back to him and got in his SUV before he could figure it out.

Blowing out a breath, he looked around to make sure all their gear was loaded and then moved over to close the back. He needed to drive and focus on something other than her for a bit like that was going to happen. Once he closed his door, every breath he took was going to be tinged with her scent, her taste. It was going to be a tense drive—the snow was the least of his worries.

Chapter Twenty-Nine

The break in the weather didn't last long, or it didn't seem like it did. They'd abandoned the idea of using the main highway to cut back on time. With the lack of plows and other drivers' lack of ability, they'd had to get off as soon as Amari had plotted a new route.

He'd been preoccupied with Amari and her stunt, the little girl's comments, and the fact that all he could smell was his mate. Now he had no time for other thoughts, and it was taking all of his focus to find and stay on the road, moving forward. The snow on the road was deep and with the amount still coming down it was only going to get worse. "You'd think it would eventually run out of steam—or snow."

"It's Ontario. The weather does not follow any norms here. Ever." He heard her shifting around in her seat but didn't dare take his eyes off the road. At least he hoped they were still on the road.

Tripp's stomach growled, reminding him he still hadn't eaten. "I'm about ready to chew on my hat." He leaned closer to the windshield, hoping that helped him not feel hypnotized by the motion of the wipers.

"Do you want some of the food they sent?"

He heard her unwrapping something and the smell of food immediately filtered to him. Tripp didn't want to stop; they may never get going again. Driving one-handed right now was out of the question. Before he could answer, her hand with food in it appear in front of his mouth.

"This will be safer, I think."

He took a bite of the sandwich and wasn't entirely sure what kind of meat it was, but it tasted heavenly.

"Nothing tastier than a Bambi sandwich." Amari chuckled.

Swallowing, he grinned, "since when do you do things safer?"

The sandwich that had been in front of him again was jerked back. "There's a time for safe and there's not."

"Jumping off a ravine was safe?" Now probably wasn't the best time to get back into that, but his mouth already said it.

"Yeah. In cat form, safe has different boundaries. While driving with no visibility, it's time to be extra safe."

Tripp grinned; he really couldn't argue much with any of that. Before meeting her, he would have jumped off the ravine too. Instead of starving from pissing her off, he opened his mouth and heard her soft snort as she shoved the sandwich in his mouth for him to bite. The back end kicked out and slid sideways. By the time he corrected it, he had the entire sandwich hanging out of his mouth as she braced for the slide.

Reaching over, she took a hold of it again and allowed him to get a bite.

"You should put your seat belt back on."

"It's driving me crazy; I feel trapped." She paused, and blew out a breath, "I don't do well in storms like this, too many bad moments when I was on my own." Out of the corner of his eye, he watched her lean forward to look out the windshield. "Are we pushing the snow like a plow?"

Tripp finished chewing and swallowed it. "Yeah, for the last twenty minutes."

She leaned forward and looked out his window and then hers. "Is this even a road?"

"Pretty sure." He had no idea at this rate, just hoped no trees jumped in their path. He saw it but didn't have time to react, some kind of blue sign. The post for it dinged off the passenger mirror and he winced. At least it was on the right side, so they still must be on the road. "See. Road."

"No, I can't and that was a little close, special operations."

"My mirror is wrecked, could be worse, could be a broken window."

"We should stop before we have to dig out in the morning."

Tripp inhaled slowly, then tried to blow some of the tension out. "Stopping in the middle is a bad plan and I can't see shit to pull us over anywhere."

"Want me to get out and lead the way?"

Tripp scowled at the snow outside, "no, I could end up running over you."

"I didn't mean I would stand in front of the vehicle, just figure out where the road ends and ditch starts." He heard the rustling of material, "the jacket is bright red, you will be able to see me."

Tripp hated this plan. Why did all of her plans make sense, but put her at risk? Every one of them. He would look ridiculous if he stopped, made her drive, and went outside himself. He glanced in the mirror but saw nothing but white. "Can you see any lights behind us?"

She chortled, "I think we're the only ones still trying to drive in this."

He sighed; she was right. He was just about to stop when her phone rang.

"That you, Z?" She sounded like she was chewing. He chanced a quick glance; she was eating the rest of the sandwich.

"Yes. Where the hell are you? You didn't check in."

Amari laughed, "I didn't know I had to when I'm with, Special operations."

"Considering the weather, yeah a check-in would have been good."

"Okay." She leaned forward and tapped the windshield. There were trees close to the road. "No idea where we are, we can't see a damn thing." Tripp inched the tires toward the tree, just enough that they'd hopefully be off the road. "We're just stopping now."

"You're still driving?"

"Yeah." She was chewing again. He hoped there were more sandwiches left.

"Everyone else gave up over an hour ago." Zain sounded tired. "Look, pullover, rest, and hope that by morning it's settled down. I need sleep and I can't do that with a member of the team out playing in the snow."

Amari chuckled, "okay. Go sleep. We're stopping."

Tripp put his window down and stuck his head out, he tried to see behind them, beside them and it was a whirl of blowing snow. Putting the window up, he gave his head a shake to get the snow off. He checked the gas gauge. Half tank. They wouldn't be able to leave it too long, considering he had no idea exactly where they were on the map. That was the problem with low visibility, you could feel like you'd been driving for hours, but hadn't really and didn't make it very far. He glanced at his mate to see her smiling at him. He'd worry about the location and fuel later—much later.

Chapter Thirty

The pain in his shoulder woke him. A stabbing pain? Inhaling, Tripp fought through the fog to wake up. Amari's scent filled him, making him smile despite the ache in his shoulder. Leaning back from her warm body, he reached to see what was causing the pain. He couldn't move it any further. Squinting, he turned to see his arm stuck in the sleeve of the red puffy jacket Amari had been given. He smirked, not even wanting to know how that happened. Jerking it out of the sleeve, he moved his hand around until it connected with cold metal. His gun. He pushed it out of the way and then opened his eyes. His bladder was also trying to get his attention. He didn't want to leave the warmth of her naked flesh pressed against his, but he knew she'd want to go for a run as soon as she was awake, and shifting with a full bladder was a 'never do that again' kind of deal.

Tucking the blanket over her, he grabbed his pants and flipped them over twice to find the right way in. Leaning back, he pulled them over his hips and looked around for his boots. He might go out in the snow with no shirt on, but he hated cold feet. Wiping his hand over the window, he checked to see if it was still snowing. He smirked; he'd be okay if it was too bad to drive. They hadn't discussed the status of being mates or spoke many words at all, just spent hours exploring each other and being close. His cat was more than happy with the outcome—for now.

Crawling carefully, so as to not wake her, he reached for his missing boot at the back of the vehicle. This was going to be a quick in and out bladder drain, his arms were already covered in bumps from the chill. Once Amari was awake, he'd start the SUV and let the heat blast to defrost all the windows. Jumping out the door, he closed it just enough that the cold air wouldn't filter into her. Snow filled his boots, he looked down at them like they'd just betrayed him.

When he turned to get back in, a movement out of the corner of his eye got his attention, his cat was right there now. There was someone out here, along the snowed-covered road. Getting back in, he shuffled over to his rifle case and popped it open. Grabbing the scope off it without having to look for the slide to release it, he moved to the back window and cleared a small spot to look out it. "Shit." He jolted back and dove for the front where his phone was.

"Amari, babe, wake up, we've got company." He brought up Kenzo's number and hit it as he jammed the bud into his ear.

"What?" She groaned sleepily but sat up at the same time.

"Tripp?"

"We've got someone coming up behind us, walking." He told both his boss and the naked woman looking better than anything he'd ever seen in his life. With automated movements, he put his scope back on his rifle and then flipped the blanket out of the way to find his gun.

"Who are they?" Amari sat up completely and leaned toward the back window.

"Maybe they're stuck in the storm." Kenzo sounded like he'd been sleeping too.

"One has a rifle," she sounded annoyed. "I can't see what's in the other one's hand."

Tripp shuffled to the back and looked out the scope, "tranq gun, it looks like."

"Not friendlies." Kenzo's tone was colder now, more business as usual as opposed to the 'why am I awake' one he'd had a few moments ago.

Amari moved past him as he snarled at the offensive people moving toward them. This was not the way he'd planned on starting the day. With slow movements, he flipped the window lock and opened the small window as much as he could. He was not shooting through his damn window, driving with an open window in this weather was not happening.

"Who the fuck are you?" He said quietly as he lined the rifle up out the window. The sound of shattering glass echoed a split second before the pain in his shoulder did.

"What the hell was that?" Kenzo barked.

Tripp dropped down from the view of the window and looked to see blood free flowing from his shoulder down his arm.

Amari was laying belly down looking at him.

"They fucking shattered my back window." He told his boss.

"Were you hit?" Kenzo hissed into the phone.

Tripp hissed out a breath and forced himself to ignore the pain, "yes. Shoulder."

"Take them out." His commander ordered.

Blowing out a breath, Tripp forced his mind back into work mode. "I need a distraction; they're going to take my face off as soon as I'm visible."

"I've got this," Amari whispered.

By the time her words registered, he was watching the door close. "Amari." He growled, but she kept moving away from the vehicle. "Fuck."

"Tripp?"

He ignored his leader. "Fuck." He hunkered down, blocking the fact that the smell of his own blood was filling his nostrils, and lined up the rifle with the bottom of where his window used to be. "She's fucking naked." He growled and then getting shot or not, he lined his scope up with the males coming toward them. "She just fucking went outside to greet them fucking naked." He snarled.

"Uh, cover her," Kenzo answered.

"What the fuck do you think I'm doing? I'm going to kill her," he clenched his teeth together, forcing his arm to stop shaking, he didn't care if all the blood drained out of it, his mate was out there. "She's sashaying through three fucking feet of snow, naked for fuck sake." Both men were looking at his naked mate like she was something they needed to conquer.

"Tripp." Kenzo barked.

"What?" He snapped back at him.

"Take the fucking shot."

A split-second decision had him take out the one with the rifle. A tranq wasn't lethal to either of them. Tripp winced from the impact of the rifle with his shoulder as the recipient of the bullet landed on the snow-covered ground. By the time he adjusted his sights, Amari was right in the other one's face, she spun around and that's when Tripp caught the flash of metal in her hand. When her hand was lowered again, it was painted red in the other one's blood. She paused and looked down at the body where it dropped in front of her and then spun on her heel and jogged back toward him.

Tripp dropped his rifle and flopped back, relief filling him. Reaching blindly, he grabbed the first material his hand connected with and held it against his shoulder. "Both targets down." He blew out a breath.

Amari climbed back in and slammed the door shut. Dropping the bloody blade, she crawled over to him and took the material out of his hand, "how bad?" She leaned around him and looked at his back, then turned and looked at the back of the passenger's seat. "Straight through, a shift should heal it." She smirked at him, "your seat, not so much."

"Fuck." They'd broken his window and shot a hole in his leather seat.

"Did she say straight through?"

Amari leaned down and licked the blood trailing down his arm, a shiver went through Tripp, and it wasn't from the cold. Lifting her face away, she looked at him with blood-red lips. His cat was almost convulsing with anticipation.

"Tripp?"

He heard his team leader, but when she gently licked over the oozing hole in his shoulder and then pressed her nose into his neck and inhaled a deep breath, he couldn't have spoken if he tried. Tripp started to lift his hand to hold her, but his cat conveyed that was a bad idea.

"I guess I better take you on, to keep your ass from getting dead." Her hot breath was against his throat and in the haze of the pain, he realized that was her way of saying she accepted him, he tilted his head to the side. Her hot wet tongue licked over the cord of muscle in his neck and then her sharp feline teeth pierced the skin. Tripp groaned and then grabbed her hair tight in his hand, wanting her to stay there longer.

"Tripp? What the fuck is happening? I thought you said it was your shoulder?"

He closed his eyes, a smirk on his face despite his commander's voice bellowing in his ear. Amari released his flesh, and he opened his eyes to see her smiling at him, she reached over and plucked the earbud out of his ear.

Licking the blood off her lips, she put it in her ear, "Tripp is busy right now; you'll have to call back later." Reaching over, she ran her finger through the blood on his arm and then raised the finger in slow motion and put it in her mouth. When she pulled it back out, she smiled, "We'll investigate that in a few minutes, Mister Dean, I'm trying to claim a mate here." Lowering the phone, she tossed it in the direction of the dash. Her gaze moved down his chest, "mmm, might want to send them in on snowmobiles." Taking the bud out of her ear, she tossed it over her shoulder.

Tripp patted along the side where he was sure he'd dropped his gun, finding it, he looked away from her long enough to set it in the door handle where it could be easily found.

Amari's expression sobered, "you really should shift and heal that."

Tripp glanced down at his shoulder, "I'll live a few more minutes," he motioned with his finger for her to come over, "come here, first."

She grinned, "shouldn't you tag our location so they can find us?" She glanced at the broken window, "we should move the bodies."

"Fuck it, they can chill out there for a few minutes."

A serious look filled her eyes. "I didn't think I'd want this." She moved closer, "but now, there's this feeling, I've never had." She licked her sexy mouth, and he had a hard time focusing on her words. "Do you feel it too?"

Fighting through the lust, he nodded, she needed words right now and whatever his mate needed, she would get. "The hollow feeling is gone."

She stopped, close enough that her breath was on his mouth. "Yeah, that's it."

Tripp could see the emotions going through her eyes, questions, and doubts. He reached with the arm blood wasn't running down and cupped the side of her head. "What's say we seal the deal, darlin?" He gave her a daring look, "then get back to work and slaughter every last one helping Tomas."

"Mmm," she smiled, "you say the sweetest things, mate."

Later he knew he'd have to contain her, as she wreaked havoc and revenge on all involved in the cruel world they were fighting to clean up, but for now, he planned to tire out his unpredictable, uncontrollable, and slightly violent woman. She bit his lip not gently in any way. She was so perfect for him.

Torment

Animal Senses Series Book 10

By Jacqueline Paige

Chapter One

As drives went, that one had been intense. Blaise put the truck in park and blew out some of the tension. Visibility at best was five feet in front of the vehicle. Her truck was built for off-roading and it was a good thing, much of the drive had been through snow that would have bogged down her Alliance ride. Even the few times she could see, she wasn't sure if she was on a road or making her own. She wasn't one hundred percent sure she was at the right location now. There hadn't been any gaps that could have been a turnoff, so she hoped this was the place. The last part of the drive was through trees, they had been the only indicator she was going in the right direction. The snow was blowing so much she couldn't see anything. Was there a house or something here? There had to be. Why did they send her here?

Grabbing her phone, she messaged her boss, Kenzo. Maybe now he'd give her some details. The cryptic instructions she'd been given were to get here any way possible, tell no one, and then she'd be filled in. It had taken her a day and the weather had done all it could to prevent her from going anywhere. She couldn't remember such a vast snowstorm before. She kept hoping she'd drive out of it eventually but hadn't. If anything, the closer she got to this mountain the worse it got.

Her phone rang, and she answered without pausing to see who it was. Not many called her.

"Blaise." It was the boss.

"I made it." She had already told him that in the message, but after that drive, she'd thought it bared repeating.

"You used your own vehicle, right?"

She nodded slowly, "That's probably the only reason I got through it."

"Good. There's no way you were tracked then."

She grinned, "good luck to anyone tracking *anything* in this weather."

"Yeah, it's a mess out there."

"Why am I here, Kenzo?" She put the window down a few inches and tried to see through the blowing snow. A gust of wind blew snow in her face. She closed the window.

"Roughly twenty feet into the bush there's a small shed. I'll send you the key code to get in. There's a sled inside to get you up the mountain."

Blaise leaned forward and caught glimpses of 'the mountain'. The wipers were pushing snow, but not able to keep up with it. She was going up there?

"Raymond says you go straight up from that shed, there's a trail cut through the trees. When you can't go any further, you hang a left and it will take you to the cabin."

"Raymond Hardy?"

"Yeah. This is his personal getaway spot."

Blaise raised both eyebrows and looked out the windshield again. "What am I doing at this cabin?"

She heard Kenzo suck in a breath and blow it out. "Watching Aiden Tomas' half-brother, a half-breed, until we can figure out what we're doing with him."

"I'm sorry, did you say Aiden Tomas' brother is a half-breed?"

"Yes, I did. Tripp and Amari got him."

Blaise stiffened, the exhaustion from her long drive was gone. She opened her mouth and then closed it. "How long have we had him?"

"Just before the storm hit."

"Does Tomas know?"

"He has to by now."

She started to ask if he wanted her to 'persuade' information out of him, but he cut her off.

"Hold on."

There were other voices in the background and wondered where her boss had gotten snowed in. All the teams were stuck at various locations and all of their plans to breach Tomas' locations and free their kind had come to an abrupt halt. No one was happy about it. Blaise had been escorting a few collared rescues when the storm hit. Fortunately for her, the center was near HQ and her own ride had been parked in an underground lot she used when in the area.

"Tell them to go see if they can find their vehicle and tag it." He cleared his throat, "sorry, Tripp saw a bit of action this morning."

"Everything good?"

"Yeah. They were somehow tailed in this storm and thought they'd catch them off guard at dawn."

Blaise smirked, "How'd that go for them?"

"Tripp took one out, Amari," he snorted, "got the drop on the other. Trying to get clean up there right now is a fucking nightmare."

Blaise had dealings with Amari a few times and she had nothing but respect for her. "Amari's out of control, I like her style."

Kenzo laughed, "well, her mate, Tripp, isn't sure he does."

Her eyes widened, "they're mates? That's awesome." She chuckled, "he's outta control too. Good match." Lately, everyone was finding their *fated* mate. She rolled her eyes at the thought. A part of her was happy for them, but then there was her reality, that didn't leave room for happy, gooey thoughts and wishes.

"You can say that because you don't have to try to control Tripp."

"I don't think anyone can control Tripp, Boss."

"Don't I know it. At least you don't openly defy *every* order. Message me when you find the cabin. Graham Watts from Raymond's team is there right now, but he is needed elsewhere. Take all your gear with you, I don't know how long you'll be up there."

She nodded, "any instructions on what I can or can not do with the prisoner?"

"Unknown at this time, we're waiting on word from Devin Addison. He is tagged though, by Tomas, so he can *not* leave the Faraday cage he's in. It's shielded from all signals."

"Tomas tagged his brother?"

"He's a half-breed, Blaise, given how the Tomas family feels about our kind, we're still astounded he's been allowed to live."

What kind of life would that be? To share blood with a man that thought of their kind as pets? "Yeah." Was the only response she gave him. She couldn't talk about Tomas or what those they rescued went through. It just sent her into a murderous frenzy. *Focus on the task.*

"Objective until further notice, keep him safe and alive. You good to head up now, or do you need a short rest?"

"I'm all aces, boss."

"Good. Probably an hour's ride in this weather, so get your bearings and head up now."

"Will do." She listened as he hung up. "Aiden Tomas' half-brother." She blew out a breath, "this is going to be a helluva ride." She glanced at herself in the mirror her green eyes were flecked with amber, telling her that her cat was close and ready for some fun. At least now she understood the secrecy. Turning the truck off, she stowed her keys in her run pack and grabbed a hair elastic. She made fast work of getting her hair braided and off her face all while avoiding looking at herself in the mirror again. The dark skin on the right side of her body from her jaw down didn't bother her anymore, but that didn't mean she wanted to *see* it either. She'd accepted her life, but then again, she had no choice. No one with a brain dared ever call her a mixed breed, but that didn't mean it wasn't true. The secrecy regarding that topic in her own family told her it was one hundred percent fact and someday, she was going to find out all the nasty details about it.

She felt the truck rock in a gust of wind and decided to go find the snowmobile before she hauled all her gear there. She stared at her phone waiting for the code to be sent before she put it in her pack. Had Kenzo purposely chosen her to do this? Get the abomination to watch the half-breed? She didn't know, but it didn't matter. He didn't treat her differently and she respected him for that. Besides, she had orders, and she'd carry them through without question. She owed Kenzo a lot, he'd recruited her when she was at a crossroads in her life. One direction on that road would have led to the end of her existence, and further humiliation for her family. Today, she'd proceed like any other day, follow her instructions and not deviate from them. If she got to beat someone or kill something along the way, even better.

KEEP READING FOR AN EXCERPT OF

The Huntress

Alterealm Series Book 1

By J. Risk

Chapter One

I didn't even get both eyes opened and focused before I knew something was wrong. Where was the color? I was only seeing sepia? Everything was brown. Blinking rapidly, I tried to readjust my eyes to see if there was any other hue. It didn't change a thing and for the life of me I couldn't figure out why.

Sitting there, I tried to decipher what was going on and why I was sitting on the ground. Looking down I ran my hand over the dried dusty surface. Why was I on the ground? Craning my neck as far as I could in all directions, I looked around. Okay, where was the pavement and cement? The buildings and streets I called my natural turf?

The why's flying around in my brain suddenly decided the top question, was what the *hell* was going on?

Squeezing my eyes shut, I struggled to recall the last thing I remembered doing. I was hunting down a bounty—a nice one with a large dollar sign attached to her. I had tracked her ass down and…

I confronted her? Yes, I was minutes away from calling Frank and telling him to get out his shiny pen and sign my check.

So what happened between then and now? Not to sound repetitive, which is something that drives me nuts, but *what* the hell was going on?

Startled, I started to check for bullet holes or the deep crevices that knives leave behind in flesh. That had to be it, I'd taken a beating and this was that in between place you sit when your near death's door, but not quite ready to see what lies on the other side.

Finding no critical injury, I slumped forward and rubbed my head. There was some rational explanation for this, there had to be. Had I been drugged? It could be some crazy hallucination. Any minute now I was going to either wake up in my bed at home or some hospital with a cheery nurse leaning over me, reassuring me we are going to be *just* fine. I only had to wait it out a little longer and all would be normal.

To kill time until I woke up, I looked around some more. Wherever this was it looked like a burnt-out world. Not the charred kind of burn, but depleted and completely used up sort.

Vacant.

Sitting still wasn't really a strong trait of mine, so I figured I'd get up and take a look around, there had to be something to see around here. If my body was actually somewhere else for safekeeping, what harm could come to me, right?

I staggered like I'd never stood before, struggling to get my balance. Whatever was going on with me, my equilibrium was totally shot. Standing there swaying like grass in the breeze, I turned carefully trying to see if there was anything around me except rust tinted dirt and nothingness.

My heart stumbled around in my chest when I spotted someone coming in my direction. Yes! I wasn't the only one in this soulless place.

The closer it got to me made me the more I questioned my original conclusion. I didn't know, exactly, but it was not some*one* it was a some*thing*. No one label could describe it. Standing over six feet, it had the shape of a man dressed in jeans and a large, very out of fashion gingham snap up shirt. When I reached the face, I can only describe it as part wrinkle puppy dog with floppy skin crossed with Freddy and Jason after the slash scenes.

It stopped in front of me and instinct had me reach around behind me under my jean jacket for my raptor claw knife, which I put on as regular as underwear when dressing; and that would be everyday, by the way. Relief washed over me when I felt the small circular handle. At least while waiting to survive I got to bring my toys with me.

Big brown eyes assessed me slowly and I wanted to make the call that it was harmless, but yeah, having tracked down anything from a sicko killer to a card shark in the last three years, I knew better than to fall for sappy looks.

"Are you a magishian? You juisht appeared."

A male voice, even though he spoke with a heavy lisp that randomly inserted *ish* into his words. Then again if I had saggy lips like he did, I'd be happy to talk at all. I sized him up for a few more seconds, trying to gauge whether he was really in front of me, or if I was having some sort of psychotic episode. Was a magician good or bad? I decided the play dumb, being blonde did have *some* advantages. "A magician?"

Those brown eyes developed a nervous quiver. Magician equaled bad. "No…"

He looked relieved. "Oh good. I didn't want to have to bash you over the head."

I grasped my raptor tightly and shrugged. "Yeah, me either."

The sky brightened and began to glow a rust orange color. When I asked for some color, I'd hoped for something out of the orange family.

"We better go, they'll be coming soon."

"They?" I glanced around quickly, not wanting to take my eyes off him for long.

He nodded and pranced on the spot, the nervous movement had me on high alert. "The daywalkers." He whispered.

Daywalkers? Did I even want to know? I didn't think so, but this bizarre nightmare wasn't going to be complete if I didn't ask.

Looking me over a few times, his eyes widened under the pressure of his drooping forehead; *that* was quite the expression. "You're not one of them, are you?"

I walked in the day, night and even at dusk, but I wasn't going to tell him that. I decided honesty might work, if not violence was always a good backup. Judging by his expression daywalker ranked on the bad list with magician. "I—I don't know what you'd call me."

Those sappy eyes looked me up and down a few times trying to figure me out. "You better come with me. It's not safe to leave you wandering around." He looked behind him and then motioned behind me and started walking.

I knew in my gut it was a mistake, but as I had no other real options… I didn't know where I was or what was going on and so far he knew more than I did. "Where are we going?"

Pausing he glanced over his shoulder and then lumbered along again. "I'll take you to Troy, he'll know what to do."

My eyes were starting to strain as the sky brightened. "This Troy, he's in charge?"

He stopped so suddenly I almost ploughed right into his back. When he turned and looked at me, his eyes weren't a sad brown any more but were leaning more towards red. It had to be from the strange color of the sunrise. "You're not from Alterealm are you?"

"Is that where we are?"

He nodded.

"Nope."

That nervous jitter of his seemed to return all at one. "How did you get here?"

A reasonable question that I had nothing to offer that resembled an answer. "I don't know that either."

His red eyes darted to the sky. "We have to go."

Turning, he began jogging toward, well, nothing that I could see. Not wanting to find out what he was afraid of, I ran along behind him. All I could think was this Troy person, if he was a person, better have some answers.

He stopped again and dropped down onto his knees. Was he hurt? Surely that short jaunt hadn't winded him that much. He began tapping his hand on the ground. What was he doing? Looking all around us, I kept watch for anything really, not wanting to meet these daywalkers in the slightest. Just when I'd had about enough of his short break, he grasped something in the sand and pulled a door in the ground open.

"We're going to have to use the shortcut. We don't have time to get to the main gates."

Looking down into a hole with a ladder, I glanced around again and despite every muscle in my body telling me to run and get the hell out of here, I started down the metal rungs into a deep hole that would take me, hopefully back to friggin' reality.

About Jacqueline Paige

Jacqueline is a multi-published author of 'all things paranormal'. Her book list proves this is her niche with stories of witches, ghosts, psychics, shifters, and more now on the shelves. Her current genres are paranormal romance, paranormal fantasy, and paranormal romantic suspense.

Her books are available in many formats around the globe, including book/reading apps. Since adding them during the pandemic, her books have had over a million reads and her 'to be written' list is growing longer each day. She can't write fast enough.

Jacqueline began her writing career in 2006 (as a joke) and her first book was published in 2009. She hasn't stopped since then. She is an avid reader and will read 'anything with words', whether it's a novel, article, or even every sign she passes.

Jacqueline lives in Ontario, Canada in a small town that's part of the popular Georgian Triangle area. Even though she can see the mountains, she does not ski.

When she's not in one of her writing worlds, she spends time with her grand-monsters. She has nine of them (so far) and looks forward to corrupting them in the years to come.

Jacqueline also writes under the pseudonym of J. Risk

Jacqueline loves to hear from her readers, you can find her at

http://jacquelinepaige.com